MY BROTHER'S HANDS
Paul Barile

Lexographic Press
1555 N Astor St, 15NE,
Chicago, IL 60610

ISBN: 978-09847142-4-7
Library of Congress Control Number: TBC

Cover design: James Sparling, Lexographic
Text design and production: Lexographic
Typeset in Minion Pro, 9pt/14.5pt.

Printed in the United States of America.

My Brother's Hands

Paul Barile

LEXOGRAPHIC PRESS

for Peter Frank and David Jeffrey

How far that little candle throws his beams!
So shines a good deed in a naughty world.
—*Portia, Merchant of Venice*

1972

Alice Campbell sat on the edge of the sagging bed in her best cotton nightgown. She continued to rub out the wrinkles, feeling the smooth fabric under her trembling fingers. Her face twitched—alternating from excited to nervous as she was waiting for her man, her brown eyes shifting from the bathroom door to Johnny Carson in his impeccable suit glowing off the massive 19-inch television screen. Then they shifted back to the solid white door. John Campbell was singing a song that was popular in their younger days—one she had almost forgotten. Alice found herself singing along even though she didn't really remember all the words.

He was a young upstart from the south. He was trying to make his way in a world where the bigger and the better got the attention, the endorsements; they got the world handed to them on a platter, overflowing with money and privilege. If you didn't bring your best every time, you'd be home by January. Now December was winding down and he figured it was a hell of a run. There might be a next year.

John Campbell emerged from the bathroom followed by a cloud of heavy steam. A damp cigarette dangled from the corner of his mouth, but he continued to sing out of the other side of it. "I-I-I-I ain't got nobody." He held his weathered arms out and skipped a slow step that may have been confused with dancing. Alice smiled up at him. She quietly admitted to herself that she loved it when he got this way. She forgot that it always ended in the same fashion. For this moment, she was ecstatic. She continued to rub out the invisible wrinkles in her nightgown.

His choices were limited. Time was ticking away there at the confluence of the powerful rivers. The enemy was advancing, but he knew what to do. There was nothing to fear now. He surrendered the last ounce of himself to the task and set the world in motion. No one watching had even the faintest idea what was about to happen. Many had left for home—others had already hung their heads in defeat. He never gave up hope. Well, almost never.

Alice Campbell pried her arm loose from the slumbering body of her husband. Once again, he had started something he could not finish. His erection didn't last long enough to keep him awake through one Tidy-Bowl commercial. He spilled his seed in her soft hand only moments before sleep overtook him. She cried softly to herself. All she ever wanted—all she ever remembered wanting—was a child. John Campbell was obviously not up to the task. She cried softly as she touched herself where he never did—never could. She allowed herself this small amount of pleasure there on that saggy, musty bed. Then she got up for a cup of coffee and a cigarette.

He watched his life—his dreams—bounce hopelessly out of his control. There was nothing he could do at this point. Then—without any warning or provocation—an angel of mercy swooped down putting an indelible fingerprint on his fate. Success was his with five seconds to spare.

Alice Campbell sat at her faded kitchen table in Orton's Cove, smoked a cigarette, and sipped her coffee. The tears came in spasms. She clicked on the television for distraction. She peered through the threads of smoke that rose to the ceiling carrying her dreams as far away from her as she could imagine. She took another sip of coffee.

There were questions. There were answers. When all was said and done, he had done the undoable. He had thought the unthinkable and was ready to step up and accept his place in history. He was preparing to step into that world of privilege. Maybe not tonight—maybe not tomorrow—but soon enough. He would be there soon enough.

Alone in her kitchen, Alice Campbell hung her head and cried. Was she asking too much? All she wanted was a child. Why was that too much? Alice hung her head and cried.

Throughout the west—in every tavern, kitchen, den, living room—grown men hung their heads and cried. The taste of triumph was as sweet as the flavor of failure was foul. They had tasted both tonight. Triumph tasted better.

John Campbell snored mercilessly. Alice eventually curled up on the couch and drifted off to an unsettled sleep. She had a dream about swimming. She loved it when she dreamt about swimming.

He never knew—was never sure—what happened that day. Decades later that night continues to linger in the memories of many—some who weren't even there, but who have heard the stories repeatedly and feel as if they were. It was a special night for everyone involved.

When Alice Campbell found out she was with child, she cried for a second time. She promised herself and her higher power that this child would never want for anything, as long as she was alive. This child—she would name him Peter—would be a gift to her and John and would always be treated as such.

"AND SO IT BEGINS"

The first time Peter Campbell's palms burst into flames was at the old Rialto Theater on Whitley Avenue.

The Rialto was hosting a Marx Brothers film festival when the brilliant flashes of light yanked everyone's attention away from the wild-eyed, piano playing Chico gesticulating across the pock-marked screen. Eager eyes searched the darkened room to see if anyone had figured out what had just happened.

The flames didn't last very long—just enough time to scare Betty Croney halfway out of her furry, pink angora sweater. She launched her buttered popcorn container over the chair in front of her as she leapt from the padded seat.

Peter sat in his seat somewhat dazed. He just stared at his hands as if he had recently woken up with these new appendages, like they weren't his and he couldn't figure out where they came from.

The beam of the usher's tin flashlight cut across his startled face. "There is no smoking in the theater," the little man yelled. "You better come on along with me, young man, because there is no smoking in here. No smoking!"

The little man in the threadbare blazer held his accusing tin flashlight in one hand and grabbed Peter with the other.

"Sit down, Frank," a voice yelled at the usher.

Frank was a natty little man. He trained his beacon of justice across the faces of the people seated nearest him. He had a few ideas who would question his authority but he wanted to be sure. His beam of light lingered on the faces of the boys he suspected were serious troublemakers. "Miscreants," the usher said.

He only looked away for a minute, but that was all the time that Peter needed. He slipped out of Frank's grip and through the emergency exit next to the screen before the old usher realized what had happened.

Chico's manic piano playing eventually drowned out old Frank's voice. "Get back here."

"Go home, Frank," a voice yelled. "We're trying to watch a movie here."

"There is no smoking in the theater," the little man yelled. "No smoking!"

The door slammed shut separating Peter from the possibility of what had happened.

Walking home, Peter was unsure what to do with his hands. He could hardly take his eyes off of them as he wound his way through the alleys and streets of Orton's Cove. He was afraid they might combust again without warning, which couldn't be safe, so his pockets were definitely out of the question.

By the same token just letting them hang at his sides as he walked could be equally dangerous because, if they decided to ignite again, Peter would have less control over the flames and where they might reach and what kind of damage they might do.

Peter Campbell didn't even know for sure if his hands would ignite again, or why they did in the first place. This made it that much more difficult for him to prepare for a second incident. There seemed to be only one place to go. There seemed to be only one man who he could turn to for answers.

He took the short cut around the Triangle Park and made a beeline for his cousin Luther's place. Peter knew he could count on Luther for some solid advice, maybe some coffee, at least a pair of gloves so that he could contain any ambitious flames.

Peter hopped over the weathered wooden fence, which abutted the alley that separated the struggling park from the well-manicured back yards. He cut across Mrs. Case's driveway and her crabgrass yard. He crossed the street and walked down the dimly lit alley that led up to the white cinder block garage that he helped Luther renovate into a small apartment. Luther and his wife Joellyn rented the building from old Mrs. Powers.

He stepped quietly through the gangway, being careful not to awaken Mrs. Powers, or worse, her mongrel dog Rambo. Rambo was a Shepherd mix, but somewhere in his genealogy laid some unknown mutant strain that didn't evolve fully, which made for one angry cur.

As he came around the corner of the garage, Peter was sure he had succeeded in reaching the door without waking either of them. It wasn't until he saw the teeth and heard the growl that he realized Rambo was waiting for him.

Instinctively, Peter put his hands up to protect his face, when the two brilliant flashes sent Rambo—now a smoldering ball of fur—scurrying under the back porch where he buried his crooked snout in the dirty gravel.

Peter pounded on his cousin's door. "Luther," he whispered. "Luther! Are you in there?"

He kept looking over his shoulder to where the dog had gone. He couldn't see the frightened animal but he wasn't taking any chances. He might have been less anxious if he'd known it would be two days before the humbled mutt could crawl out from under the porch and that was only to get food.

The door creaked open and a pale, thin face, framed in the bright orange mane of hair poked out.

"Whodat?" he asked.

"It's me," Peter whispered.

"Who me?" Luther asked stepping out and closing the door behind him. The moon cast a sickly light on the skinny hairless chest of Peter's cousin. The faded monster truck tattoo on his chest glowed against the pallor of his flesh.

"It's Peter," came the reply.

"Where's the dog?" Luther asked peering around nervously.

"I don't know," Peter lied. "Let me in?"

"Yeah, but you gotta be quiet, Dude. Joellyn is sleeping."

The harsh white exterior of the little building completely belied the interior. The walls inside were painted a soft tan and there were framed photos occupying just about every inch of open space.

There was Joellyn's family and Luther's family posing at picnics and parties. Peter's favorite was the one of Joellyn's little sister, Maureen, sitting on the back of a motorcycle that Peter appeared to be riding. He didn't own the bike, nor had he ever taken Maureen on a bike. It was a prop from a short-lived photo studio that had opened at the strip mall out on Route 7.

Peter dreamed of one day riding a motorcycle like the one in the picture. He often pictured himself riding down Route 7 with Maureen Davis or Betty Croney on the back. Steppenwolf music filled the air as he opened the throttle and left Orton's Cove behind him.

With the exception of the overflowing ashtrays and the empty cigarette packs that littered the room, everything else was immaculate. The books, mostly auto repair manuals and video game cheat guides, were lined up neatly on the shelves. The tapes, mostly heavy metal, were organized in alphabetical order in the racks next to the stereo.

The carpet was spotless, which couldn't have been an easy task when you consider that it was on top of the countless automotive fluid puddles.

"You want a Pepsi?" Luther asked.

"I can't stay, Lu," Peter said. "I need to borrow some work gloves for a couple days."

"Dude, you got a job?" Luther asked.

"Not exactly," Peter said. "I just—ah—I really can't explain right now. I'm not sure I understand myself."

"Give it a shot," Luther said.

Luther listened closely as Peter repeated the story ending with the unfortunate canine incident. When he was finished, Luther just shook his head and reached for the nearest cigarette pack.

The first one was empty so he put it back where he found it and grabbed another pack. This one had two cigarettes in it, one for himself and one for Peter.

"Can you light it with your hand?" Luther asked.

"Probably," Peter responded uncertainly. "I don't know for sure."

"Try, Dude. It'll be *boss*—if you can do it I mean."

Peter stuck the filter of the cigarette into his mouth and brought his hands up to his face. Luther watched with almost enough intensity to light the cigarette himself.

"I don't know about this," Peter said.

"Just do it, Dude," Luther prodded.

"I just don't feel so good about it," Peter said.

He never took his eyes off of his hands.

"I'll give you two dollars," Luther offered. He jammed his hand into the pocket of his jeans and produced a wad of wrinkled bills.

"I don't want your dang money, Lu," Peter said.

"Then just do it," Luther said.

The money fell off Luther's lap and landed on the couch.

Peter finally stretched his fingers back as far as they would go and aimed his palms at each other. The flash of light was quick, but Peter was quicker and soon enough the tip of his cigarette was burning.

"That was *BOSS!*" Luther shrieked. "Do mine! Do mine!"

Peter stretched his fingers back again and aimed his palms at his cousin. By the time they extinguished the fire, Luther had no eyebrows at all. They were both grateful and surprised Joellyn had slept through the whole thing.

"That was so *BOSS!*" was all Luther could say.

"So, do you have some gloves I could borrow?" Peter asked. "I'll get 'em back to you in a day or so."

Luther got up and walked into the area they had converted into a kitchenette. Inside one of the drawers was a pair of white gardening gloves with sunflowers on them. He pulled them out and tossed them to Peter, who was not exactly happy about the flowers.

"That's all I got," Luther said. "And be careful with 'em. If Joellyn finds out that I gave you her new gloves, I'm up the creek."

"Thanks, Lu," Peter said as he slipped his hands into the gloves and got up to leave.

At the door, he turned and thanked Luther one more time. He stepped into the night air keeping an eye out for Rambo who was hovering under the back porch. Peter made his way around the garage and into the alley.

He walked down the dimly-lit alley at a leisurely pace. His home was not very far and he needed time to think about what he was going to tell his mother if he came in wearing gloves with flowers on them. Ever since his father died, he had had no male role model and she constantly worried about him. The gardening gloves alone would serve as a dismal reminder of the tragic loss the family had suffered.

❀

There had been a record heat wave that summer and most of the rational people were in their homes sitting in front of a fan with their feet in a bucket of ice water. Peter was not much more than a baby at the time and his mother Alice doted on him. One afternoon, she drew him a cool bath. She slowly introduced small shards of ice into the water.

She wanted him to be cool but she couldn't bear the idea of the rough gooseflesh on her sweet baby's arms. The water was cooled at a sensible rate so the loving mother and her son—there in the cluttered pink-tiled bathroom—could both remain comfortable.

"You're turning my son into a baby," John Campbell yelled from the backyard where he was dripping clear sweat down the sparse hairs on his chest and into the dingy band of the boxer shorts that hung below his waist line, just above the belt loop on his dingy gray trousers.

In one hand he held a brown paper grocery bag overflowing with weeds and other undesirable garden refuse. The other hand held a steel

Stroh's beer can.

"He is a baby," she called back through the open window.

"Get him out of that dang tub before he turns into a prune," John Campbell yelled again, running his sweaty forearm across his sweaty forehead, drawing a gritty streak of gray dirt across his face like a slash.

"He'll be out in a minute," Peter's mother said again. "Just give him some time."

The old man turned and headed back toward the pitiful little patch of dirt he had come to call his garden. There were two tomato plants and a pepper plant, but if there was anything else alive it was purely accidental.

"I'll give you a minute," he muttered under his breath. "I'll give one dang minute!"

He didn't have the energy to get into another battle over the boy's future. The garden needed tending and no small amount of heat was going to rob him of the pleasure he received witnessing the miracle of vegetal growth.

The sweaty John Campbell lowered himself to one knee and began to yank at anything that didn't look familiar. The wild flowers nature had placed in his path were doomed to end up in the brown paper bag with the carrots he had forgotten he planted.

By the time the old man saw the baby carrots and realized what he was doing, they were jammed into the garbage bag and hardly fit for eating.

"Maybe I can give them to that baby of a son of mine," he muttered to himself.

The still air and the merciless sun were John Campbell's only companions that day, and when he gripped his tired heart and fell face first onto one of the healthier of the tomato plants, the squashed skins and pulp were the only witnesses to the old man's last moments.

When Alice found him in the garden, she called the hospital over in Riverton. They knew it was too late for an ambulance. The hospital called the county coroner who sent a car to pick up the old man's body. Peter's mother did not want her baby to see his father this way, so she dressed him in his best striped shirt and overalls and brought him down the street to her sister's house where he could play with his cousin, Luther.

The coroner said John Campbell's heart just "up and quit" on him. There was no wake and there was surely no expensive funeral. John Campbell wouldn't have wanted one. He was cremated and his ashes were sprinkled over his patch of earth just before the harvest. This was what John Campbell wanted and no one was going to deny him his last wish.

❁

Now, all these years later, Peter crossed the area his father had worked so hard to maintain. It was overgrown with every manner of bush and wild flower because no one was allowed to disturb it. His mother always told him that allowing the wild growth was his father's last wish.

The boy looked at the gloves on his hands and decided it would be easier to try to hide the incendiary palms than to explain the gloves. He loved his mother, as all good boys should, and he didn't want to upset her.

As usual, she was sitting on the couch in her curlers and blue cold cream when he walked in. The television was on but the sound had been turned off. When she saw the look on Peter's face, she reached for him, but he immediately recoiled.

"Are you okay, Junior?" she asked getting up from the couch.

"I'm fine, Mamma. Just tired, I guess, and hungry." Mamma always knew when her boy was lying.

"Didn't you take that nice Betty Croney out for dinner after the movie, Honey?" she was already making her way into the kitchen on her thin worn slippers.

"I was going to, but I was so tired I just wanted to come home."

There was no way he would be able to explain to his mother that Betty Croney had probably spent the last hour burning up the wires on the telephone with every girl in Orton's Cove crying about her new sweater and his flaming hands. His dear sweet mother would never understand that it wasn't really a date in the first place.

"Well, you come on in here," she called from the other room. "I'll fix you a nice grilled cheese sandwich."

By comparison to Luther's family museum, the house Peter shared with his mother was sparsely decorated. The living room had a few knick-knacks and mismatched odds and ends.

The sole conversation piece was a picture of Peter's Aunt Trudy standing next to former Vice President Dan Quayle at a Republican-sponsored spelling bee. The former Vice President barely even realized she was standing there but that didn't stop her from beaming like a fool.

The dining room was slightly more cluttered with stacks of books and folders overflowing with patterns for dresses and skeins of various materials. The two sewing machines set up near the windows were quiet for the evening, but with the first light of day, Mrs. Campbell and her machine would be humming away alongside Maria Beltran, the Mexican girl from down the street.

This week it looked like new uniforms for the band, last week it had been costumes for Miss Kolinsky's dance school recital. If he stopped long enough to look at the calendar, he would see his mother and Maria were booked well into the future with orders for every type of costume, uniform and gown imaginable.

❀

One Halloween, when he was 13, Alice Campbell made her son a spaceman outfit out of metallic silver material. Maria had made an amazingly uncomfortable headpiece to go with it. Peter was mortified when he saw himself in the mirror but he didn't want to hurt his mother's feelings, so he kept his opinions to himself.

The costume she made was easily the coolest thing in Orton's Cove but Peter didn't have the nerve to be so gaudy. He was never comfortable with too much attention. Any other kid in town would have killed for that suit (not necessarily the headgear). Peter had other ideas.

Before leaving for school that morning, he grabbed his plastic gym bag, the one with the Indian head on the side of it, and threw in a pair of denim pants and a black shirt. This package was dropped out the window at the side of the house when he knew no one was looking.

"I'll drive you to school today, Peter," Alice said. "We wouldn't want you sweating up your new costume."

"I'd rather walk, Mom, but, thanks," he said. "I have to meet Luther on the corner. We're going to walk together."

"Okay, Baby," she called back at him. "You be safe."

He nodded, smiled, and thanked them both for the hard work they put in on his costume as he slipped out the door. Once he was sure he was out of their line of vision, he tiptoed back across the yard and into the hedge and unzipped the plastic gym bag.

The shirt came out first, which he hung over a branch. Then the trousers, which he hung next to the shirt. The anxious young boy slid out of his silver suit just as Mrs. Dockery was passing.

Had he noticed her, he probably would have tried to hide himself from the old woman's view but he was so worried about the safest and best way to store the headpiece while he was gone, he didn't see her until it was too late.

She smiled and waved at him before walking away. He blushed with his entire body as he pulled the trousers over his knees and buttoned them up.

"Where's your costume?" Luther asked when they met on the corner.

Luther, for his part, was dressed in oily jeans and a stained denim shirt with a John Deere baseball cap on.

"I see you are going as a mechanic again," Peter said.

"Mechanics are cool. They get to work on cars and no one makes them wash their hands or nothin'," Luther said.

"But it's not really a costume," Peter laughed softly. "That's what you wear all the time."

"Not so," he said. "It's all about the hat."

"Luther, that's your dad's Deere hat. If he catches you..."

"This hat makes me more of a mechanic than my baseball hat," Luther said, taking the hat off for a moment and looking at the patch on the front with reverence. *"This is a John Deere."*

"Your cap is from Snap-On Tools."

"But that's my cap. This cap belongs to a real live mechanic. So where is your costume?"

"In the bushes," Peter replied. *"I just couldn't wear it. I have to get home early enough to slip back into it before I go in the house."*

"Dude, what if your mom finds out?" Luther asked as they entered the crowded playground. The sea of clowns and ballerinas and monsters screamed, ran, and played all around them. No one even noticed Peter.

"She'll never know, unless you say something,"

❀

The steaming cheese sandwich in front of him offered temporary solace but he knew it was only temporary. He dug in nonetheless.

"I'm going to have to start working Sundays," his mother said as she lowered herself into the seat across from his.

"That busy?" he said trying to sound interested as he jammed the lightly toasted bread and gooey cheese into his mouth. The cheese burned the roof of his mouth.

"Slow down, Peter," she said. "No one's going to take it away from you."

"Sorry, Mom," he replied, setting the half-eaten portion on the plate.

"That's better. Do you want milk?" she asked.

"Thanks, Mom," he answered.

"Get a glass down while I get the milk out," she told him.

He stretched his arm out to reach his favorite milk glass, the one with the football helmets etched in the surface on each side. The reach was just long enough for the sparks. Two quick flames shot out from his hand singeing the cloth flowers in the terracotta sitting on the cabinet shelf.

"What the hell was that?" his startled mother asked as she spun around. She dropped the milk bottle on the linoleum floor shattering the glass.

"I dunno. What?" Peter asked wringing his hands together under the table.

"That! Those flashes of light! Didn't you see it?"

"Probably that heat lightning," the boy said.

He couldn't even look at his mother when he lied. They both knew he was lying but neither knew what to do about it on those rare occasions when it happened.

"Aw, now look at the floor," she said when she realized she was standing in a puddle of milk and broken glass.

"I'll get it, Mom," said the dutiful son, getting up quickly from his chair, glad for a reason to get up and move.

He pushed the sponge mop over the pool carefully so the unseen chunks of glass wouldn't scratch the floor. He still couldn't even look at his mother who began preparing a second sandwich.

"I can't figure it out," she kept saying to herself. "If the flashes were lightning, where was the thunder?"

"It's that heat lightning, Mom," Peter said. "There's no thunder with heat lightning."

She pulled the large plastic pitcher of Kool-Aid out of the icebox to pour a glass for her son to drink with his second sandwich. When she reached for a glass, she noticed her cloth flowers were crispy around the edges.

"That's odd," she said pulling the small vase off the shelf and looking closer at it as she turned it slowly around in her hand.

"How's that sandwich coming?" Peter asked quickly hoping to distract her. He had finished the mopping and was carefully picking up the last pieces of glass.

"Now you go wash your hands before you finish eating, Junior," she said, setting the pot and the singed plant back on the shelf.

Running his hands under the water, Peter knew he would

eventually have to tell his mother about his condition. He wasn't sure how and he wasn't sure when, but he knew he would have to do it eventually.

Only when drying his hands did he realize that, if he kept them wet, they would probably not be as likely to ignite. He set the towel down and walked back into the kitchen.

He eased back into his chair. His wet grip didn't help the sandwich at all but his peace of mind made it worthwhile.

Alice sat across from him and pulled a long, slim cigarette pack out of her robe. Next came the long, brown cigarette. She lit it and drew the smoke deep into her lungs.

"So, is this Betty Croney thing serious?" she asked as she exhaled.

"Aw, Mom," Peter moaned. "I can't get serious about a girl until I get a good job so that I can get a nice car so that I can—well—you know, Mom."

"Well, why don't you go down to the Rialto tomorrow and apply for a job? Elvis Hart says they're looking for an usher, and you like movies."

"Yeah, but my friends will think there's something wrong with me if they see me hanging around with old Frank."

"You don't have to hang around that old man," his mother laughed.

"I don't know, Mom," he said finishing his sandwich. "Can we talk about this tomorrow?"

"Sure, Honey," she said taking his plate from the table and setting it into the sink.

"I *do* have something really important to talk to you about," he said. "But I need to borrow a cigarette before I can tell you."

She pulled the long thin pack out of her robe again and slid it across the table. "You know I don't like it when you smoke," she said handing him the lighter.

"Mom," he started. "If something happened to me—I mean if I changed. What I mean to say is..."

"I will love you no matter what choices you make, Peter," she said patting him on the hand. "It's your life and I'm your Mamma. I only wish that your Daddy was here for you."

"This has nothing to do with Daddy," Peter sighed.

"A boy needs his Daddy around when he is growing up. He needs a positive male role model so that he can be a man when the time comes."

"Mom," he interrupted. "You've been watching Oprah again. I've asked you not to watch that stuff. It puts weird ideas in your head."

"Well, what is the problem, baby? What is it?" she asked.

"It's probably better if I just showed you," Peter said. "Come with me."

He stood up and led his mother out onto the back porch. He guided her over to the corner away from the staircase on the chance she might get startled and jump. She would be safer farther away from the stairs.

"Ready?" he asked.

Peter stretched his fingers back and aimed his palms at each other. The flash of light was quick, but Peter was getting better at the game. The tip of his cigarette was burning soon enough.

His mother crossed herself quickly before pushing past him and running back into the house. Peter stood still with the twin golden flames smoldering in his hands but not burning the flesh.

He was still there when she returned with the cordless phone.

"Who are you calling?" he asked.

"The Good Reverend Crenshaw," she replied. "This is a miracle and a man of the cloth should be here to document it for the church."

Reverend Harland Crenshaw was only a man of the cloth by virtue of a variety of tax breaks, and his uncanny ability to abuse the position of authority and trust. He also had an ingratiating way of being there for the town's women when they needed something done while their husbands had gone to work or just plain gone.

"I don't want him here, Mamma," Peter protested.

"He's a man of the cloth and he needs to be here," she said sternly. "I want him here and I'm your Mamma."

It was Peter's turn to push past her although he did it gently. He could hear her voice turn cheery when she addressed the leach on the phone. He walked upstairs to wash his hands.

By the time Crenshaw arrived, Alice was back at the kitchen table sipping fresh brewed coffee and wearing her hair in a tidy bun. There was a small spot of cold cream on her chin, but other than that, she was dressed for Sunday morning. Peter begrudgingly sat by her side smoking a cigarette.

The man in the black silk suit entered the house without knocking. He moved down the hall with practiced stealth startling Peter and Alice when he stepped into the kitchen. He swabbed the cream off Alice's chin with his left hand while he offered Peter his right.

"Maybe that's not such a good idea," Reverend Crenshaw said pulling his hand back quickly and laughing too loudly.

He didn't even notice Peter had not attempted to accept his hand.

"Reverend Crenshaw, would you like a cup of coffee?" Alice asked.

Peter watched the con man lower himself into the chair across from him. His look was disapproving and Crenshaw was all too comfortable with it. Men—in general—did not welcome the phony preacher into their homes and this boy surely did not welcome him either.

Crenshaw wondered what Peter would think if he knew about the widow in Kansas City. Crenshaw had promised to make her boy walk again in exchange for a small donation to Crenshaw's "mission in Uganda".

Once her bank account was drained and she was sufficiently smitten with him, Crenshaw disappeared. He didn't stick around to see the widow or her son who would never walk again. They woke up one morning to find him gone—back on the bus taking his musty tents to the next town. There was no way of him knowing for sure, but Harland Crenshaw knew stories tended to follow a man.

At the very least, the young boy had probably heard about the high school cheerleader, down in Amarillo. The bubbly little blonde the Good Reverend had to take to that clinic in Corpus Christi. Her family found out about the tryst, and the devastating results, and the man was once again, forced to slip out under the cover of night while the little blonde waited tranquilly on the back porch swing for him to return as he promised he would. By the end of the summer, she left Amarillo with an alcoholic rodeo clown named Oliver.

Crenshaw thought there might be a chance Peter didn't know anything about his despicable past or unsavory behavior. With any luck, it could be something as simple—and familiar—as the fact that the honest men of Orton's Cove didn't seem to have any use for the man without a family who made a home amongst men and their families.

To have a man of the cloth who wasn't necessarily welcome at family picnics or events was something the generous people of Orton's Cove had trouble reconciling. The expectation they held of his position just didn't seem to match his actions. Rather than try to figure it out—they just thought it better to leave well enough alone. It wasn't that he wasn't respected; he flat out was not welcome.

❁

St. Agnes of the Fields had a gay vicar named Neil McDermott. He was more popular than Crenshaw in a town where the average opinion was that homosexuality was a curable condition. The women loved his attention to detail. They took small pleasure in the royal purple trim of his stole matching the royal purple of his cassock.

The men loved the fact that he could hit a sixteen-inch softball over the centerfield wall at the intra-parish intramurals every year up around Trinity. He could drink a cold can of beer faster than even Al Simpson, the catcher, who kept a cooler in the dugout.

When the church decided the attendance at St. Agnes of the Fields didn't warrant a full-time vicar, Neil McDermott was transferred to a small primitive village in Central America. The softball team was hit the hardest by the loss.

McDermott was replaced by a ruddy-faced fire-hydrant of a man who basically ran the church into the ground—then ran out of Orton's Cove. The building sat empty until Crenshaw came to town, talked to Billy White over at White's Real Estate, and got the building for a song.

❀

Whatever the reason, if what Alice had told him on the phone was even remotely true, Crenshaw knew there would have to be more than one way to make a large pile of money out of Peter's condition. It wouldn't be unreasonable to give the kid and his mom a few bucks.

"Son, let me talk to you about stigmata," Crenshaw began.

"Don't call me son, Mister," Peter said evenly. "I ain't your dang son."

"Peter," his mother admonished.

"The boy's right, Alice," the Good Reverend said, patting the woman's hand.

"Don't touch my mother again," Peter said. He had not taken his eyes off of the preacher's hand.

"Peter, that's enough," his mother scolded.

Crenshaw smiled at Peter. "Perhaps I was out of line. Like any good shepherd, I have been known to get a little too familiar with my sheep. I do need to mind my wandering hands."

"It's quite alright, Reverend Crenshaw," she said. "How about that cup of coffee?"

"Yes, please. With cream and sugar," he said softly never taking his eyes off Peter.

Peter immediately recalled the day his Uncle Marv pulled him aside at the church social to give him the facts of life. These— according to Uncle Marv—were basically work hard and be a real man. They also inexplicably included something about not diluting your coffee with confections.

Peter wasn't even sure he understood the wisdom imparted to him that day but he always drank his coffee black—always.

❁

The junior high and high school-aged kids were pairing up to go off in the woods to neck, one of the more popular traditions at church socials. Peter found himself under the heavy hairy arm of his dead father's brother.

"Now I know I ain't been as good an Uncle as I should be," he started. Peter's eyes darted around the small room hoping he wouldn't be stuck with Marcia Black. No one ever wanted to neck in the woods, or anywhere, with Marcia Black.

More than her breath always smelling like salami, the most unsettling aspect of Marcia Black's necking was her tongue, which was as thick and rough as a slab of wet granite. Not a model of subtlety or finesse, Marcia tended toward jamming that huge appendage into her partner's mouth mercilessly. This battering was known to loosen teeth, crack jaws, and cause severe headaches.

"I'm gonna tell you a couple things that your daddy, my brother, taught me when I was a kid and if you remember them, you'll be better off than either he or I ever was."

Peter nodded his head and tried to focus on his uncle's words.

"The first thing to remember is that if you love a woman, never let her see you cry. Once she sees that—woo boy—she knows she's got you by the short hairs and she'll make you miserable for the rest of your natural life.

"The second thing you gotta remember is a two-parter. First, never be late for work, and never talk back to your boss, and you will be rewarded. We all come into this world with a potentiality of some kind or another. We have to find it and be all we think we should be.

"The other thing is that you should always wash yourself when you

are in the shower—you know your... self. Keep it clean and it will never let you down."

Peter looked around at the thinning crowd and realized it was being narrowed down to the dreaded Marcia Black and the (barely) less than dreadful Lisa Tobin. Lisa was a sloppy kisser and she always left the boys' lips raw. Lisa's most attractive feature was that she let the boys put their hand under her sweater—over her bra—but at least feeling that silky padded material was always more exciting than just rubbing against the front of the other girls' sweaters.

"The other thing your Daddy told me to tell you," Uncle Marv continued.

Peter watched Joe Rogers offer Lisa his hand. She stood up and smiled as he led her out the door.

"Are you listening to me, boy?"

Peter nodded weakly.

"The other thing is never—ever—trust a man who doesn't drink his coffee black. He has no grit. If a man has to put something in his coffee, he's likely hiding something. That or he's just a plain liar."

"Thanks, Uncle Marv," Peter said casting a cheerless eye around the room.

"Don't mention it," the older man said.

Peter turned to where Marcia Black was sitting by herself next to the battered upright piano. He resigned himself to his fate and began walking toward her when he was nudged out of the way by a beefy arm that was somehow familiar to him.

He paused when he saw his Uncle Marv offer Marcia Black his hand. She looked at Peter for a moment then back at Uncle Marv before taking the beefy hand and following the man out the door.

She looked back at Peter and shrugged before allowing the man to lead her out of Peter's sight.

❀

Reverend Crenshaw raised the cup to his lips and drank the tepid tan liquid. Peter's mother lit a cigarette as the young man stood up and walked out of the room.

"G'night, Mom," he said over his shoulder. "I'll be just upstairs if you need me."

"I'm sorry you had to drive all the way out here," Alice said. "You just wouldn't believe what the boy can do. It is a miracle. *My Peter* created a *miracle*. You believe me, don't you Reverend Crenshaw?"

"Oh, I believe you, Mrs. Campbell. I believe you completely. I will see it for myself when the time is right. In the meantime," Crenshaw said, "Is there a Mr. Campbell?"

"IT'S NOT A TRICK..."

The news about Peter's hands spread through Orton's Cove like a wildfire. By the time Peter crawled out of bed the next morning, the front lawn of his mother's house was littered with people hoping—expecting—to witness the miracle.

As for Peter, he dragged his hands through his hair as he tried to pry his sleepy eyes open. The whole thing felt like a dream. He had eaten a frozen pizza before going to the movie and there was probably a shaving of processed mozzarella cheese lodged in his duodenum. The bacteria created a toxic effect causing him to have the horrific nightmare that ended with him leaving his mother alone in the kitchen with Reverend Harland Crenshaw.

When Peter peered out the front window and saw the people gathered there on the front lawn, the realization—and the heaviness of what it surely meant—settled into his stomach. He felt like he was moving in warm, thick water as he tried to step away from the window. Last night was not a dream. What happened last night would surely ignite Peter's life as much as it did his hands.

Peter dashed to the back window in time to catch Reverend Crenshaw slinking through the crowd that was collecting in the backyard. No one seemed to notice him. Travis Dodson was standing on Peter's father's garden patch. The preacher furtively glanced up at the window hoping to make eye contact with Peter. When he saw the frightened young man staring down at him, he shifted his direction and headed toward the front of the house where he might get lost in the crowd and have a better vantage point to watch Peter without Peter seeing him.

He heard his mother's footsteps padding up the carpeted stairs. Realizing he was still in his briefs, Peter called to her as he scrambled for something to cover himself with.

"I'll be right down, Mom," but she was already at the top of the stairs and turning into the little room where Peter kept his model cars and airplanes.

"Peter," she said attempting to restrain excitement. "There is someone here who would like to meet you."

She was completely oblivious to the way her son was dressed—or in this case not dressed. Alice stepped aside and let Megan Nichols and her camera crew into the cramped room. Megan Nichols was a waspish but pretty television news reporter.

Peter liked to watch the news if only to see the young Miss Nichols. More than just a pretty face—Peter felt that Megan was talking directly to him whether she was doing the weather or recapping last night's ball scores. Now that she was here—in his room under these conditions—he was horrified.

"Excuse me," he said, pushing past them and hotfooting back into his little bedroom. He slammed the door shut behind him.

"Peter," his mother said softly to the door. "You're not being very polite."

"I'll be down in a minute, Mom," he yelled. "Let me get dressed."

"Coffee?" she asked Miss Nichols and the cameramen sweetly.

Megan Nichols and the crew hesitated before walking down the stairs. The story was there behind the door and it was difficult to walk away from it.

"Are there windows in that room?" Megan asked.

"If Peter says he'll be down, he'll be down," Alice said. "Let's just have some coffee. I'm sure he'll be down soon enough. *He is kind of sweet on you*," she whispered.

"I'm flattered," Megan Nichols responded, looking at the closed door one more time.

The camera crew settled in around the table. Megan Nichols took up her position by the back door, which gave the make-up girl more natural light. Alice was scurrying around trying to fill coffee cups and juice glasses when Peter entered the room.

"Do you want some toast, Peter?" Alice asked.

She dropped two slices onto the paper plate in front of the little bearded man who was fiddling with a light meter.

"Just the coffee," he muttered.

Peter was never considered bold by anyone he came in contact with, so being seen by Megan Nichols in his underwear—with bed head no less—made him even more sheepish than usual. He couldn't look anyone in the eye.

"Now Peter," Megan started. She was looking at him sideways while the make-up girl dusted her face lightly. "We're going to live in just a few minutes. Why don't you grab a seat and we can go over what I am going to ask you and what you are going to say."

Alice eyed the chair. Peter caught the look and decided that he would do it—for her.

Peter sat down at the table across from a guy who got busy setting a short microphone stand on the table in front of him. The bearded guy with the light meter whisked his little instrument around Peter's face and shoulders. Alice was beaming with pride as she set a cup of black coffee in front of her pride and joy.

"Now Peter," yet another man said. He was holding a clipboard, which he was studying intently while he spoke. "Let me assure you that your comfort and dignity are our priority here. We are only here to get the truth—to get your story. We are professional journalists. Are you with me?"

"Ed," Megan Nichols called over the head of the make-up girl. "I need mascara. You know how the camera simply despises my eyes without enough mascara. Send someone to find me mascara right away."

"Yes, Megan," he said without looking up from his clipboard. His coffee was nearly as blonde as she was. "Right away, Megan."

Ed motioned with his forehead to the microphone guy, then

toward the door. The microphone guy vanished. Their unspoken communication was intriguing to Peter.

"As I was saying," Ed began.

"I don't have a story, Mister," Peter said sipping his black coffee.

"Sure you do, Baby," his mother cooed.

"Are these the flowers?" the bearded guy asked pulling the singed cloth flowers off the shelf and placing them in front of Peter.

"The very ones," his mother replied watching the man set the flowerpot down.

"All right people," Ed said. "We're going to begin."

"What about my mascara?" Cynthia asked.

"We'll do Peter's close-ups first," he replied. "You ask your questions off camera and we'll shoot him over your shoulder."

"You're brilliant, Ed," she whispered.

"Rolling… Speed…"

Peter sat completely still in his chair. He didn't even bother to look at the camera or the woman holding her own microphone behind it. His only movement was the hand that brought the cup of coffee to his mouth.

"Ladies and Gentlemen," Megan Nichols started, in a voice altogether different from the voice Peter remembered—the voice that made him swoon. "This is Megan Nichols reporting for WWOC. I am standing in the home of one Peter Campbell, the young man who shocked the tiny town of Orton's Cove last night when his hands burst into flames during a showing of a Three Stooges movie-"

"It was the Marx Brothers," Peter corrected her. "It wasn't the Stooges, it was the Marx Brothers. There's a difference, ya' know."

"Cut!" Ed yelled.

"What's the dif?" Megan asked Peter.

"No *Stooge* could ever play the piano like Chico Marx," Peter said firmly. "That's one difference."

"Let's try it again. Speed…"

"I am standing in the home of Peter Campbell, the young man who shocked the tiny town of Orton's Cove last night when his hands burst into flames while he was enjoying *a movie* with friends."

34

"I was alone," Peter interjected.

"Cut!" Ed yelled even louder.

"Seriously?" Megan asked Peter. "Can we try one more time?"

"One more," Ed called out to his crew.

"I am standing in the home of Peter Campbell—the young man who shocked the small town of Orton's Cove recently when his hands burst into flames. Tell us how you feel, Peter."

"I feel like being left alone. Listen, Lady," was all he could force out before bolting out of the room.

"Cut!"

"Can't we just interview his friends?" Megan pleaded with Ed.

"What about his mother?" Alice chimed in. "Who knows her boy better than the mother?"

"Pack it up," Ed said and they did. Within minutes, Mrs. Campbell was standing alone in her kitchen. Her smile faded slowly.

Peter left the house and pushed his way through the growing crowd that was now spilling onto his front porch like visitors to Lourdes. He walked down Hubley Street with no real destination in mind—just distance from the house—distance from the crowd taking up residence on his front lawn.

He felt terrible for embarrassing his mother in front of Megan Nichols and the news crew but he had already been through more than he could handle. He just wanted to go to the movies last night—he didn't ask for this. He never asked for anything that would draw any attention to him. Now it seemed that was all he was going to have until he could figure this out.

He surely didn't choose to be visited by this new incendiary talent nor did he think he was equipped to deal with the complications it would surely bring. Peter Campbell wanted to get on with his simple life in the uncomplicated manner he had become accustomed to—the way his father would have expected. The plan—which he did not intend to deviate from before last night—included graduating from Orton Central High School, going to work for Carlsbad Freight, marrying a woman like his mother and living plainly ever after.

A regular, ordinary life was good enough for John Campbell; it was surely good enough for Peter Campbell. Now, however, Peter Campbell found himself in a situation he felt ill-prepared to handle. The timing of his new unanticipated talent couldn't be any worse. There was only a week before Peter was to begin his senior year at Orton Central. This was supposed to be the best year of his life—and now this.

He stopped at Kaucky's soda fountain for a fresh pack of cigarettes and a cup of coffee. Old Man Kaucky was always good for a joke or two—maybe a story about the war. Today—more than ever—Peter needed the distraction to take his mind off of the people milling about in his front yard.

Peter swiveled onto one of the vinyl-covered rotating stools and opened the package of cigarettes the old man had slid down the counter.

"Coffee—black, just like-a you dad," Old Man Kaucky said.

"Coffee—black," Peter replied. "And a piece of pecan pie."

The old man poured a steamy cup of hot black coffee into the cup with one hand while he set a small cellophane-wrapped pecan pie in front of Peter with the other. He smelled like inexpensive after-shave, which Peter found reassuring.

When Peter reached for his wallet, he realized, in his haste to get out of the house, he had left his wallet on his bureau. He began to push the coffee away but Old Man Kaucky just smiled and nodded.

"Next time, yeah?" he said. "You pay next time."

Old Man Kaucky was always a soft touch when the boys were between jobs—or forgot their wallets at home in a mad rush to elude the paparazzi waiting to pounce. Almost no one really worked in Orton's Cove until after high school but the tabs were always—miraculously—paid. The few kids that did work before they finished their schooling did so because their families needed the money and Old Man Kaucky was especially generous with them.

Peter sipped his coffee between puffs on his damp cigarette. He played with the cellophane wrapper but wasn't ready to eat the pie. He looked up at the television mounted in the corner opposite the picture window.

There on the screen, Peter was afforded an unobstructed view of himself running through the upstairs hallway at his house. Old Man Kaucky looked over the edge of his newspaper at the TV as Peter ran from one room into the next in his underwear. Megan Nichols looked flustered and his mother looked confused, but to Peter, he felt that he looked like a fool—bed head and saggy underwear and all.

There was a quick shot of Betty Croney who was holding her purse against her chest and stammering. Besides Peter's cousin and his mother, she was the only one who had witnessed the flaming hands.

"It was so sudden," Betty wept. "One minute we were watching Harpo play the piano-"

"Chico," Peter interrupted half-heartedly.

"And the next thing I knew, my new angora sweater was on fire."

The next cut revealed Frank the usher. He tugged his toupee into place on his wrinkled pate as he forced out the words, "There's no smoking in my theater you see!"

"You're a minimum wage usher," Peter yelled at the television.

Old Man Kaucky laughed and went back to reading his paper.

"So when I saw the flashes of light, I knew it had to be something else," Frank, the usher concluded. "You see, because no one smokes in my theater."

"Could you please turn this off, Mr. Kaucky?" Peter asked the old man, who appeared rather comfortable reading his paper and smoking a small green cigar. "Could you please change this?"

"You no wanna be the star?" Old Man Kaucky laughed. "Everyone wanna be the star."

"Not me, thanks just the same," Peter replied. He tugged at the corner of the cellophane wrapper but was still not ready to commit to opening the package. He sipped his coffee and twirled the pie around in his fingers.

"Ima no wanna be star, too," the old man said.

"Me, *too*," Peter laughed.

37

The old man walked over to where the television set hung above the ice cream freezer and picked up the flyswatter that hung on a nail. He swatted the on/off button until the screen went dark. He replaced the flyswatter on the nail and went back to his newspaper.

The eerie silence was deafening. It seemed they were trapped in a vacuum—an absence of sound. Peter spun slowly around on his chair and looked outside. He hadn't realized that he had been followed; now he was suddenly aware he was being watched. The first few faces pressed up against the shiny picture window almost amused Peter. It took him a minute to comprehend how just about the entire town was standing outside on the street looking in at him—watching him—hoping to witness the miracle with their own eyes.

Some rubbed their hands as if this simple action might make them better understand what had happened. Some just stared, slack-jawed.

Luther knew his cousin well enough to know that they could talk. They had been through a lot together from the time they could walk. Peter's first beer was out behind Luther's mother's garage on the Fourth of July when they were 11 years old. Luther's first hickey was from a girl that Peter introduced to him. Neither could imagine a life without the other. Luther knew it was up to him to reach out to his newly famous cousin in this time of crisis—despite the singed eyebrows.

Luther walked out of the crowd and into the pristine little store. The glass on the display cases was flawlessly polished, as were the acres and acres of perfectly oiled and burnished oak that wrapped around the room. The huge mirror that served as a back bar reflected Peter's face back at him as Luther sidled up, pausing for a moment to check his hair.

He took a seat next to his cousin and pulled out one of the cigarettes in the package that lay near the almost empty coffee.

"You gonna eat that?" Luther pointed to the pecan pie.

"G'head," Peter responded quietly. He tossed his cousin the little pie.

"You can't stay in here forever," Luther added.

"I'll go out when *they* all go home," Peter said.

Luther tugged at the wrapper of the pie. The cigarette dangled from his lips but he was focused on the cellophane between him and the pie. It was not giving in as easily as he had hoped it would.

"Just give 'em what they want and they'll go home. They's just curious is all."

The ash fell from Luther's cigarette. He rubbed it into his pants while he ripped at the pie's protective wrapper.

Peter turned slowly on his seat and looked at the gaping faces of the same people who wouldn't even have given him a second look twenty-four hours earlier. The women, who are typically braver in these types of situations, were the closest to the window. The men hung back and sipped root beer out of brown bottles. Peter searched the crowd for Betty Croney.

"Are you saying that if I show them how my hands fire up, they'll go home and leave me alone?" Peter asked Luther as he turned back around.

"That's what I'm sayin', Bro," Luther said with confidence. "They just want to see something they never seen before. What the hell else happens in this town? Show 'em your trick and let's go catch some fish."

"It's not a trick," Peter said. "A trick is something that you learn and do by choice like pick-a-card or pulling rabbits out of hats." Peter held out his hand and a little flame ignited in the center of his palm and flickered. He said, "This isn't a trick and I didn't choose this."

"It's a figure of speech, Peter," Luther chuckled. "Now, let's go. Your public waits."

Luther snubbed out his cigarette and tossed the still-wrapped pie onto the counter. He walked toward the door with Peter in tow. Luther actually believed in the simplicity of his plan. He figured Peter could whip up a little fire and the boys would be free to go down to the ravine for some fishing.

Peter stopped at the door to thank Old Man Kaucky for the brief moment of solace he had provided, and to remind him he would be back by nightfall with the money for the coffee, pie, and cigarettes. Peter walked back to where his pie sat unwrapped. He scooped it up and slipped it into his pocket for later. He walked back toward the door.

"You no worry, Peter-boy," the old man said as he wiped the counter with his threadbare, white towel. "You no worry 'bout a ting."

Peter stepped out into the doorway of the old drugstore. The light glared in his eyes. When he put his forearm up to block the sun, a woman shrieked. Peter looked to see if he could find Betty Croney.

"Show us your trick, Fire-boy," someone yelled from the back of the crowd.

"There is no cause for name callin'," Luther called out. "If'n you can't behave like civilized folk, I'm afraid my cousin'll be tempted to go fishin' and leave all y'all to your own."

"Shut up, Luther," someone else called out. "We here to see Fire-boy do his thing and we ain't 'bout to leave until he does."

"Who said that?" Luther snapped looking over the crowd.

"Forget it, Luther. Let's just get this over with," Peter said.

Peter was still adjusting his eyes as he stretched his arms out dramatically.

"Show us the trick, Fire-boy," someone else yelled out.

Peter couldn't figure out who was saying what . He leveled his gaze at the crowd; he focused on Johnny Simmons just the same.

"This ain't a trick," Peter started.

"We want to see the fire," Johnny Simmons' little brother Jimmy said.

For reasons they alone knew, the Simmons family gave all of their children names that began with the letter J. The oldest was Joachim, next came Jiselle, followed by Jasmine. Then there was Johnny and the twins, Jimmy and Joey. That their father's name was Clark and their mother's name was Mabel would have puzzled the amateur genealogist but somewhere, in the lineage, there had to be a very important J.

"Stand back," Peter said. "Please. Stand back!"

He stretched his fingers back in the way that was going to become very familiar to him and when the little balls of flame burst forth, the crowd murmured their approval. Some of the children cheered aloud. One of the men whistled really loudly causing the entire mob to laugh—releasing the tension.

Peter laughed nervously to himself first. He looked at Luther and they both laughed out loud. They weren't sure what else to do so they just laughed and watched the little balls of flame.

Peter saw the cameras—especially Megan Nichols' crew—on the periphery of the crowd. He was glad he had had a chance to comb his hair. He smiled weakly as the balls of fire began to change color. First, they were red; then they were green; then they went back to red. Peter couldn't believe what he was seeing himself. He had no idea how or why this was happening, but he hoped he could learn to control it—at the very least, the colors and their appearance.

There was a smattering of applause from the people closest to Peter. Eventually the whole crowd began to cheer loudly. Peter took a self-conscious bow, which Old Man Kaucky saw from his place in the window of the pharmacy. Old Man Kaucky just smiled to himself before going back to wiping the immaculate counter.

Peter's mother quietly wept with pride in the midst of the crowd. She scanned the faces in hopes of memorizing the people who were so fascinated with her son. If only John Campbell were alive today to witness this. Who would have ever believed her little Peter would become so popular?

The entire spectacle was not wasted on Reverend Crenshaw either. He sat low in the seat of his old Riviera and watched until the balls of fire finally extinguished. He watched as Peter took another weak bow and disappeared around the corner with Luther.

The crowd didn't disperse immediately. This was the crux of the entire event. The same people who had seen Peter everyday of his life never really noticed him until he became a fire hazard. Now they were standing in groups and cliques talking about him as if he were going to save the world.

Crenshaw saw this as an opportunity that should not be wasted on the simple minds and limited checkbooks of Orton's Cove citizenry. He started the car and drove slowly away. There was a new day dawning for Peter Campbell and the Good Reverend Harland Crenshaw was going to guarantee everyone capitalized on it—whether they were willing or not.

"HER NAME IS MAKI"

Orton's Cove was not so much misnamed as the name it was given was misread. The founding father of the little town, Forrest Orton, had originally decided to name the town Orton's Orchards but felt the alliteration might be confusing to the immigrants who were coming to build the railroads.

Sitting at the wooden table behind his log home one spring afternoon, Forrest noticed the trees for what seemed like the first time to him. There were so many and they were so beautiful he couldn't imagine how he had missed them before, but there they were.

He decided Orton's Grove was a good name for the settlement. Orton's Grove was a name that reflected the pastoral beauty of his little slice of paradise. The trees that grew in abundance along each of the little roads leading away from his home enhanced the beauty he had only recently begun to appreciate.

Forrest Orton had come over from England just before the War Between the States broke out. He was a hard-working man with a pleasant disposition and a cunning sense for business. He was barrel-chested with thick tufts of hair sprouting out of the open collar of his shirt.

His raven black hair constantly had a wind-blown look making Forrest Orton appear as though he were continuously in motion. Truth be told, he likely was continuously in motion except in the evening when he sat by the fire smoking his pipe and reading the Bible.

By the time the first snowflake lit on his sweaty nose, Forrest had built a small two-room log cabin in the clearing he created. He dug a crude path from his front door to the main artery that cut across the countryside. Forrest knew there was money to be made by the stagecoaches and horseback riders heading from the east to the unknown frontier out west; and he set his sights on how best to establish a trading post, where to position it, and what to sell.

Forrest served food to travelers, later to soldiers, who were passing through. He sold them toiletries and medicine he had bartered from those who came before them. Less a cottage industry, Forrest's log cabin industry boomed as people felt the need to see for themselves what all the fuss on the west coast of the country was about.

By the end of the war, the industrious expatriate had added three more cabins and a smoke house. He rented the cabins to travelers who were unaccustomed to sleeping under the stars and provided food to those who slept outdoors. His business sense was evident from his thriving trade with all of the trappers, hunters, and alchemists he had come to know so well.

As the settlement grew and developed into a town, Forrest was elected the first mayor. Along with his general store, he maintained his political position until he passed away many years, and many children, later.

It was Mrs. Whitley, in her application to the state's recorder of the deeds, who misread Forrest's handwriting on the town's charter. She felt terrible when the paperwork came back addressed to Orton's Cove, but by then, it was too late to do anything about it.

Ironically, the nearest body of water was the Creek Neck River in Riverton—one half day's journey south on foot. Things being as they were, Creek Neck River was barely more than a dribble down the center of the quickly developing town but Forrest didn't see it as a reason to visit Riverton. He was always happiest right there in Orton's Cove.

A historical note: academic topographers and hobbyist mapmakers have not even acknowledged Creek Neck River. The omission was less down to malice than seasonal comfort. The engineers and recorders of the necessary map boundaries and borders tended to work in the south during the cold months. By the time they made it far enough north to do Forrest Orton, or the people of Riverton any good, it was midsummer and the Creek Neck River was nearly dry.

Had someone come in March or April, when the thaw created an almost respectable stream, the tiny tributary might have ended up on a map, then people purchasing riverfront land would have altered the entire economy of that region of the country.

 Orton's Cove didn't even make it on a map until sometime in the middle of the 20th Century. But by that time people were passing through it on their way to the bigger, slicker cities. The lure of the small town's modest domesticities were passed over in preference of indoor plumbing and the convenience of a grocery store which was eventually replaced by a Wal-Mart. Not many people remembered when Orton's Cove was just one man at a crossroads.

In the days before the boom, a stagecoach from the East Coast made an incidental visit to Orton's Cove. The rickety wooden carriage held four Chinese women and one tough Irish broad who planned on opening up a house once they made it to the lawless plains out west.

One young woman, in particular, caught Orton's eye. She was young and slender and spoke little English. Forrest knew from the moment she stepped off that stagecoach, she was the angel God had sent for him.

"Her name is Maki, my friend," the tough Irish broad said. "Virginal."

Forrest didn't sleep a wink that night. When he felt he might be having impure thoughts, he turned to the Bible, reading passage after passage late into the night, smoking more than one extra pipe as he paced the floor quietly so as not to disturb his sleeping beauty.

In the early morning light, as the women were getting back into the stagecoach, Forrest stopped the tough, old Irish broad and lead her to the back of the coach.

The strong independent man begged the old broad to allow Maki to stay with him there in Orton's Cove. The leather-faced Mick placed her callused hands firmly on her hips until she saw Forrest Orton pull out a bundle of cash. Her beady eyes no longer saw Maki as anything more significant than a commodity she could profit from.

The first few bills off the roll loosened the old woman enough to encourage Forrest to peel a few more off. When all was said and done, Forrest paid $100 for his angel. They stood arm in arm and watched the stagecoach rattle off down the road.

Forrest swept his young, sweet lover up in his big strong arms—arms that had only known work up until this moment—and carried her into his own cabin where he laid her gently on the overstuffed mattress. He pulled back her layers and layers of lacy petticoats with one hand while he yanked his denim trousers down with the other.

The man who only knew solitude before this moment was about to step into a world the likes of which would keep him beguiled for the rest of his days. He threw his head back in ecstasy. He threw it back a second time. Then, like a drowning man, the third time was golden for him. Maki just smiled up at him and purred.

Afterward, he was only a little disappointed to learn he wasn't her first. Surely, he should have known that by her previous employment there might have been a man or two before him.

He was a little less than understanding—initially—when he learned she was already pregnant on the night he took her for the first time. Not only was she pregnant, but either the language barrier or her shame prevented her from disclosing who the baby's father was. Not that Forrest would or could have done anything about it, but he would have rather been prepared for what she might deliver.

When the baby boy was born, Forrest forgot all of his questions and lavished on the infant all the love a father would lavish on his own child. Maki asked that they call him John. Forrest agreed, and the next preacher who passed through the little settlement baptized baby John Orton.

Not long after young John was beginning to walk on his own, Maki found herself with child again. She and Forrest were both joyful this time because she was sure it was her husband's child. (Maki had hardly spoken to another man since John was born. This was not by Forrest's choice; Maki made the decision herself. She was as dedicated and loyal to Forrest as he was enamored and smitten with her.)

When the baby girl came prematurely, Forrest and Maki feared for her health. She was so small and weak that when a carpet-bagging doctor named Pepper, heading south to cure a paternity itch (*his own*), stopped at Orton's Cove for a night, Forrest and Maki convinced him to stay on until the baby was out of danger.

The delicate child was named Faith. She would spend her life smaller than the other children, almost fragile. She would spend her life cradled in God's loving hand.

The following spring, a large family asked Forrest if they could clear an area of his land and build a homestead. Forrest saw the opportunity to begin to expand his little piece of the country and make some money in the process.

Over the years, the town grew slowly and steadily. Each innovation brought a little more activity and ingenuity from the outside world into the sleepy little town. Men and women went off to college or to war only to return home bringing souvenirs from their travels. The ones that didn't return often sent postcards, which the first Old Man Kaucky regularly hung in the first apothecary.

The pictures of the men in dirty green uniforms standing around a jeep or a tank—smiling for the camera—puffing on little white cigarettes were treated with the greatest reverence. The young boys who emulated the men in those pictures had a certain fondness for the pictures the girls sent home from college. They cherished the creased snapshots of cheerleaders sailing through the air—short skirts waving like beautiful felt flags.

Most of the people who lived in Orton's Cove were born there and would die there. Even though it eventually was listed on the map there was little to recommend in visiting Orton's Cove, let alone settling down there.

Over time the town did achieve some note of fame when they fought tooth and nail to keep Wal-Mart on the other side of Riverton, sacrificing a few low-wage jobs for the sake of the local merchants. Eventually all of the small businesses in Riverton were shuttered and most of the town's citizens wore blue vests with desperate smiles plastered onto their faces.

Orton's Cove was a lot like its founder. The work ethic was strong. The bonds of loyalty were unshakable. When a hand was offered, it was open and welcoming not tight like a fist. The irony is that a town that was unquestionably the perfect place to raise a kid was so because there were just enough kids for the neighbors to keep an eye on. Very few were ever really aware of what a little slice of paradise Orton's Cove was.

"LIKE A SALVATION SHOW…"

The evening that followed Peter's public debut in front of the drugstore, as the sun was setting behind the trees that lined Whitley Avenue, Peter sat on the roof of his mother's house on the thin stretch of shingles, with his legs hanging over the gutter. This was where Peter came to think and to smoke cigarettes, and sometimes to dream about his future or think about life outside Orton's Cove—a life he never expected to know.

He sat alone on his perch watching the infrequent cars move down Hubley Street. Occasionally a head would appear—the neck craning—to see the house where the Fire-Boy lived. For the most part, though, Peter sat in the dusky silence. Most of Orton's Cove was home by now—certainly talking about what most of them had seen—wherever they were, they had finally deigned to leave Peter alone for a while.

Luther's voice echoed in Peter's head. "Show 'em your trick," he'd said. "Show 'em and they'll leave ya alone."

Peter had shown them all—everyone gathered out on the lawn and in the street in front of the pharmacy. He showed them his trick and they did leave him alone—completely alone. Now Peter was wishing he had never let them get away.

Solitude was something Peter had become accustomed to, but even he had to admit it felt kind of nice for that few minutes when he had all of the attention of the entire town.

Even Betty Croney looked at him differently now. He wasn't sure exactly how to take her glances but at least he was finally getting some of her attention.

Now he was back on his little roof and back to being plain old Peter Campbell. The only difference being that he was plain old Peter Campbell who could ignite his hands at will. He hoped that counted for something.

"Pssst..." he heard from below. " Peter."

The startled young man hung his head over the rusted gutter and looked down into his yard. There stood Reverend Crenshaw looking up at him. Next to the snake-oil salesman in the silk suit was a round balding man in a white linen suit and an even whiter, brighter felt fedora. They looked quite the suspicious pair lurking in Peter's mother's side yard at dusk.

"Peter," the Reverend continued. "This here is a friend of mine—a business associate—his name is Clayton McDaniel. Why don't you come down and meet him? He's gonna do you, and your mamma, a lot of good. He's on your side, Peter."

"Call me Mac, Son," the fat man wheezed. "My friends call me Mac."

"Good evening, Mr. McDaniel," Peter said, climbing in the window to his mother's bedroom. "I'll be down in a minute."

As Peter descended the stairs, he could hear the dialogue on the television show being censored. Every few seconds there was another beep. Peter never understood why his mother watched talk shows where they had to take out all the talking.

"These shouldn't be called 'talk' shows, Mom," he said. "They should be called 'beep' shows."

If she heard him, she gave no indication of it. He smiled to himself as he walked out into the last of the fading light.

"Son, you'd be doing me a favor if you called me by my given nickname," McDaniel said over his extended hand. "Please, call me *Mac*."

Peter took his thick hand and shook it heartily. The fat man's fearless demeanor and steady handshake drew Peter to him instantly. His suit was so white—and there was so much of it—McDaniel almost glowed, like a rotund angel or a southern chicken salesman.

The young man ignored the feeble hand of the preacher. The rejected preacher jammed his hand into the pocket of his silk pants and looked away. McDaniel noted the non-exchange of pleasantries.

"Peter, I'll get right down to brass tacks," McDaniel said. "Harland, here, told me about your affliction—if that's the word you wanna use. Fact of the matter is I think we shouldn't think about this in a negative way. This is a golden opportunity," he said. "Would you agree with me Peter? I mean, I think you have been given the license to print money. Are you with me?"

"Peter, what *Mac* is trying to say is..."

"I know what he's saying, Crenshaw. I ain't *completely* stupid."

"No, son, I don't believe you are. But I also don't believe you have the contacts or the wherewithal to take full advantage of your new—shall we say—gift?" McDaniel laughed aloud.

"What do you want?" Peter asked.

"Standard finder's fee," McDaniel answered. "Maybe a little more, but it'll come out of my cut. You don't have to worry about cutting this old rascal into a slice of your pie. Whyn't we go find your mamma and negotiate some kind of arrangement?"

"Not yet," Peter said. "This whole thing, the television lady and, well, everything has been a lot for her to take in one day. She's resting. I don't want to bother her. Let me sleep on it. Come back in the morning and if I decide I am going with you, we'll talk to her then. I ain't goin' anywhere tonight anyway."

"Why, that's fair enough," McDaniel said. He laughed again and his entire body bounced. "I'll come around in the morning to hammer out the deals. Will your sweet mother be making coffee or should I bring some?"

"She'll make coffee. Next to my dad, she makes the best I'm told," Peter said.

Peter turned to walk back into the house. He intended to leave the two men there to watch him walk away. Standing there in the side yard, the fat man in the ice cream suit and his skinny shadow made an amusing sight. Instead, Peter stopped, spun and looked Clayton McDaniel right in the eye.

"Mr. McDaniel," he started. "How do you take your coffee?"

McDaniel started to speak—then he stopped.

"I'm just curious is all," Peter said.

"Black, Peter," the fat man said positioning his hands on his fleshy waist. "Is there any other way?"

"No," Peter said. "No, there isn't," Peter replied looking long and hard at Crenshaw. "I was just wondering."

The two men walked past Peter. Crenshaw hardly looked at him especially when McDaniel offered that beefy hand and Peter shook it again. The two men slid into the biggest, whitest El Dorado Peter had ever seen. The car glided away from the curb and moved easily down Hubley Street. McDaniel honked once—quickly—before the car disappeared. The brake lights flashed at the corner before the car disappeared.

Peter thought about going back up onto the roof where he could think through the proposition. He had his mother to think of, his future, and his hands. There was money to be made –strike while the iron is hot—money that would buy him a nice car.

With a nice car—he might impress Betty Croney enough to get a date. One date could lead to another date—then to holding hands—maybe kissing.

He could buy his mother some new sewing machines, lots of shiny fabric, and books of patterns for boys' clothes. He got lost in a reverie that included gas operated lawn mowers and snow blowers. The whining of the engine and the patter of the snow were interrupted by the footfalls on the soft ground as they approached him.

"Pete," Luther said.

"Pete," Joellyn echoed.

"Hey y'all," Peter replied.

"Wanna go shoot some pool?" Luther asked.

"Not really," Peter said fishing for a cigarette.

"Milkshake?" Joellyn asked.

"No. Thanks," Peter answered still looking for his cigarettes.

"Smoke?" Luther asked extending his pack.

"Thanks," Peter said pulling one out and lighting it with a disposable lighter. He took a deep drag on it and held the smoke in his lungs for a moment before letting it out into the clean night air. He took another deep draw and smiled quietly at Joellyn and Luther.

"Was I right?" Luther asked. "Are they leaving you alone now?"

"What does it feel like?" Joellyn had to ask. "Your hands I mean. Does it hurt?"

"Not really like too much at all," Peter replied. "It's kind of like having your hands in warm wet mittens like Auntie Lilly used to knit for us. Kind of thick and heavy—maybe a little itchy but that's about it."

"Wow!" Joellyn stretched her body completely as she released the syllable into the air. Peter and Luther watched as her slender fingers mingled with the stars.

"So," Luther started. "Was that old Reverend Crenshaw out here just a minute ago? What'd that ol' *sumgun* want?"

"Him and this guy, Clayton McDaniel, want to make a traveling freak show out of me."

"Like a salvation show?" Joellyn asked. "I love a good salvation show."

Joellyn's daddy had been a preacher. At least that was what her mamma had always told her. He was off doin' the Lord's work.

❀

It was an early autumn tent revival they were holding out near Judah's Field. This was the mid-harvest revival so it was packed with hayseeds and farmhands praying like hell for a bumper crop.

It was muggier than usual considering the season. The air was heavy and moist. The tent was bursting at the seams. Striding purposefully back and forth in front of the congregation was a barrel-chested man with huge white teeth and slick black hair. His black silk suit shimmered in the soft light.

His wide swinging gait brought him back and forth across that sagging little plywood stage. From time to time, as if to draw emphasis on his point, the howling messenger of the word would stride down the center aisle and reach out to the hands and shoulders of the people lucky enough to have an aisle seat.

There were three boys behind him in matching purple robes leading the congregation in song. One boy waved and banged a tambourine. The next held a hymnal. The third just rolled his little head back on his shoulder and sang as if his life depended on it.

"And He walks with me and He talks with me."

In a way, their lives did depend on their performance because these three boys knew if they failed to ignite the crowd, they'd be back in the boxcars and the state-run homes. They could be replaced as easily as a flat tire on a bus.

Striding down the aisle, careful not to kick any dust up onto his silk suit, the man paused for a moment at the sixth row. He was looking at the faces of the women sitting shoulder to shoulder when he froze in his tracks. Every eye was on him as he moved down the aisle, which caused every mouth in the tent to fall silent except for Mr. Shimmins who was so overwhelmed by the spirit, he just kept singing as loud as his creaky voice would carry.

"And He walks with me and He talks with me."

When Mr. Shimmins realized he was the only one singing, he stopped and looked around at everyone. Even the three singers had become eerily silent.

He was grateful to see they were completely captivated by the big man with big teeth and slick hair.

The man had stopped at the sixth row for a better look at the stunning redhead who sat two seats in. Her face was barely visible under the wide brim of the white straw sun hat, but her face wasn't what had captivated him.

Her luxurious red hair spilling over her shoulders combined with the angle of her porcelain chin peeking out from under the hat were mesmerizing. Three stray freckles fought to be seen through the lace that concealed her perfect bosom. He couldn't even look any further for fear that his old heart might seize up and he wasn't about to die out here—not this way.

As he made his way back to the stage, he turned to look at her one more time. From this angle he could see more of her face which was stunning—to say the least. He was ready to end the service right there—send everyone home. This could be the most glorious night of his entire career. He knew this to be as true as the need to restrain himself until the time was right.

She would surely be worth the wait. The old fool never even thought of the possibility that she might rebuff him. He was already planning his post-coital serenading. He was thinking Air Supply. She looked like an easy sell for Air Supply.

She waved a white-gloved hand at him and smiled.

The Judah Fields Daily News called the rest of the service "the most inspiring sermon since Moses came down from the mountain. The man was so excited he almost forgot to pass the basket at the end."

The Judah Gazette said "His mind and soul seemed to be on the same mission—to lift our souls out of the tent to follow him into the Promised Land."

He had the Promised Land in mind but had no desire for company of any kind other than the woman with the straw hat and three freckles.

As the crowd thinned, the desperate man of the cloth stood at the entrance of the tent nervously shaking hands with the congregation. He had not even thought about their picnic. He had restrained himself enough to get through the service, who could ask any more of him?

Now he combed the crowds for flowery dresses and big straw hats, looking for the young woman with three stray freckles. She had a powerful impact on this man who thought he was impervious to things like emotions. He needn't have looked far as she never left her seat. She clearly wanted to be found as badly as he wanted to find her.

He walked across the tent slowly to where his vision of perfection sat. She was the only person in the tent who did not shed a drop of sweat that day. She sat there like a perfect porcelain doll waiting to be taken off the shelf.

When he saw her there, he ran to her and swept her up in his arms and whisked her out through the back flaps of the striped tent and right into the cluttered converted school bus that served as his office and his living quarters as well as his transportation.

His clothes were quickly reduced to a pile on the floor next to the bed he had fashioned out of mattresses in the back of the vehicle. The silk suit that he considered the trademark for his profession was discarded and forgotten about for the first time in his career. He rolled back on his shoulders and tugged his socks off while never taking his eyes off the woman.

The woman insisted on folding her clothes and hanging everything neatly over a chair. She knew what she had and what he wanted. She was completely aware of why she was there. She was not about to rush into anything. There would be time. There would be plenty of time.

The man watched achingly as the woman undressed deliberately and carefully arranged her clothes. He still couldn't believe what he was looking at. He thought—for a moment—about the Polaroid he kept for such occasions but she didn't seem the type and he didn't want to create any speed bumps on this magical journey. When she was finally and completely ready to be taken by him, he was far too ready for her.

Despite his restraint—or perhaps because of it—the entire union lasted less time than it did for the woman to undress. One short poke and one grunt and he was singing, "You're Every Woman in the World to Me."

Soon he was snoring. She had gotten what she came for so, as he slept, she slipped out into the darkness taking his worn Bible with her.

That spring, Joellyn was born. She never knew the man but, even as a child, she loved to thumb through the heavily outlined pages of that battered old black leather-bound book.

❀

"Are you going to do it?" Luther asked Peter. "You gonna take your show on the road?"

"I don't know," Peter responded. "I just want to finish high school and have a normal life and do normal stuff."

"You're not a normal guy anymore," Luther said. "You're… Well… You're…"

"You're Fire-boy," Joellyn said with a giggle. "You're Orton Cove's very own Fire-boy! I think that's just beautiful."

"I need to think," Peter said heading back toward the steps.

"You go ahead on and think, but while you're up there being all normal, remember how hard your mamma worked and did right by you. This is your chance to do right by her, Bro. You better take it," Luther said.

"G'night, Peter," Joellyn said. "Think about it. Think about doing something better for yourself. Just think about it."

Joellyn rested her hand on his shoulder letting that one sweet motion make her point.

"Yeah. G'night," Peter murmured closing the door behind him.

"I WAS WRONG"

The news of Peter Campbell and his incendiary hands was carried around the world on every wisp of smoke he produced that day. The barely believable story dropped into all the right—or wrong – ears, as the smoky carriers made their way across the sky.

The fresh new light of day brought the media wolverines to the front door of his mother's house. When the front yard was full, they scrambled around the sides of the house and into her backyard. Others set up base camp just outside the big glass foyer of Orton Central High School where they waited with uncountable cameras and large intrusive microphones.

Peter peeked through the curtains while he dialed Luther's number. The faces didn't register any emotion at all. They weren't angry or malicious as he imagined a mob would be. They also weren't happy to see him or particularly excited about being there in Orton's Cove. The only thing he knew for certain was they had come in numbers and would not be as easily appeased as yesterday's little crowd.

"I thought you said they would go away," Peter whispered into the phone when his cousin finally answered. Unbeknown to Peter, Luther was just sitting down to do an interview for a major network affiliate.

"I was wrong. Gotta go." Luther said quickly. He dropped the phone into the cradle. "Where do we begin?" he asked the beaming mustachioed host in the herringbone jacket.

Peter forced a large chunk of his own pride down his throat and thought about calling Reverend Crenshaw. Peter was sharp enough to know that he wasn't sharp enough to handle what was building up around him. Crenshaw and McDaniel would at least provide some type of buffer between Peter and the people trying to get to him.

He was dialing the number of the church when he heard a rustling on the roof of the bay window. He dropped the receiver back into the cradle and reached for something to put on. He wasn't going to be featured on the news in his underwear two days in a row.

Slipping into a pair of gray sweat pants, Peter walked toward the window that let out over the roof. As he eased the curtain back, the flash from the camera knocked him back against the wall. Instinctively he put his hands up in front of his face to try to protect himself. He had no idea what was happening, but the twin spheres of fire returned the flash sending the photographer tumbling off the roof. He hit the ground with a solid thud and his camera landed next to him with a crunch.

Meanwhile, the lace on the drapery began to smolder. Peter grabbed the smoking material and pulled it off the thin metal rods. The sight that greeted Peter made him swoon. He had no idea just how insane things were about to turn for him. Both sides and the middle of Hubley Street were lined with people all the way down to Whitley Avenue.

There were more people out there looking up at him than there were when the Orton Central Pirates were in contention for state championships in football. Peter placed his hand on the wall to support himself.

Interspersed throughout the crowd were news vans from every network that Peter had ever heard of and some that he hadn't. Photographers and videographers, and voyeurs of all stripes hung from heavy branches on the stronger trees. The more resourceful of these people rented prime space on porches and roofs belonging to Peter's neighbors.

People were already beginning to cash in on Peter's talent and there was nothing anyone could do about it.

Some of the younger people—Peter's classmates—waved homemade signs while the older people looked on the proceedings with the suspicion obligatory to small town people when news cameras and correspondents in expensive suits begin to show up uninvited.

Mr. Meyers told one of the reporters that he was friends with Elvis Presley. Everyone knew that Mr. Meyers had never met the rock 'n' roll singer, but they all agreed his stories were harmless. And if Mr. Meyers got a cup of coffee out of it from a naïve reporter, what was the harm?

Peter remained still with his hand against the wall. With every passing second, the sensations continued to overwhelm him. When he was finally able to move, he staggered back to the window that opened directly onto Hubley Street. If what he had seen before was devastating, it had hardly prepared him for what was going on below in the street.

There amid the circus atmosphere was his mother. She was selling T-shirts. He noticed they weren't shirts with his likeness on them. They were his *actual* t-shirts. They were the shirts he wore to school and to play ball and they were *his clothes.*

Strangers were throwing their money at Alice Campbell faster than she could collect it. She was jamming it into the pocket of her brown smock—the one with the pink and yellow flowers.

Next to her stood Crenshaw. He was beaming like a beacon in the night protecting the lost and lonely souls—and the cash in Peter's mother's pockets. Clayton McDaniel stood behind Crenshaw. The money signs were in his eyes but Peter could see McDaniel wasn't comfortable with the higgledy-piggledy way the whole thing was being handled.

The T-shirts gone, Alice walked back into the house and began scouring the front room for something else she might be able to sell—anything that belonged to Peter. He had made it downstairs by then. He grabbed his denim jacket—the one with the motorcycle patches on it—just in time. Alice had placed a hand on it. She tugged a little but when their eyes met, she let go.

"What are you doin, Mom?" he asked slipping an arm into the sleeve of the jacket.

"This is for your college fund, Peter," she said.

With stealth neither knew she possessed, Peter's mother grabbed his Metallica jersey off the chair next to where he was standing. By the time he realized what she had grabbed, it was lost in the folds of her frock. She blew him a kiss and exited the front door.

"I ain't goin' to no dang college," he yelled but Alice didn't hear him. She was too busy haggling over the price of the never worn Orton Central baseball jersey. The buyer—a short, bespectacled 14-year-old—was locked at $15. Alice would take no less than $20. This was surely a seller's market.

Peter made it as far as the door. The inevitable roar was as embarrassing as it was loud. Peter realized, in that moment, he did not miss the attention after all.

"There he is!" a young woman's voice called out.

"He looks...different," yelled the chubby kid from his gym class.

"We was always best of friends," yelled a kid that Peter had never seen before.

Peter forgot all about his clothes as he backpedaled into the house and slammed the door. The house fairly shook as the decibel level got louder. The people in the back and in the side yard began chanting, "Peter Peter PETER!" The mob began to push toward the porch. Everyone was jostling for a better position. They clearly wanted to know exactly why they were cheering.

Peter fell into a chair and pulled out one of his mother's cigarettes from the pack on the end table. He lit it and took a deep drag. He held the smoke in his lungs for a moment and exhaled slowly. Exasperated, the young man reached for the television clicker. He needed to get his mind off the wave of humanity that was churning outside the door.

The major networks were running more personality pieces on him this morning. Mrs. Humphries, his homeroom teacher for the past three years, who couldn't have picked him out of a crowd, was being interviewed for the CBS cameras.

"Peter has always been a poet. He is sensitive and sweet. It is no surprise to me he has been given this great gift. He has always had a spiritual side and now he has the opportunity to use it."

Peter couldn't hit the red rubber button on the remote control fast enough.

But then he saw his cousin, Luther, on NBC.

"You see, Gerry. Can I call you *Gerry?* Peter and me, we are not just cousins. We're like best friends, too. Hell, I'm the one who told him to show everyone his trick. I mean it ain't a trick, but it ain't something everyone around here can do either." Luther rattled on, a satisfied glint in his eye.

Peter clicked the red rubber button again.

Coach Van Der Wooten was on ABC. Peter had never known the coach—never spoken to the coach. Coach Van Der Wooten taught Industrial Arts and coached girls' track. He knew even less about Peter than Mrs. Humphries, but that didn't stop the square-jawed man with the impressively large forehead from taking his time in front of a rolling camera.

"He was a disciplined athlete. He always gave a hundred percent and put the team's needs before his own. America needs more young boys like Peter Canfield."

The red rubber button again—faster.

Peter couldn't understand what they were saying on the Spanish station but his likeness, an old high school yearbook photo, was enlarged and placed behind the anchor's head. His crooked grimace and his stubborn cowlick were magnified and being broadcast into the homes of millions of Spanish speaking people all over the world.

The distraction tactic definitely wasn't working, not that Peter had expected it to. He pulled himself up out of the chair and began pacing back and forth across the carpet, stopping occasionally to pull back the curtain and check on the crowd but he never had the heart to go face the crowd. He just walked across the room, then back to the window again.

Admittedly, there was a side of Peter Campbell that wanted to bask in the glow of the adulation. He almost relished having the power to command fire with his bare hands. This was the time to make the world see Peter Campbell was someone—not just anyone but someone.

There was also the other side of him—a more realistic side—that was scared. It was actually well past scared, but Peter's limited vocabulary often restricted his articulation of his range of emotions. An idea of what he needed to do was beginning to form for him, like a fireball.

He picked up the phone and dialed the operator. His mother would, doubtlessly be angry with him for not using the phone book, but he figured he could splurge this one time. He asked for the numbers for CNN and William Morris.

"Do you mean the cigarette company, or the talent agency?" the voice squawked.

"Both." he said.

"Well, I can only give you two numbers today, Sir," she squeaked. "If you want CNN, then you have to choose between the cigarette company and the agency."

"The agency," he muttered pulling a red plastic pen out of the Flintstones jelly-jar-cum-pencil-holder.

The William Morris Agency seemed right. He remembered seeing the name in an Entertainment Weekly magazine he found in Luther's bathroom the day of the chili eating contest.

"Hold for the number please."

His mother came in through the door wearing a white T-shirt with his likeness printed on the front. She modeled it for him as if it was a new Easter dress from Korvette's department store.

The picture on the back was of two open hands with fire rising from the palms. She continued to spin around slowly and she smiled at her son. "Jack Harvey made them."

Peter tried to return the smile but the best he could do was a grimace. He returned his attention to the telephone.

"I got one for you," his mother said sweetly, draping the crisp white T-shirt over his shoulder. "They were only $10!"

He dropped the phone and spun around, grabbing the shirt from his shoulder and throwing it on the couch.

"You paid money for shirts with my picture on 'em?" he screamed.

"Actually, I got 'em at cost," she said. "He also has a design with the burning cloth plant in the pot. That one costs $15.00."

Peter shoved past his mother as he stormed out the front door and right into the mouth of the waiting crowd. The enormous cheer was stifled by the look of rage that had crossed his otherwise dull face. The people at the sides and out back were slower to because they hadn't seen his face, but they figured if the people in the front were stifled, then they should probably be stifled too.

Peter stood—rooted to the weathered wood of the old porch beneath his feet. He stood face to face with faces that didn't even see him yesterday. These people couldn't have picked him out of a crowd 24 hours ago. Now they couldn't seem to get enough of him.

"MARMADUKE KILLED HIMSELF"

There was only one other time in his short life that Peter had known such overwhelming anger. And, like then, he wasn't sure if he would be able to control it now.

❀

It was early spring, a time when most of the kids at Orton Elementary school were focused on the annual science fair. Peter was nine years old, in the fourth grade and looking forward to the fair as much as anyone.

Throughout the academic year, the children were encouraged to keep extensive journals of the experiments they had conducted in the classroom. They charted everything from calculating weight to dissecting a mealworm. The remedial students worked with magnets— the advanced students with Bunsen burners.

On the first day back from spring break, the students would each sit down with Mrs. Harlow and discuss what their project would be for the spring fair. The grade for the year depended heavily on the project each student presented at the fair, in addition to the few tests and quizzes they had taken throughout the semester.

That semester, Peter decided that he was going to present something about electricity because he had found he enjoyed taking radios apart.

He couldn't put them back together, which wasn't always pleasant, especially when his father wanted to listen to National Public Radio while he tended the garden. Poor Peter just couldn't resist the way all the little diodes and transistors resembled a small city of the future.

Another contributing factor to Peter's curiosity about electricity came from the time when his younger cousin, Sam, tried to take a Lite-Brite set away from Peter while he was playing with it. Sam tugged fiercely at the cord but Peter wouldn't give up.

Sam decided if he couldn't play with the Lite-Brite then no one could and he chomped down on the cord. Had he realized that biting a cord that was plugged into the wall socket would have had such cosmetically devastating results, he probably would not have done it.

In that flash—Sam's face resembled the insane blur that they had both seen on highway billboards advertising Krazy Kaplan's fireworks superstores. Peter never got to finish his red-white-and-blue tug boat—but this was admittedly much better.

The doctors did what they could, but Sam's mouth will always be soldered shut on the left side. He grew up a very quiet and patient boy. Peter never forgot the sight of his little cousin's hair standing up, and the smell of the burning flesh.

Over spring break, Peter scribbled in his notebook just how he might demonstrate the power of electricity. He didn't want to do some lame pull-a-lever-turn-on-a-bulb trick. The young man wanted to impress his friends and earn the highest grade possible.

After several designs and re-designs, Peter asked his mother for help.

"I wish your father was here today," she sighed. "You could do a nice horticulture project together."

"Mom," Peter said slowly. "I want to do my project on electricity."

"I'm sorry, Petie-boy, maybe your Uncle Marv can help you."

"Forget it," Peter said. He really didn't want to work on his project with Uncle Marv. Peter sulked up the stairs and into his room thinking about Uncle Marv sitting alone in his Ford Pinto outside the school at lunch time every day.

That night he lay in bed with the window open listening to the sounds of nature as they harmoniously combined with the rural din. He fell asleep thinking about currents and voltage and when he woke up he scribbled something from a dream he'd had. The plan, it seemed, was right there in front of him.

He was going to make an electricity safety chart. The chart would light up with colored bulbs based on varying degrees of danger in any given electric situation. He was filled with a certain sadness that he hadn't thought of the idea in time to save his cousin Sam years of embarrassment, but if his illuminated safety chart could save one kid, it would be worth it.

Peter found a grimy old ball-peen hammer, a box of rusty nails, and an old wooden onion bin in the garage. He used the material to create a box to house the circuits. The top of the box was lined with the sockets the little bulbs would go in. The circuits for the sockets led to a series of doorbells he had mounted onto a chunk of a two-by-four.

Peter drew one large diagram outlining the flow of the electrical currents. He plastered this into the center of a bigger sign, which was lined with the light bulbs that would illuminate when he pressed the corresponding doorbell.

Mrs. Harlow loved the idea, which was all the motivation Peter needed. He spent every waking hour in the basement of his house creating his masterpiece. The uneven rhythm of her son's hammering became Alice's lullaby that spring.

On the day of the fair, Peter packed his creation—his labor of love—into the trunk of his mother's car while she put on her make-up and straightened the seams of her hose.

He was so excited he could barely contain himself. The young inventor had already sweated through his undershirt and the moisture was making its way through his white school shirt. His mother told him they wouldn't be leaving for school until he ate something—anything—at least a grilled cheese sandwich. He folded it in half and choked it down while she twittered about between the kitchen and her bedroom touching her hair and pulling at her dress where it was snug around her hips. She was as excited as he was.

When they walked into the front door of the school, the smell of education clung heavy in the air. Young bodies scurried back and forth setting up projects, performing last minute adjustments, and posing for pictures with relatives and friends. Older bodies clutched flimsy paper cups of coffee and watched the kids—offering advice or encouragement.

Peter and his mother looked at the wonderful and exciting things that lay before them there in the room. Everyone was there in their finest clothes putting their best scientific foot forward.

Luther had done his annual piece on capillary action.

The Palmer twins had created a dizzying three-dimensional optical illusion.

There was a half-finished model of the human body (organs and all) someone had left unguarded by the door.

Peter carried his project over to the table that had been pre-assigned to him. He wasn't as close to Luther as he would have liked but he didn't have a choice in the matter. He carefully set the project on the table. The sweat was beginning to show down the middle of his back and under his arms.

He swiped his hand across the table to remove any dust or debris that may have settled there. His mother came behind him and dropped a cloth that she had made next to the circuit box. The material was metallic—it was on sale. She always bought extra metallic material when it went on sale. This piece was nice. It was shiny like a spacesuit from a science fiction movie in the 1950s.

Peter held up one edge of the project while his mother slid the tablecloth across the table. Then he held up the other end so that she could cover the rest of the table.

They straightened the edges together before placing the project directly in the middle of the table. Peter stepped around to the back of the box and uncoiled the thick, black electrical cord. He took two more steps back to the little bone colored outlet on the wall and plugged his creation in.

He began to attach the wires to the external connections and tested each of the doorbells. He seemed almost surprised himself whenever one of them worked. He smiled long and hard while he worked until his face cramped and long after he connected the final circuit.

"Peter, your face is going to freeze like that," his mother said. But she too was smiling. She had never seen her boy so focused and so ready to claim his place in the annals of the school science fair. One lone tear trickled down her cheek as she thought about how proud Peter's father should have been if he were standing here.

The last doorbell Peter touched activated the little bell he had placed on the side of the sign last night. The soft tone that emanated from the bell startled a few of the passersby, but the subtle illuminations calmed their concern and turned it to curiosity.

Meanwhile, across the aisle, Robin Butler was preparing the maze he had created to show how a mouse might find its cheese. The only discrepancy in this plan was that Robin's "mouse" was his pet rat Marmaduke, and Marmaduke was pretty well trained to run mazes, to sit pretty, to crawl up the bed post of Robin's sister's bed, inevitably bringing forth a shriek that would delight Robin and his friends.

The maze itself was too small for Marmaduke, but no one figured there would be any problem. Robin was performing a test run and so he rang the hand-held bell. Marmaduke pushed open the gate and ran through the maze as he was trained to do, if only occasionally getting stuck in a tighter section of the maze.

When the rodent had completed the maze, he got a small piece of cheese wrapped in bacon. This wasn't so much an experiment, but a trick the boy had taught the rat. And the rat was happy to perform.

The boy got a grade. The rat got the treat. Everybody wins.

As Mrs. Harlow entered the room, accompanied by Principal Jacobs and some of the other teachers, everyone fell silent. Each nervous student and proud parent watched eagerly to see which table the group of educators would visit first. They were equally concerned with how long they stayed at each exhibit.

The group made their first stop at the table opposite Peter. The sweat stains became visible from across the room but his mother told him not to worry.

"You're a shoo-in for a perfect grade." Alice rubbed Peter's head and added, "My little Alva Edison."

Peter wanted to believe her but he just wasn't sure. He knew that

Mrs. Harlow liked him fine but Principal Jacobs was another story entirely.

Principal Jacobs didn't like the boys who lived in the town proper. They were too common for him—too unwashed. He preferred the boys who lived "up the hill", the ones who had soft hands and impeccable manners.

Principal Jacobs was the oldest living bachelor in Orton's Cove. With his pinched face and his haughty air, it was no wonder.

When Mrs. Harlow and her group stopped at Robin Butler's exhibit, they mistakenly expected a small mouse to come burrowing through the maze. No one was prepared for the hulking rat, when Marmaduke came barreling out the shoot in search of his culinary treat.

Mrs. Grossman from Home Economics nearly did a back flip as the feral-faced creature careened off the walls of the too-small maze. She finally fainted, as Marmaduke entered the second half of the maze, sending her frightened body crashing toward the floor.

Mr. Van Der Wooten from Industrial Arts tried to catch her, but in bending down, his forehead hit the edge of the table, which upended Robin Butler's maze, catapulting Marmaduke in an arc across the room while the awestruck children and their families moved quickly away. No one took his or her eyes off the flying rodent.

Most of the children were shrieking and fighting to get under tables. Peter—for his part—was so aware of his own project and the dripping sweat pooling at the top of his trousers and the base of his back that he hadn't realized there was a rat flying through the air with no accessible landing gear.

When Marmaduke hit the floor, it was with a scratchy thud. This development sent the children scrambling. Some of the women followed Mrs. Grossman's path directly to the worn linoleum floor. The smart men caught their wives mid-swoon. Robin, Luther, and some of the boys began to crawl around on the floor looking for Marmaduke.

"Mom," Peter whispered, still quite immune to his environment and focused on his own project. "I have a secret surprise at the end of the presentation. I added it last night."

Just then, Marmaduke jumped onto the table and bumped the button that Peter had attached to the bell that, in all the confusion, sounded like the bell at the end of the maze.

Marmaduke looked for his food, but there wasn't a morsel in sight. Peter stared at the rodent. The rodent glared at Peter with malice in his beady little eyes.

"Do it again, Honey," the proud—albeit confused—mother cooed.

It was Marmaduke that hit the button a second time. The bell sounded and Marmaduke stared at Peter. When Peter did not present a treat, Marmaduke bit through the thin plastic casing around the wires that carried the electrical current from the wall to the bell.

Peter screamed, not in fear, but in anguish as the sizzling rodent was again sent into the air in a smoldering flash of light that began at the base of Peter's own project. The rat careened off of a terra cotta tiled rafter beam and landed at Peter's feet. It bounced once—but without enthusiasm.

Standing over the dead pet, Peter felt no remorse at all. He just knew he wanted this to go away. He wanted this moment in his life to be over. He wanted to pack the remains of his project into his mother's car, go home, and start the whole day again.

When Robin Butler approached him, things deteriorated.

"You killed Marmaduke," Robin said evenly.

"Marmaduke killed himself," Peter responded with the same tone.

"Listen SPAZ!" Robin said grabbing Peter by the damp collar of his white shirt. "You killed Marmaduke! You gotta pay for that!"

"I SAID, 'MARMADUKE KILLED HIMSELF', OR DIDN'T YOU HEAR ME?" Peter yelled back. His eyes flared and a small vein bulged on his sweaty forehead.

Peter grabbed Robin Butler's collar. Robin, who was not used to anyone yelling back at him, released Peter's shirt and began to back away.

"YOUR RAT KILLED MY PROJECT!" Peter screamed.

He screamed it evenly and repeatedly.

Peter's first punch caught Robin Butler under his right eye. The second grazed his ear. Peter didn't have much talent for this kind of thing. He tried to throw a third punch, but by that time, he was too tired.

He let go of Robin Butler's shirt and walked slowly out of the gym and then out of the school. Alice made apologies for Peter as she scurried after him, tugging on the seams of her dress.

It took five days to get the smell of fried rat out of the gym.

❀

Peter stared at the mob that had gathered on his own front lawn. There were people standing in the street in front of the house. There were people sitting on branches of the trees. There were even those who were standing on his neighbors' cars for a better view. Someone finally yelled, "Fire Boy!"

Peter walked directly into the crowd.

He wasn't sure what he was going to do. Somehow, he found himself transported back to that fourth grade science fair. Only now he was the rat in a cage—but he had no intention of staying locked up, or following a maze. Not now—not ever—and especially not for a nibble of cheese wrapped in bacon.

"He doesn't look any different," someone whispered.

"He kind of looks mad," said someone else.

"Who is he?" asked the very small, very old lady who was wearing his old Foghat shirt.

When Peter saw the Reverend Crenshaw, he could feel that little vein begin to bulge in his forehead. He hadn't trained for this. He surely wasn't equipped to deal with what was going on around him.

That was when Peter saw Betty Croney's brother, Scottie, selling swatches of material from her scorched sweater. Many of the people in the crowd were wearing the T-shirts Jack Harvey had made or Peter's own clothes that they had bought from Alice. He missed his Knight Rider T-shirt, but was happy to see Melanie Anderson give the car a certain three-dimensional appearance.

Peter turned and staggered back to the porch.

Reverend Crenshaw and McDaniel squeezed through the crowd. They wound up on the porch. The man in black and the man in white stood behind Peter on either side of him.

McDaniel held his lapels and beamed at the mob like a proud poppa. Crenshaw dug his thumbs into his belt like John Wayne did in the movies.

Three chubby boys in camouflage cargo shorts and Star Wars T-shirts were standing on the plot of land where Peter's father had planted flowers. It aggravated Peter.

"This is my land, my father's land," Peter shouted. "All-y'all are trespassin'. If you don't go home, I'm going to make you wish you did."

The crowd gasped collectively. The two men who flanked Peter couldn't have been more pleased. He was turning out to be a regular fire-and-brimstoner. Given some tutelage and the proper motivation, this kid was a license to print money. The two men knew it—they just had to harness it.

"Mr. Harvey, you give my mother every penny of profit you made offa them shirts. You understand me?" Peter continued to shout. "That's me on them shirts and she made me first so she gets the money. You understand that Mr. Harvey?"

Mr. Harvey was a wiry man in tight jeans and faded flannel. He offered the large wad of wrinkled bills up toward Alice who was coming off the porch to meet him. She tucked the money into the large pockets of her housecoat.

Mr. Harvey moved quickly away from the porch, back to the safety of the street. He had another pocket with a small handful of bills that he had kept for himself. He considered it commission. There was maybe enough for a carton of cigarettes and a quart of beer. When Mrs. Harvey found it in his pocket on laundry day, she considered it a tip for doing his laundry.

"Now all y'all git, go on home," Peter yelled. He turned around and, stepping in between McDaniel and Crenshaw, the young man walked toward the door of his house.

The crowd began to disperse—hesitantly. Peter stopped and turned around again. "Betty Croney can stay," he called out, surprising the crowd and himself.

He walked into the house.

Crenshaw and McDaniel tried to follow him in, but Peter's short pause and the look in his eyes quickly discouraged them. They contented themselves by sitting on the porch watching the crowd mill about on the lawn. As the men discussed the situation, neither believed that it was over.

Both men had been around enough to know that everyone has a price. They just needed to figure out what Peter Campbell's price tag might be. Whatever Peter's price, it would surely be worth it when all was said and done.

Betty Croney walked warily up the rickety wooden stairs and into the house followed closely by Mrs. Campbell. The older woman paused to glance at the preacher briefly.

"You two must be hungry," she said to Peter and Betty, as if they had just arrived home from school. "Should I make some grilled cheese sandwiches?"

"That'd be nice Mom," Peter said softly.

"Thanks, Ma'am," Betty said, offering Peter the handful of money her brother Scott had earned selling sweater remnants to the others.

"Keep it," Peter told her. "Use it to buy you a new sweater."

"Thanks, Peter," she replied. "I'll do that. But can you answer one question for me?"

"Sure, Betty," he said putting a cigarette into his mouth. He lowered himself onto the couch. He offered Betty a cigarette. She declined. He took the one out of his mouth and stuck it back into the pack.

"Why am I here, Peter? Why me?"

"We gotta talk, Betty."

"SOUNDS LIKE A PLAN"

Always the dutiful mother, Alice set two plates with steaming grilled cheese sandwiches on the table in front of Betty and Peter and returned to the refrigerator for a pitcher of ice cold milk.

On Alice's last trip to the table, she folded and placed napkins printed with pastel flowers and filled two frosted glasses she had pulled out of the freezer. Then she vanished noiselessly like an indentured servant.

"I'm flattered you asked me in, Peter," Betty started. "But I can honestly say I'm not quite sure why you did." She looked at the grilled cheese masterpieces in front of her, but her upbringing forced her to nibble not devour.

"Neither am I, Betty. Neither am I," the frightened boy responded gingerly running the crust from the toasted bread across his lips.

He finally took a deep bite.

He sat back in the chair chewing slowly. The hot cheese was burning the inside of his mouth, but he never let on. He simply sipped his milk and sat looking at Betty. In a way he hoped that she might have some kind of answer for what had been happening to his quiet little world.

One minute Peter was following Betty into the movie theater. The next, she was aflame and he was the center of attention. He was *just* bright enough to know that he would need someone as bright as Betty to make some sense out of everything that had happened in the last 48 hours.

⚛

Betty Croney was the kind of girl every boy in Orton's Cove wanted to spend his every waking hour with. There was nothing the boys—and some men—wouldn't do for a little of her lovely attention.

Betty's family moved to Orton's Cove when she was in the fourth grade, just a few short years before her fluffy angora sweaters began to take on new dimensions. For her part, Betty never saw what all the fuss was about. Most who knew her agreed that her humility might be one of the reasons they loved her.

She had blue-black hair and sharp green eyes, which blended exquisitely with her flawless white—nearly transparent—skin. Even at the youngest age, she was striking while most of her peers where simply cute.

As Betty continued to mature, the women in the town were constantly poking their husbands in the ribs for gawking at her when they went to Jolly's for pizza. Betty never noticed. She set the pizza on the table, offered a winning smile, and collected the bill when they left. It was a job, not a social club.

She easily made three times what the other girls made in tips and every penny went into her college fund, except for a modest allowance she permitted herself to spend at Old Man Kaucky's, where she liked to buy movie magazines, and occasionally splurge on a new lipstick.

Jolly's was Betty's first and only job. She started working at the pizzeria when she was fifteen. She worked there throughout high school except for the three-week stretch every summer which she spent in Arizona at Blue Skies Cheerleading Camp. Betty was planning to be in the Human Pyramid of Leadership program next summer. The leadership program was a gateway to college scholarships.

Peter was convinced he was in love with Betty. He knew that in his heart this was the only true love he had ever known. When he found himself behind her in line at the cinema, then sitting next to her at the movies, he thought it was luck. He was sure there was a reason God put the only empty seat in the theater next to Betty.

Historically, Betty had only a vague memory of Peter. In the memory, Peter was with a friend of hers, but she didn't really realize the two young men were in actuality the same until she saw him on the porch that morning.

The movie theater spectacle was actually their first physical encounter beyond the daily passing of each other in the halls of Orton Central High School. Peter relished these chance meetings, although if you looked closely at the tardy slips for certain classes, they looked less and less like chance meetings. Peter deliberately found himself standing in the hall long after the classroom bells had rung.

Betty wasn't one of those obnoxious rich girls from up on "the hill". She just ran in different circles to Peter. She was a cheerleader. She sang in the girls' choir, and was the editor of "O", the school's literary magazine. Peter's social circle consisted of Luther and Joellyn. Their activities included walking along the railroad tracks and reading comic books at Old Man Kaucky's place.

As small as Orton's Cove and the school were, the sad truth is that no one had really noticed Peter Campbell until two nights ago. He just fitted in so completely, everyone overlooked him.

❀

"Do you remember when Lulu Anne Burns and me were supposed to be dating?" Peter asked Betty softly. Lunch done, he pulled out his pack of cigarettes.

"Well," Betty started. There was a small dab of cheese in the corner of her mouth.

Peter offered Betty a cigarette. She declined. He sheepishly slid one into his mouth and lit it, relishing how adult he felt with it hanging out of his lips. He puffed tenderly.

"Thanks," she said as he set the napkin next to his on the table.

If either of them had known Peter's mother had her ear pressed against the door, they would have changed the subject quickly. She was struggling to hold her breath and Peter and Betty had no idea she was listening.

"I know. I know. Lulu Anne lost a bet," Peter said. "But when the bet was over she dumped me. She would pass me in the halls at school and bury her face in her book or something. She wouldn't even look at me. Can you imagine how that felt?"

"I remember feeling bad about that, Peter. Honest I did!"

"Did you know I have never actually kissed a girl in my entire life?" Peter pressed on. "I didn't kiss Lulu Anne. I never even kissed Marcia Black. Every dang boy who has ever passed through this town has kissed Marcia Black. Every one but me."

"I'm sorry, Peter, but why are you telling me this now?"

That's when they heard Mrs. Campbell sniffle. She ran into the bathroom, slamming the door and turned the radio on.

"Dang," Peter whispered. He wanted to wipe the cheese from the corner of Betty's mouth with his napkin.

Betty interrupted this thought.

"Is she all right? Do you want to check on her?"

"She'll be fine," Peter said. "There's just a lot of stuff going on right now."

"Peter, you still haven't told me why you called me in," Betty said.

She gave up nibbling on her sandwich and began to destroy it. She ripped through the sandwich with a hunger that made Peter hesitate for a moment.

"I'm thinking about leaving the Cove," Peter said.

Betty stopped eating and wiped her mouth. "Really?" she said.

Peter continued. "Reverend Crenshaw and Mr. McDaniel are talking about putting me on some type of church tent revival circuit. They want me to share my *gift*. They think I'll be able to reach the masses with my fire. They think the fire will change things for people."

"What do you think?" Betty asked.

"I don't really know," came the timid response.

Peter looked toward the bathroom door. The tinny music from the little radio obscured any sound his mother might have been making. He took a long drag on the cigarette.

"You would be doing the Lord's work then?" she asked.

"More than likely I'll be doing Mr. McDaniel's and Reverend Crenshaw's work. They say that they'll be sending the money home to my mother," he said, exhaling smoke.

"And you believe them?" Betty asked.

"I just don't know," Peter said.

"And?" Betty said.

"I guess I wanted your opinion, is all," Peter said, spinning the cigarette between his fingers. "I can't figure this stuff out so well for myself. I was hoping that you would help me make sense of the whole thing."

"Me?" Betty said. "I'm not sure what I can do."

"What do you think I should do?" Peter said. "Be honest."

Had Peter been alert, or at least quick enough to grasp the obvious, he would have noticed the flicker of betrayal in Betty's eyes. Not betrayal of Peter, but of her own image. In Peter, Betty now saw an opportunity to shake up people's perception of her. Peter—his hands—might be the best chance she would ever have.

For a moment, she pictured herself riding around the country without the pressure of being Betty Croney. She could visit exotic places and meet interesting people. She could just relax and be.

She had no problem with the idea of working the tent revival circuit. This type of experience would far outweigh the Human Pyramid of Leadership program at the Blue Skies Cheerleading camp, of which she was beginning to get a little tired anyway.

Betty Croney was anxious to do the exact thing no one in Orton's Cove would have expected from her, to hit the road and never look back—at least not until summer was over. She could forget about Jolly's Pizza and all the assumed trappings of being Betty Croney. She could see some of the country and experience life on her own terms—without her parents, without her friends, without expectations.

It was right there and then she decided that if Peter Campbell and his incendiary hands were the ticket to something new and unpredictable, then so be it. She could think of worse ways to get out of town.

There was Jemma Plumber who got herself into some trouble with the Magalia brothers. Then there was Alex Feldman, who realized he was just more comfortable in women's shoes—and clothes? He moved out east and no one had seen or heard from him since.

Betty was not about to do anything irreversible. She estimated that this was the safest way to get while the getting was good. She would come back and finish high school in the fall. She would surely go on to college and do all of the things she was expected to do. This was her chance to sample a taste of life outside of Orton's Cove.

She sat for a minute and looked at the boy sitting across from her. The cigarette dangling from his lips made him look older than he was. The cigarette was not attractive, but the warmth that she knew lived inside of those hands—and that heart—was more than enough for her.

"I'll go with you," she said.

The very thought of it—now given breath—excited and terrified them both.

"You'll go?" Peter stammered. The cigarette dropped from his mouth into his lap. He jumped up and grabbed it.

"I'll go with you," Betty repeated. "I'm sure that I could be lots of help to you when you start to get homesick. I can also help keep an eye on the books to make sure that your mother gets the money that's due her. What was I going to do this summer anyway? Learn the proper execution of a full-lay-out twist? This seems so much more important."

"You'd do that for me?" he asked sweetly. Then he added, "Why?"

"I can honestly say that I don't know why but I'm here and there is a reason that you invited me in."

Peter was flush. The cigarette was broken and he had a new hole in his pants, but these things were far from the words he needed to say.

"Before today—before my hands—I wouldn't have had the nerve to say 'Hello' to you."

"Well," Betty said, realizing she had a hand in this game now too. "Something has obviously changed in you. I'm glad you started my sweater on fire. I'm glad you invited me in."

Her smile made Peter light-headed. "Call Mr. McDaniel and the Reverend," Betty said. "Tell them we'll be ready to leave when they are. That will give me time to go home and convince my parents to let me go. I'll be ready when you are."

"Sounds like a plan," Peter said. He stood up to walk Betty to the door.

Neither of them saw his mother standing in the bathroom doorway. She was rubbing the tears out of her eyes and smiling so richly and so completely that she began to cry again.

"The tears," Alice said to no one. "They are not sad tears. Not this time."

"SO YOU BROUGHT A LITTLE"

Mr. McDaniel navigated his shiny Eldorado up to the curb in front of Peter's house. Betty and Peter were sitting on the front steps. On Peter's left was a battered canvas duffel bag stuffed with some of his clothes (whatever his mother hadn't sold) and a couple of books, family classics mostly. He also had his father's soft bristle hair brush even though most of the bristles were long gone. Then—of course—he carried his extra Captain America tooth brush, and his bubble-gum flavored toothpaste.

To Betty's right sat a small cosmetics case and two matching faux-denim suitcases. They were embroidered with flowers trailing up and down each side. *Betty* was embroidered just above the handle on each bag.

Her bag was as organized as her life—everything having a place and everything in that place, including *days-of-the-week panties*—in order. She brought her collection of romance books, with a picture of her parents marking the page where she would continue reading once they were on the road.

To Betty, Mr. McDaniel was a rotund figure who reminded her of how Santa Claus might look to the children in Texas. He was clad all in white with bulging, shiny red cheeks.

Reverend Crenshaw—the slender character in black—was someone she was familiar with but never comfortable around. The two men pulled themselves out of the car as if synchronized with the opening pop of the trunk. They ambled toward the house laughing out loud.

McDaniel's laughter was hearty and honest—if only driven by opportunity. Crenshaw, on the other hand, wheezed suspiciously. He cupped a hand over his mouth and wiped something on his trousers.

"You ready to go, son?" McDaniel asked.

Peter and Betty stood up. McDaniel slapped Peter on the back with great gusto. The sound was like a wooden bat on a fresh baseball. Betty winced. Peter barely seemed to notice.

Reverend Crenshaw stepped around the kids and up onto the porch. He checked his hair in the reflection in the glass pane in the center of the door before he rang the bell.

Peter's mother came and opened the big wooden door, but she wouldn't open the screen door, not even for Crenshaw—not this evening. She tried to speak but her voice cracked, making both of them that much more uncomfortable. There was no way that he could understand how she felt—what was going on in her tired old heart, seeing her son on the steps with his bag packed and his back to the house. Crenshaw had never been a parent. She wasn't sure if he *ever* loved anyone enough to feel like this. Alice Campbell was overwhelmed by the sad realization that she wouldn't be seeing her precious baby for a while, if ever again.

"You know you can come along, Alice," Crenshaw said. He knew she wouldn't go.

She hesitated for a moment as if she was weighing up the option of leaving her home and the Orton Central Marching Band and all the little girls at the dance academy behind.

The flicker of doubt that danced across her eyes gave Crenshaw a start for a moment. But then Alice Campbell closed the door completely, without so much as a word, and disappeared down the long dark hallway into the confines of her home. Crenshaw exhaled heavily. He turned and walked back toward Peter, Betty, and McDaniel.

"Let me help you with these bags," Crenshaw told Peter as he grabbed Betty's suitcases.

Peter was left to wrestle with his own duffel bag. He stopped and looked back at the house, hoping to catch his mother's face in a window. He was sure he saw her at the one on the second floor. Whether she was there or not, he waved, weakly, at the house. He began to walk toward the car. Peter gazed around himself at the now-quiet street. There was no one around.

Peter was the only one who noticed how quiet things were. Still, he had trouble believing that just a few hours earlier this same street was packed with people who wanted to see him do his trick. Peter imagined they were all home now, grilling burgers and hot dogs and listening to old Louis Prima records.

"So you brought you a *little something-something*," Crenshaw arranged Betty's bags in the trunk. He never took his eyes off of Betty, specifically her new sweater.

"My friend," Peter said. "She's coming along to look after me."

"Is that what they're calling it these days?" Crenshaw laughed and slapped Peter on the back. "If that's your story, we'll stick to it."

As they rolled past Old Man Kaucky's place, Betty and Peter waved at the aged proprietor. He, in turn, looked up from his polishing cloth and waved back at them. The old man had a sadness about him, but not because Peter owed him money. He was sad for what he feared the two men might turn Peter into. He wouldn't have worried about most of the boys in Orton's Cove, but to Old Man Kaucky, Peter was someone who needed to be worried about.

"LET HIM EAT"

The Valley View Motel offered very little view of the valley, or anything else for that matter. The scenic vista from the back door offered a barren brick wall with a rusted basketball rim that drooped sadly. The whole thing swayed with the slightest breeze. The ground around the hoop had at one time been painted with a free throw stripe and lane markings but decades of neglect and vegetation made the area appear unusable for any type of regulation basketball game.

The window on the side of the building was pressed up tightly against Snuff's Bar-N-Grill. Various birds occupied the higher levels of what precious little space there was between the buildings. Betty shuddered to think about what was housed on the lower levels. She sure wasn't in Orton's Cove anymore.

Neither Crenshaw nor McDaniel was enthusiastic about spending the money for the extra rooms. They weren't even convinced an extra room was *completely* necessary. They acquiesced though, because Betty would demand privacy, which was expected of a young girl. There might be some merit in that.

McDaniel and Crenshaw also knew *they* would appreciate the privacy if—by chance—they made any new *friends* at Snuff's or at the Glitter Gulch directly across the street from the motel.

They agreed dinner would be the first order of business. There were plans to be made, duties to delegate. The men knew they worked better on a full stomach. This visit to the restaurant would also give them a chance to explore their immediate surroundings and get a feel for the local community. Crenshaw knew the value of spending money in little towns in order to raise attendance at any future revivals. His collar—and his demeanor—resulted in the occasional complimentary meal. Crenshaw came to expect it as a valuable benefit. He came to expect much as valuable benefits and took them where he found them.

The Glitter Gulch—with its ceramic deer our front and its twinkling tiny Italian lights around the frames of windows— appeared to be the perfect place to begin the process of introducing the sleepy burg to their little party. Sitting on the patio would afford them a view of the local traffic, which Crenshaw always looked at in terms of a potential audience. The patio was also a prime spot for allowing the audience a sneak preview of Peter and—if he could tempt the Gods—a small sneak preview of what was to come.

The four hungry travelers entered the cozy little lobby with a flourish that embarrassed Peter but emboldened Betty. She spun herself around like a child in a fun house making certain she didn't miss one crocheted owl or etching of a reindeer in its nature habitat that covered every open space on the walls.

"Four, for the patio," the Reverend said to the blonde hostess.

To Betty, the hostess's skirt was too tight and the buttons on her blouse were too strained, but the men in her entourage leered approvingly. McDaniel pretended to be interested in the food options. Crenshaw was doing his best to uphold a laudable worldview. Betty caught Peter looking at the hostess's sway as she led them to their table.

Peter saw Betty watching him watch the hostess and was embarrassed. He couldn't raise his eyes to look at Betty. He just stared at his worn brown shoes and wished he could go back in time thirty seconds and do it over again.

"How's this?" the hostess asked, pointing four menus at a clean, glass table on the patio.

"This will be perfect," Crenshaw told her as he lowered himself into the chair facing the door they had just entered through. This way he could watch the young woman exit back through it on her way into the restaurant. This was the kind of *traffic* he was interested in.

"Thank you," she smiled too sweetly. "Annie will be your waitress this evening. She'll be right with you. Can I get you anything while you're waiting?"

It was hard to believe the wait would be long. The patio, as well as the rest of the restaurant, was empty at the time. It was either too early or too late, but there weren't very many cars passing by either. The place was a ghost town.

"I'm all right," Peter whispered.

"Can I have a Cherry Coke?" Betty asked.

"Coffee," McDaniel said. "Black."

"I'll have coffee as well," the Reverend said. "With cream and sugar."

"Thanks," the hostess said, repeating their orders.

She turned and was gone.

"Well, this is exciting," Betty chirped.

"Yeah," Peter said, with less enthusiasm.

"We might as well enjoy a good meal," McDaniel said. "Tomorrow morning, you are going to meet Lester. He's driving the gear up from Kentucky. He'll meet us here."

"Who's Lester?" Peter asked.

Lester was McDaniel's right hand man when it came to setting things up and breaking them down. As a child, Lester was a wildly popular child tent attraction. He had the misfortune of growing up ugly, which minimized the time he could spend in front of an audience. The very attributes that made him a cute little boy, made him relatively unsightly as a man.

Lester had grown used to the gypsy lifestyle and, rather than give it up, he continued to work for McDaniel as a stage-manager-cum-roadie. It was a great deal for the both of them. Lester made a decent living and got to travel, and McDaniel got a reliable assistant—one who couldn't fight for the spotlight.

❀

When Lester Pringle was four years old his family realized he had the gift. He could save a barnyard animal's life with the touch of his hand and he could sing "How Great Thou Art" before he could even talk. He also saved a boy who had a stalk of wheat lodged in his throat simply by touching the boy on the neck.

This was also the time the Pringle family realized their dirt farm was careening into bankruptcy. When McDaniel offered to take the boy off their hands and give them money, Mr. Pringle had no trouble packing his boy's little cardboard suitcase with the promise that, in exchange for the boy, their farm could be saved.

Now nearly three decades later, the dirt farm was paid off, Lester's sister Annie Lou had a college degree and Mr. Pringle finally got some dentures that were actually made for him. His first two sets were hand-me-downs from a departed uncle.

❀

"Lester will handle the tent and the chairs and all of the paperwork needed to obtain a permit, if the town requires it."

"What can I do?" Crenshaw cut in. He was already being edged out and didn't like playing second fiddle.

"What'll I do?" Betty asked.

"You'll not worry too much," McDaniel laughed. "Maybe a nature hike, or a little shopping. Until we get closer to show time, you can relax, or help Peter relax. When the service gets under way, we'll be expecting you to help."

Annie, the waitress, showed up with a black plastic tray full of coffee cups and the necessary condiments. There was a large sweating glass of red-tinted cola with two cherries floating at the top, just above the ice.

She wasn't as pretty as the hostess but she wasn't exactly tough on the eyes either. Her hips were spreading a little and her eyes drooped a bit in the corners. Long hours on her feet and the steady temptation of the bread baskets were beginning to take their toll on her.

If only out of habit, Crenshaw sized-up Annie as she set the coffee cups in front of them and arranged the red-tinted cola in front of Betty. Annie pulled a little green pad from the pocket of her clean black apron and asked if the team was ready to order.

"We'll take four of whatever is on special," Crenshaw said.

"Meatloaf with gravy and mashed potatoes for everyone?" Annie asked.

"That will be just fine," McDaniel said.

They all watched in silence as Annie walked away. Crenshaw cleared his throat while McDaniel wiped his brow as they turned their attention back to the table.

"Lester may or may not be bringing Viola Rogers with him," McDaniel continued.

Peter watched as Crenshaw poured a generous amount of cream into his coffee. He looked over at McDaniel who was sipping his coffee—black. Peter's gaze fell to his feet. He couldn't help thinking this was a mistake—and he missed his mother. He didn't think he was strong enough to go through with this. He didn't look up again until Betty spoke.

"Who is Viola Rogers?" Betty asked between sips of her sticky sweet soda.

"They call her the *Tennessee Twister,* Miss Betty," Reverend Crenshaw responded. "She's a singer. She can really get a crowd fired up and on their feet when she wants to. And can she ever dance! Why she dances around the room like the angels were Fred and she were Ginger."

"Fred?" Peter asked. "Ginger? Who are all these people?"

"Never mind, *son,* before your time," McDaniel laughed. "Let's just say that our young Viola will have the congregation in a right fit and fixin' to fly by the time you take the stage!" McDaniel slapped

Peter on the back and smiled, nodding.

"Did you say 'young'?" Betty asked.

"She'll be fourteen come October," McDaniel added quickly.

"Isn't she kind of young to be doing this type of thing?" Betty asked.

"The Lord don't ask for no identification cards, Miss Betty," Reverend Crenshaw laughed. "He don't care how old you are. If you speak the good word, then the good word will be spoken. Amen."

"Amen," McDaniel echoed.

Annie returned with a large black plastic tray, which held four plates of steaming food.

She set the tray on a table behind Peter. One by one, the white porcelain plates holding slabs of meatloaf and mounds of mashed potatoes were carried from the tray to the table where the hungry quartet was waiting.

"That was fast," Peter said. "Thank you."

"The specials usually are, Honey," Annie replied setting the last plate down. "Can I get you all anything else?"

"I think we're fine for now," Betty said.

"I'll take a warm up on the coffee," McDaniel said.

"I guess I'll have a root beer," Peter said.

Peter used the last piece of bread to wipe up the last spot of gravy from the white porcelain plate in front of him. He would have stopped there, but he noticed Betty had hardly touched her dinner. She removed his plate and replaced it with her own the way couples who have been married for a long time do.

Peter reached across her, picked up the half-eaten dinner roll, and dug in wordlessly. The two older men ate at a healthy, leisurely pace as they watched the glass door to see who was coming in and out. Crenshaw watched the hostess grab her purse and a light sweater and head toward the door.

"The restroom's this way?" he asked no one in particular as he made a hasty beeline for the door.

When Crenshaw was out of earshot, McDaniel chuckled softly

to himself. He wiped his mouth with the white linen napkin and reached for a cigar in the expensive leather case in the inside pocket of his coat.

"That's got to be the only preacher I ever met with a forked tongue," he said. "Well almost the only one."

He laughed quietly to himself.

Peter didn't respond to the comment, he continued eating. Betty and McDaniel watched the silent production play out—almost as if for their amusement—just beyond the glass door. Crenshaw was all smiles and affected hand gesticulations as he tried to hypnotize the young hostess.

For her part, she just listened, giggled, and snapped her gum, but she would not be buying any of the snake oil Crenshaw was offering. Not even a drop. It was only when Crenshaw pointed toward their table, at Peter particularly, that the young boy looked up from his plate.

"He better not," McDaniel started, but he stopped when Crenshaw and the hostess crossed the threshold and made their way to the table.

"Peter," Crenshaw beamed. "I have been telling Elba..."

"Elmira," the hostess interrupted.

"That's what I meant." Crenshaw forced a laugh. "I've been telling Elmira about you. She would like to see first-hand and up-close what you can do."

"I'm eating, *Reverend*," Peter said between forks full of food.

Peter tried to conceal his disdain for Crenshaw but the task was getting increasingly more difficult. He promised his mother to remember his manners, but Crenshaw didn't make keeping his word easy.

"Let him eat Harland," McDaniel said.

"Yes," Betty chimed in. "Let him eat."

"I guess your friends want the boy to eat," Elmira said.

"I'm not a dang boy, ma'am," Peter shot back, quickly correcting his delivery.

"I didn't mean anything by it," she said.

"Peter, don't you think you're being rude?" Crenshaw asked.

"No more rude than you interrupting my dang dinner," Peter replied.

He immediately regretted the tone. It was as if his mamma was there and she'd heard him.

Elmira was getting noticeably uncomfortable. She shifted her weight from high-heeled foot to high-heeled foot. "I've got to go, Reverend," she said quietly, and turned to leave.

"Can I call on you tomorrow for lunch?" the dejected Crenshaw asked.

"I don't think that would be a good idea," Elmira said.

She made her way quickly to the door and through the restaurant. The young woman was barely out the front door when she broke into an uncontrollable gale of laughter. That had to be the second worst attempt at getting into her panties she had ever experienced.

"A boy who could throw fire, indeed!" she muttered under her breath.

She decided the phony preacher would have been more amusing, or at least more original than Helmut, the last groper who tried to slide his hand up her skirt. Now Helmut was a real winner.

❀

Helmut was an odd old man with an accent. She only remembered his name because by the third martini she was calling him Helmet. He told her he was a photographer and he would like to do a study on her. It would have to be nude of course, but it was purely in the interests of art.

Helmut asked Elmira to come to the house on the lake he was renting and sit for him one evening. He promised there would be no funny business. He would pay her for her time and he would make a print for her of the image she liked best.

He was only planning to stay in the country through the autumn. He would be going back to Germany in September. The old guy was cute—

probably harmless—but she wasn't about to pose naked for some old guy she didn't even know.

"Helmut," she said to herself. "What the hell kind of name is that?"

She was shaking her head and giggling to herself at the idiocy of men, as she descended the wooden stairs of the restaurant. As she pulled her keys out of her purse, the bright flash of light exploded behind her.

⚘

"I DIDN'T DO IT ON PURPOSE"

Charlie, the frantic manager of the Glitter Gulch, descended on the table quickly with a shiny red fire extinguisher in his arms. Thinking a *saganaki* presentation had gone awry, or perhaps a tipped candle had caused the burst of flame, he was filled with apologies and grace.

"I assure you this type of thing never happens on my watch," he blurted out. "You just sit there and relax. I'll take care of this."

Charlie stopped talking for a moment and looked at Peter. The fire extinguisher fell to his side as his arms went limp. He stood, slack jawed, the black rubber horn of the fire extinguisher now pointing toward the ground. He couldn't take his eyes off Peter, who was standing over the table—his palms still flickering with a gentle blue flame.

"What's going on here?" Charlie finally uttered.

No one said a word. They were all looking at Peter, who was looking at the manager. Annie and a couple of people who worked in the kitchen came through the door and stood in a huddle—close enough to see, but far enough from any certain danger—whispering to each other.

One of the men was wearing a sweaty red bandana twisted around his neck. He held the largest knife Peter had ever seen. The other men, while dressed similarly, were unarmed.

"I'm sorry," Peter said. "Sometimes, it just...happens."

"I have to ask you again," the manager started, as he set the fire extinguisher on the ground without taking his eyes off Peter. "What happened here?"

Crenshaw stretched his neck as if to show off the clerical collar he was wearing and said, "Please *do not* upset the boy. We'll pay for anything we might have damaged, but I insist that you and the rest of your staff remain calm."

"Calm," Charlie mumbled to himself. He wasn't quite sure how to handle this—not with his staff watching.

He finally lowered the fire extinguisher gently to the patio and jammed his hands into his pockets. When he looked up, they were still watching him closely.

"Eladio," Charlie said. "Take the extinguisher back to the kitchen. The rest of you get back to work!"

No one moved.

"*NOW!*" he shouted.

The crew shuffled back into the kitchen, leaving the manager and Annie alone to face the four guests, who weren't even looking at each other now.

Annie approached the table cautiously. "Does that hurt?" she asked.

"Not really," Peter said.

"Will there be anything else?"

"I'm awfully sorry," Peter added. "I'm still learning how to control my dang…"

"No need to apologize," Annie said. "Would you like some dessert?"

"Do you have any sherbet?" Peter asked. "I would really love some sherbet with chocolate sauce on it."

"Right away," Annie said. "Can I get anything for anyone else?"

"Betty?" McDaniel asked.

"No, thank you," Betty replied.

"Reverend?" McDaniel asked.

"Oban, rocks, twist," he replied.

"You want single malt on the rocks?" McDaniel laughed.

"Oban, rocks, twist," Crenshaw repeated.

"I'll take whatever Zin Port you are serving this evening," McDaniel said.

He continued to look at Crenshaw and shake his head slowly. His amused smile lingered longer than necessary.

"Very good," Annie said.

The men watched her walk away. Betty stared at the stars.

"Impressive," Crenshaw said to Peter. "Why couldn't you do that when Elba was here?"

"Elmira," Betty interrupted.

"Whatever," Crenshaw shot back at her.

"I didn't do it on purpose," Peter said.

"What do you mean?" McDaniel asked. If this was a new development, he needed to be able to strike pre-emptively. He just assumed Peter could control the pyrotechnics.

"I'm not sure how it happened that time," Peter said. "I thought I could control it or I at least knew how to make it happen. That time, it just happened before I could stop it."

"Like it has a mind of its own?" Betty offered.

"Yeah, something like that." Peter hesitated when he spoke.

He was grateful she was along. She understood him better than anyone did.

"Well, we have to figure out a way to not let it happen by accident again. We don't want to be giving away anything that we can charge for," the Reverend said.

This earned him a steely glare from Peter.

"I am more concerned with the safety factor." Betty was being helpful again, which softened Peter but was wasted on the Reverend. "I wouldn't want to see Peter hurt."

McDaniel was caught somewhere between Peter's current predicament and Crenshaw's alcohol abuse. He was sure that Peter would figure out how to get his hands under control eventually. He was just puzzled over the idea of a single malt scotch on the rocks—with a twist.

"Here we go," Annie said setting the drinks down in front of the two men and the little silver dish with the brightly colored ice cream in front of Peter. The oranges and the greens were muted by the shiny streaks of chocolate sauce.

"Thanks," Peter said.

She set the black billfold containing the check between the two older men. Crenshaw pretended not to see it. McDaniel picked it up and opened it. He read the little ticket and set it back down in front of Crenshaw.

Annie watched the exchange with a weak smile.

"Harland?" McDaniel said.

"Clayton?" Crenshaw answered.

"What exactly is it you're waiting for, Harland?"

"I didn't know it was on me," he said.

"Right, you wouldn't have ordered Oban if you thought you were paying," McDaniel said with a laugh.

"I always…" Crenshaw started.

"When you travel with Clayton McDaniel, there are two restaurant rules; the first is you take turns paying the bill if you are over 18-years old. The second rule is that the tip starts at twenty percent."

"The kid eats free?" Crenshaw asked.

"The kids eat free."

"And twenty percent? To start?"

"It's only fair, Harland," he said.

McDaniel lowered his voice so that Annie couldn't hear the next part.

"That twenty percent comes back to us before we leave town. You play 'em cheap here; who do you think is going to make the trek out to the tent? Don't worry I got this one—Oban and all."

McDaniel took the billfold with the check back and began to pull money out of his own billfold. Crenshaw slipped a *Sacred Heart* money clip out of his jacket and began to slide a few bills from it.

"With tax the bill comes out to $52.18," McDaniel said.

"What's the bill before tax," Crenshaw asked. "I always tip on the net."

"You'll leave $10.60 and be done with it," McDaniel said.

Peter and Betty exchanged embarrassed glances. Peter was not used to eating in restaurants so he was unsure what Crenshaw was quibbling about. Betty's time spent at Jolly's made her appreciative of a good tip.

"That's 20% of $53," Crenshaw griped.

"Perfect. Then we're agreed," McDaniel said.

"I don't have the sixty cents," Crenshaw said, mistaking this shortage of change for a victory.

"Make it $11," McDaniel said. "See, I knew you were generous in spirit."

Crenshaw gave McDaniel eleven dollars. McDaniel slipped the cash into the billfold with the rest of the money and handed it back to Annie.

"Do we need change?" Annie asked staring Crenshaw down.

"We're good," Crenshaw replied. "Thank you for a marvelous dinner."

"Everything was really delicious," Betty chimed in.

"Sorry about my dang hands," Peter said.

"Think nothing of it, Sugar," Annie said.

She brushed a soft hand across Peter's shoulder as she made her way back into the dining room.

Peter shivered. Betty smiled. McDaniel sipped his wine. Harland Crenshaw shifted uneasily in his chair.

"IT SOUNDS LIKE CHURCH"

Even in the womb, Viola was a restless soul. She couldn't sit still for more than a few minutes. She kicked. She stretched. She fought to get out as early as possible. This was the only discomfort she ever caused her mother.

No one was surprised when she burst into the world long before her mother was ready for her. Viola made her grand entrance like a tiny, shiny pink doll. It would be several months before she actually grew into a full-sized infant.

By the time Viola was eighteen months old, she was talking in full sentences and moving about the home she shared with her mother, Fiona. She displayed grace unknown to a child of that age. And it wasn't long before Viola was spinning and dancing around the cozy, little house in her tiny diaper, singing along to her mother's Loretta Lynn records. Her long, curly red hair reflected the sun that made its way through the gaps in the curtains. She illuminated the room as much as the sun did.

Soon enough—perhaps too soon for Fiona—Viola developed into a strikingly beautiful young girl. To be quite honest, she was a wonder to behold. Her face—framed by a mane of curly red hair— had grown delicate and pale by the tender age of twelve. Her rapidly developing body had sweet, strong curves where there should have been straight-aways of bone and sinew.

Her body was unquestionably vintage Bettie Page while her

mind was still somewhere between tea parties and hopscotch. This delicate balance—this unabated beauty—is what attracted people like Clayton McDaniel to people like Viola.

❀

Clayton McDaniel found Viola, quite by accident, when she was just ten years old. He was chasing the sunrise after a night of cards and bourbon when the need for coffee and gasoline landed him in a one-horse town a few years after the horse had got wise and left.

He knew he should've waited another 20 minutes before getting off the highway. They'd be setting up the tents and they'd have hot coffee brewing, but something made him exit one town early and pull into the gas station at the bottom of the exit ramp.

As he pumped the gas he heard a choir singing from the small wooden church across the street. He looked up to heaven for a minute— before turning his attention back to the church.

He paid for his gas and took his cup of coffee across the street and up the rickety steps of the Friendship Church. Viola was singing in the Friendship Church Choir. The stunning, young beauty sounded as much like an angel as she looked like one.

This detail was not overlooked by any of the men of the Parish of the Friendship Church. As word got out about this attractive new alto, attendance at the noon service increased gradually, but noticeably. Necks craned and heads bobbed when the angelic Viola walked out of the back room with the rest of the choir and then again when she sang.

Reverend Shekels was convinced his stirring and passionate sermons were the reason for the increased attendance. Mrs. Prince—the choir director—was convinced the crowd was growing due to the popularity of her heavenly choir. She was closer to the truth, but the fact of the matter was, it wasn't the choir's singing that dragged the men out of their easy chairs on Sunday mornings as much as it was young Viola in her shimmery silver choir robe.

As the service ended that sunny, summer Sunday morning, McDaniel watched which parent young Viola ran to. As luck would have it, she went right to the back of the church where a woman sat alone. McDaniel's heart skipped briefly when he saw Fiona Rogers. It was easy for him to see where the child got her stunning looks. He took a breath and then it was right back to business as usual.

"Good Afternoon, Ma'am," he said as he approached Fiona with one hand extended. "My name is Clayton McDaniel. You can call me Mac. All my friends call me Mac."

"Good afternoon, Mr. McDaniel," the woman replied shaking his hand firmly.

"I'm sorry, I didn't catch your name," he smiled, easing into the lacquered pew next to her.

"I didn't offer it, Mr. McDaniel," she said.

"Please, call me Mac," he said.

Clayton McDaniel made a vow to himself at that moment—in that pew—that if he got through this, he would find himself someone slicker who could talk to the ladies without breaking into a world class sweat. This was too much for his tired old heart anymore.

Viola approached her mother as she spoke with the stranger. Her face was aglow and curious. She had never seen her mother speak to strange men. Now she was—and in the church—and the man was wearing a hat. Viola knew enough to keep her mouth shut and her ears open.

Fiona stood up and stepped into the aisle and unzipped Viola's robe. Viola slipped out of the robe and then folded it. McDaniel was obvious about not being obvious. The woman wrapped a white angora sweater over her child's small shoulders.

"You sing very well, young lady," he said.

Viola wasn't sure if she should respond. She looked to her mother for confirmation. Her mother nodded. It was okay to speak her mind. "My mamma says that you shouldn't wear your hat in church, Mister." This was Viola's response.

The large-faced man blushed as he removed his hat and set it on the seat next to him.

"What can I do for you, sir?" Fiona asked.

"I was just wondering if you and your lovely daughter might be my guests to the tent revival meeting tonight. We got some really nice singers, too. And lemonade."

"I don't think so," Fiona said.

"Well, if you change your mind," McDaniel said standing up and slipping his hat back on his head.

Viola looked up at him. Her sweet little face became a reminder to him he was still in a church and he shouldn't be wearing his hat. He slipped it back off his head and walked toward the door. The bait was set.

"If you change your mind, we'll be in Mosley Field out on the old two-lane just off the highway—up the road apiece," McDaniel said without turning around. "We'd really like to see you there. It will be an evening of joy and music and discovery."

He exited gracefully, only stopping to turn and wink at the little child he knew was watching him. She tried to wink back but it looked more like a squint or a fragile sneeze.

"Mamma," Viola said. "What's a tent revival meeting?"

"It's a place where people go and sing and pray and then put all of their money into a basket. Then that man and his friends take all of the money and leave town."

"It sounds like church, except the leaving town part," Viola said. "I'd like to go."

"We'll see," Fiona said. Viola knew what that meant.

She shrugged her angora-clad shoulders and they headed toward the back door of the church.

Walking home, Viola and Fiona began to see the signs tacked to all of the lampposts and street signs. They looked innocent enough to Viola, but Fiona knew better. She had seen these things come and go over the years and she had no interest in wasting her entire evening in a mosquito-filled tent filled with sweaty people jumping around and carrying on.

She turned the corner on Pilster Street and was heading toward her house when she saw Lester. Had she any idea who he was, or why he was there, she would have put her head down and kept walking.

"Ma'am," Lester stammered. "My name is Lester—Lester Pringle and I'm here to tell you about our revival meeting tonight."

The young man was so hopelessly caught between adorable child and ugly adult, that Fiona was overcome by her maternal instincts. There was nothing dishonest or planned about this guy. He just was.

By the time Lester was done rattling and stammering, she knew she would be watching the sun set over Mosley field that night.

Lester graciously declined the invitation to walk Fiona and Viola home and share a glass of ginger ale. This, coupled with the fact that his gaze on Viola was truly innocent, only strengthened her resolve to see him that night. She watched him walk away.

"Who was that?" Viola asked.

"That's Lester," Fiona answered. "Do you still want to go to that revival meeting?"

"We get to go?" Viola shrieked.

"I don't see why not," Fiona said.

When Lester was out of sight, Fiona took Viola's hand and led her up the street and into the house.

This tender interaction did not escape the watchful eye of Clayton McDaniel. Not much ever did.

As the sun was just beginning to make its descent behind the barn, Fiona dressed Viola in her other Sunday dress. Then she dressed herself in her Saturday night dress and she put on just enough make-up to highlight her prominent cheekbones, but not so much that anyone would notice.

They drove out to Mosley Field where they were among the first to arrive. While Fiona scanned the crowd for Lester, McDaniel scanned the crowd for her. Viola just scanned the crowd.

The tent began to fill and the buzz of excitement crackled through the rows of wooden chairs. The pretty hats dotted the landscape between the Brill-Creamed scalps and the perfect flattops. Crenshaw paced out back, puffing on cigarettes and slicking his hair into place.

The low-wattage light bulbs tethered to the tent stakes dimmed as Harry Hillborn appeared in a tiny pool of light on the makeshift stage.

This year's preacher was a spindly man in a black suit and a wide-brimmed hat who moved with uneasy grace.

McDaniel took his customary place at the stage left flap—just outside the tent. Blue—the mute stagehand—took his place behind the portable spotlight.

"Brothers... Sisters..." Hillborn started.

Blue hit a button on an oversized boom box and taped organ music filled the air.

"We have come here tonight, of our own free will, to offer our praise and grace to our Lord and our Savior. Can I get a witness?"

Ricky Donner, who normally wouldn't speak unless spoken to, became a witness that day. He jumped up and pumped his fist in the air. Next he spun around awkwardly and kicked up his feet.

"Amen!" he screamed.

"We have come here tonight to witness, in front of family and community, to sing His praise. Can I get a witness?"

Everyone looked to Ricky, but he had regained his control.

Sadie Sundstrand whispered "Amen."

Sadie was just grateful to be out of the house for a couple of hours. She left her husband Lars with four large pizzas and their three large sons.

"Now I am going to bring out a young man," Hillborn continued. "I am going to bring a young man out here tonight who is going to take you down that garden path where you'll walk close with Him. You will walk closer with Him. Are you ready to walk down that garden path?"

The excitement began to build. Hillborn knew Lester would steal his thunder—but not before he whipped the crowd into a frenzy. He still wasn't sure why the kid was back in the show—but he had learned to not question McDaniel—just to do his job and collect his money.

For now Hillborn would have to increase the tension to a pre-ordained level before McDaniel would let the show go on. By the time Lester made it to the stage, the congregation would have to be ready to throw their wallets at him.

"I was once hesitant like you—I was once a non-believer," Hillborn began. "It's true! I thought I needed to be shown—I thought I had to be given a sign. Then one night—one sad night in the pit of Satan's' belly—I heard this boy sing and I was lifted up and delivered to a place where even Satan fears. This boy's voice shielded me from Satan like he wants to shield you tonight."

"Are you ready to offer your voices to the Heavens and take that closer walk with him? Can I get a witness? CAN I GET A WITNESS?"

People shouted "Amen" and "Hallelujah" at the top of their lungs as Hillborn stepped off the stage and gave McDaniel the signal. All went quiet as Lester entered the tent from the side, a beat-up guitar with a string for a strap slung over his shoulder. Blue turned down the main overhead lights and flooded Lester with a soft light.

He hit the first chord looking out at the faces. They could see him clearly but, mercifully, he couldn't see them. Their reaction was strangely unsettling, just less than inviting, except, of course, for Fiona. She never took her eyes off Lester as he strummed the chords repeatedly.

Then with a voice so rich and pure, he began to sing: "I walk to the garden alone. Where the dew is still on the roses. And the joy we share— as we tarry there. No other has ever known."

The stuffy tent went silent save for his remarkable voice. Gone were the stuttering and stammering of a man unsure—uncomfortable in his own skin. Lester sang with a voice that completely defied the face from which it poured. It was as if his voice was capable of bringing the angels down into the tent. There was no one in attendance that evening that didn't have their heart softened by the brilliance of Lester's voice, his words, his gentle playing.

By the end of the third verse, the ones who weren't crying were singing along. Fiona was doing both while Viola stood on her chair and sang the loudest. She looked up to heaven and sang her little heart out. Lester, it seemed, knew all of her favorite songs.

With each new song, the crowd sang louder. Tambourines materialized, courtesy of Blue, who never stopped running the lights. People were clapping loudly. It was during the sixth or seventh chorus of "Swing Low Sweet Chariot" that Viola jumped from her chair and ran to where Lester stood on the stage.

Fiona did not attempt to stop her child from singing and dancing. It was as if she were guided by celestial beings on gossamer wings. Lester stopped playing for a moment in which he shouted "Praise the Lord!"

His sentiment was echoed by everyone with a view of the beautiful child who was dancing as if filled by the Holy Spirit.

For the rest of the evening, the audience yelled and sang and clapped until their hands stung and their throats were dry. Lester's fingers were raw from playing the guitar, but Viola was not ready to stop dancing and the congregation was not about ready to let her stop. The tent was filled with the Lord. It would be impolite to stop the entertainment now.

When Lester could no longer play, he simply set the guitar down and walked to the back of the tent. He joined Fiona at her seat and let Viola continue to dance and sing. No one seemed to notice Lester anymore.

The little red-haired beauty had transfixed the congregation.

It was as if she were made for revival. Viola sang "In Times Like These" and "I Believe in Miracles" and other songs that she had forgotten until this moment.

Here, in the presence of the Lord, she was able to sing every word and chorus of every song she had ever learned. It was only when exhaustion overtook her that the crowd also realized how late it had become. Viola wavered twice before McDaniel stepped onto the stage and swept her up with as much effort as lifting a new down pillow. He carried the child off the stage and delivered her to her mother's loving arms.

Lester figured this was his cue. He left Fiona's side and prepared the baskets off stage. When the baskets were ready, he handed one to the person on the end of each row. Then he walked to the back of the tent to wait patiently to receive the baskets.

As the baskets were passed around, McDaniel went back to the front, to the spotlight. He spoke gently.

"We understand that some of you are less fortunate than others, and we understand if you can't give much." McDaniel positioned himself for the punch line. "We can only ask that you don't take anything out of the basket as it makes its way past you." There were a few chuckles in the audience, but the point was received and the baskets continued to make their way toward Lester.

When the collection was complete, Hillborn returned. He wiped the sweat from his brow as McDaniel disappeared again into the folds of the tent flaps. Hillborn paused for a moment before he asked everyone to bow their heads for a moment of silent prayer. The only sound that could be heard was the change jingling in the baskets as Lester and Blue brought them out the back door of the tent and walked them over to McDaniel's car.

"Heavenly father, we ask that you come into this tent tonight and fill our souls with your love," Hillborn started.

Every time he paused, he opened his eyes to take in the attentive crowd and reminded himself that this preacher routine was going a lot better than he thought it would. One minute he's playing Claudius in a community theater production of "Hamlet" and the next thing he's traveling the country doing his fire and brimstone act. Nice work—when you can get it.

"May your love and generosity continue to grow in your hearts and remain a great and powerful influence on us as we go through every day of our life. We welcome the opportunity to share your love with others."

"Amen," someone whispered.

"That's right, brother, Amen. Now go in peace," Hillborn told the congregation. "There'll be coffee and pound cake available in the morning with our sunrise service for those of you who can make it back out here tomorrow. I'd love to see each one of you. Go in peace and may God go with you."

The crowd was slow to exit the tent. Some were physically exhausted while others wanted to stop and thank McDaniel personally for bringing such an inspiring revival to their neck of the woods. No one seemed to notice exactly how little he did.

There were some versions of the revival where he included more musical acts, particularly the morning services when Hillborn was hung over or just not in the oratorical mood. McDaniel was never happy with the short services. There were others where the man was given to more long-winded sermonizing—particularly the midnight services after a few drinks. McDaniel preferred these.

That night McDaniel decided he had to secure Viola Rogers and her lovely voice quickly enough to get back on the road. There was a woman waiting at the end of the next sunrise and he was anxious to shake the dust off of his boots and settle in for a day or two before hopping into his car and starting it all over again.

Viola had done more to secure the faith of the audience that evening than the man could have ever done. The way he figured it, Viola should be the one shaking hands and greeting people. She was the future—his future—but he was distracted by his need to hit the road.

"Business is business," McDaniel repeated to himself. It was a phrase he knew all too well, but life on the road can get so lonely. He only hoped she saved him some bourbon for the next go-around. These were his thoughts as he made his way through the gauntlet of hand-shakers and shoulder-slappers with sweaty palms as he moved ever closer to Fiona and her daughter.

As McDaniel approached Fiona and Viola, he said, "That's some singer you have there, Miss…" McDaniel was fishing for her name, for a way into her heart.

"Rogers," Fiona said. "Fiona Rogers and this is my daughter, Viola."

"It is wonderful to finally meet you… formally, I mean," he said offering his hand again.

His eye was on the back flap opening of the tent.

Fiona took his hand this time and shook it firmly.

"I'm sorry about earlier," she started. "We don't usually trust strangers."

"No need," he said. "Have you seen Lester, by the way?"

"He's putting the collection baskets away," Viola offered. She pointed her delicate finger at the moonlit figures of two men hoisting baskets into the trunk of the Cadillac.

"That's good," McDaniel said. "He is such a responsible boy."

"Yes, he sure seems to be," Fiona agreed.

"I know we've only just met, but I wonder if you can suggest a good restaurant in town where Lester and the boys and I might enjoy a light supper."

McDaniel could feel that his woman-in-waiting at the end of the road would have to continue waiting as he stood there looking at Fiona and Viola and his future.

"Don't be silly," Fiona said. "Everyone is welcome at my house tonight. I'll cook for Lester and the boys and you." In this moment, Fiona could hardly believe the words that were coming from her heart and she blushed.

"That's mighty generous of you, Miss Rogers," McDaniel said.

McDaniel weighed his loneliness against his success and decided that securing this little girl for the rest of the season was too much to resist. His evening was set.

"Call me Fiona," she replied.

"That's mighty generous of you, Fiona," he said "Let me gather everything up and we'll follow you to your place."

"We will be by the car," she said.

Dinner included leftover meatloaf with gravy and potatoes, leftover chicken and rice, and some ham with pineapple. Lester, McDaniel and the boys devoured the home cooked food that—even as leftovers—far surpassed the restaurant fare to which they had become accustomed.

Blue preferred a cup of coffee and a cigarette, which he took on the porch before walking back to the tent and falling asleep on some chairs.

"More biscuits, Lester?" Fiona asked holding the basket under his nose.

"Thank you, ma'am," he said reaching into the basket.

"So where did you learn to sing like that, Viola," McDaniel asked.

"I don't know, Sir," she responded. "I just sing. That's all. But I am in the choir too. They teach me the songs. My heart does the singing."

"That honesty—that purity—is so refreshing," McDaniel said to Fiona.

"Viola is a very special child," Fiona said.

"I can see that," McDaniel said. "If you don't mind, I'd like to speak freely for a moment."

Fiona agreed, out of curiosity.

"Miss Viola's talent is unique, wouldn't you say?" Fiona agreed.

McDaniel continued. "You said she sings at the local church once a week?" Fiona confirmed that she did.

"How many people would you say are in the congregation?" Fiona estimated a number close to seventy.

McDaniel landed his point, saying, "She should be witnessing for as many people as she can as often as she can. Think of how many souls she could uplift with her precious gift!"

"I don't know," Fiona said, looking at her daughter. "She's so young."

McDaniel went deep into his archive of meaningful philosophies derived from scripture. "The book of Matthew talks about hiding a light under a bushel," McDaniel said. "Do you know what he means?"

Fiona said, "Viola is an illuminated light of the Lord's word. To keep her here—under a bushel—is to deny the Lord's gift to his flock."

McDaniel didn't have to say anything more. He let Fiona's own words settle over the table.

"Viola needs to finish school," Fiona said.

"What if we offered her an opportunity for the summer, to sing for the Lord, with our revival, with the explicit promise to bring her back here to this very table with plenty of time for school," he said. "I fully agree that school is very important."

"We would have our own rooms?" Viola asked.

"If that's what you require, you would have your own room," McDaniel said.

Somehow, he surmised it wouldn't be long before Fiona and Lester were sharing Lester's room, but for now, he knew that he needed to promise everyone exactly what they wanted.

By the time the leftovers were gone, the plates were cleared, the dishes were done and tea had been had, all the plans were in place. Fiona would call her cousin, Tina, to watch the house for a couple of months. Fiona would go everywhere Viola went. The entourage would leave after the morning call to prayer.

Walking back toward the tents McDaniel was almost light on his feet. Lester was more shuffling—plodding along as if his body was resisting being pulled away from Fiona.

"Is she the reason you brought me back on the stage tonight, Mac?" Lester asked?

"Does it matter?"

"It kind of does, Mac," Lester continued. "I'll sing any time and any where—and I'll do whatever you think I should do," Lester said.

"But... I hear a but in there," McDaniel laughed.

"There is no but," Lester said. "Just don't ever use me."

"Fair enough," McDaniel said.

"You owe me one," Lester said smiling.

Mac retuned the smile as he put an arm on Lester's shoulder—the short fat father and the tall thin son. They walked the rest of the way in silence.

The following morning, McDaniel broke the news to Blue that he was no longer needed. McDaniel would provide a bus ticket—and a few dollars—but he just didn't need the extra hands. The stagehand settled for a carton of cigarettes, $5.00 and a bus ticket to Chicago.

He let Hillborn go as well—the actor who played the preacher would have to find new work. His days in the collar, under the dim bulbs in the canvas tent were over.

McDaniel liked both men; they were good at what they did. Somehow he knew his own career was about to turn a corner. He just needed that one piece—a real, honest-to-God preacher who could spit fire and brimstone and salvation—so he could do what he did best—sell tickets and get butts in seats.

The Friendship Church Choir, specifically Mrs. Prince the choir director, would surely miss Viola, as would the men who had come to see her on a weekly basis. Not surprisingly, several of the men marked their calendars for Viola's return once word got out that she would be singing with the revival.

❁

"WE'LL HAVE NO SHENANIGANS"

The blare of Lester's truck horn startled Peter out of his light and restless sleep. He jumped up—disoriented alone in a strange room far from home. Betty was slower to rise in her cramped little room. McDaniel didn't budge. He was snoring nearly as loud as the horn that cut through the morning air. He was used to hotels and he was used to getting a full night's sleep.

In his room, Reverend Crenshaw scurried about like a guilty husband. He needed to find clothes for the lifeless body of the girl who was still sleeping, hanging off the side of the bed like a half-stuffed scarecrow. Her panties were under a chair and her bra was wrapped around the light shade. As for her outer layer, he couldn't even begin to imagine where those clothes were. The sticky sweet smell of cheap rum mingling with her dime-store perfume caused Crenshaw to gag when he got too close.

He stopped what he was doing long enough to call McDaniel and apprise him of the situation. The groggy response told Crenshaw that he'd woken McDaniel up, which would not bode well for him. They agreed it wouldn't look good if the Reverend were in such a compromising position—especially with a local. McDaniel also let the Reverend know this would be the last time he would be covering for him like this.

By the time Lester and Viola got out of the truck, McDaniel was most of the way down the steel-grate stairs. He was able to cut them off and steer them around to the front of the hotel and across the street to Glitter Gulch where he would outline the day's events over coffee and breakfast.

"Peter and Betty will be joining us in a moment," McDaniel said, hustling Lester and the young girl across the parking lot. His trademark white suit glowed in the morning sun.

"Where's Reverend Crenshaw?" Viola asked.

"He'll be along in a minute," McDaniel said quickly. "Morning meditation, you know. Where's Fiona?"

"She'll be along soon," Viola told him. "She had to assist in a birth at Richardson's farm."

"What about the kid—Peter?" Lester asked. "When are we going to meet him?"

"I have an idea," McDaniel said, sweating through his white shirt and into the seams of his white suit coat. "Why don't you take Viola in and get us a table? I'll go back to the hotel and wrangle everyone."

"Whatever's clever," Lester said brightly.

He took Viola by the hand as they crossed the street. The few passers-by looked strangely at the couple—a man of his age holding hands with a young girl who was not yet a woman. It never even occurred to Lester how it looked from the outside. He was so blindly in love with her mother, and vice versa, his only concern was the little girl's safety.

McDaniel walked back toward the motel and knocked loudly on Peter's door, then on Betty's. Making the final turn to Crenshaw's door, McDaniel found the preacher setting the girl in a deck chair in front of a room three doors down from his. Clad only in her bra, panties, and red cowboy boots, she was obviously still quite drunk. She cleared her throat and burped lightly; other than that, there was very little proof of life.

"Jesus, Harland!" McDaniel said. "What did you do to this poor girl?"

"Nothing she didn't already know how to do," Crenshaw said. He quickly composed himself and the two men walked toward the parking lot.

They were joined by Betty as they passed her room, and then Peter as they passed his. They walked to the restaurant without saying a word to one another.

The day crew at the Glitter Gulch was clearly different from the night crew. Crenshaw and McDaniel were obviously disappointed. There was no sign of the hostess or Annie.

The women on duty for lunch were plump and shiny with grease-painted faces and crooked wigs. Crenshaw and McDaniel put their heads down and walked through the restaurant.

They were led back out to the patio where a short dark-skinned man was pushing two small tables together. Next, he swung two more chairs into position and disappeared into the kitchen.

A severe looking woman in a tight business suit and a red Beehive hairdo approached the table quickly. "You are welcome to stay, but we'll have no shenanigans," she said in a gravelly voice. "I do mean *no shenanigans*."

She looked at Peter as if he were America's Most Wanted. He hung his head—but a smile played on his lips for a fleeting moment as he recalled something that he had once heard about bad attention or good attention being attention nonetheless.

"Shenanigans, my dear lady, we can assure you, are not a part of our repertoire," McDaniel said, reaching to tip his hat which, due to the morning's circumstances, was not present.

The severe-looking woman looked at McDaniel as if he were trying to sell her a rainbow. "Uh-huh," she said. She turned to leave as a server with less Beehive but more face paint waddled up to the table. She had bags under her eyes that almost swayed when she walked. She pulled a little green pad out of her apron and looked over the group. She looked the group over once, then again, as if she were going to sketch them on her little green tablet rather than take their orders.

"My name's Rose. I'll be your server," she squawked. "Can we start with some coffee for the table or a soda from the fountain?"

Everyone ordered what it was they needed to ease into another day. Betty took advantage of her freedom by ordering a cherry cola.

Her father never would have allowed that if she was still in Orton's Cove. Peter watched Reverend Crenshaw pollute his coffee and grimaced to himself.

"Viola and Lester," McDaniel started. "This is Peter Campbell and Betty..."

"Croney," Betty offered.

"Miss Betty Croney," he finished.

"Hi y'all," Lester said shaking hands over the condiments and the silver napkin holder.

"Hi," Viola echoed, but she never took her eyes off Peter.

"Nice to meet you both," Betty said.

"Yeah, hi," Peter returned.

He reached into his pocket and pulled out a crumpled cigarette pack. He hadn't smoked much since the trip began, but he wanted to impress the young girl who sat across from him. He repeated her name to himself—*Viola*. To his own astonishment, he lit the cigarette on the first try.

Suddenly sounds of sirens filled the morning air. Crenshaw did what he could to hide his discomfort. He shifted his weight back and forth in his seat. McDaniel began to count the cracks in the patio floor.

The two cruisers pulled into the parking lot of the motel across the street. Crenshaw excused himself to go to the bathroom. It was McDaniel's turn to shift his considerable weight as he watched the miscreant preacher walk away from the table to hide.

Rose brought the drinks on a large circular platter and set them on the collapsible stand she carried under her other arm.

"What seems to be all the ruckus?" McDaniel asked her.

"Looks like they found Deacon Feller's daughter on the stoop over at the Valley View again," she said putting the drinks on the table.

"You don't say," McDaniel said.

"Yes," Rose whispered, so that Viola wouldn't hear the profanity. "She's a bit of a hussy. This ain't the first time Roy and the boys been called to get Miss Feller off the stoop, and it sure won't be the last. I only hope *her* party didn't disturb *your* rest. That is where y'all stayed last night isn't it?"

"Didn't hear a thing," McDaniel said smiling broadly. "Was quite happy with the room, too."

"Between us, she's been known to get looped on tequila at Snuff's and wander around in her underwear when the weather allows. Nice enough girl though, just likes that tequila too much. Well, what can I get you?" Rose finally asked.

The special was a gypsy skillet with hash browns and an egg over a bed of fried peppers and onions. The skillet included a side of Texas toast with grape jelly. The drinks were all included except for the small up-charge for the cherry syrup in the cherry cola.

McDaniel answered for everyone.

"We'll all have the special," he said.

Peter stuffed his cigarette into the little glass ashtray.

As she waddled through the glass door, Crenshaw held it for her before stepping through it himself. He walked back to the table.

"Did you order?" he asked.

"Got you the special," McDaniel said.

"Thank you," Crenshaw said, sitting down, still a little preoccupied with the police and the young girl across the street.

"Good choice," he replied, pouring his sugar and cream into his cup.

"Now, after breakfast, Viola, you and Betty are free for a few hours to wander around town a bit. Try to see what places are the most popular so we can hang posters. Reverend Crenshaw and I are going to find a secluded place to work with Peter on his—our— presentation."

Peter grimaced. He was not looking forward to spending time with McDaniel and Crenshaw.

"We'll meet back at the hotel at three o'clock," he continued. "Lester will give you some money for lunch and incidentals. I don't think I have to remind you to avoid talking to anyone you don't know."

"What about me?" Fiona asked.

"We're going to need you to find a printer to make us some handbills to announce the revival tonight. Lester and Crenshaw are going to secure the location and hire a few locals to help erect the tent.

"When we meet at three we'll divide up the town and distribute the handbills. Lester will take Viola and Fiona in the truck. Peter and Betty will go on foot, and Crenshaw and I will go in the car.

"We will meet back here at six for a light dinner before heading over to the tent. We want to be there and ready when the people begin to arrive."

"This is so exciting," Betty said.

She reached over and pinched Peter's arm.

Peter didn't even notice; he was still watching Viola, who was busy watching him. He reached for another cigarette, but the crumpled pack was empty. He let the pack fall onto the table.

"Chaw?" Lester offered, pulling a dented tin out of his back pocket.

"No, thanks," Peter passed. "I'll just get some smokes."

Peter stood up and walked toward the glass door. He got there just in time to hold it open for the woman who was carrying an even larger tray with their breakfast on it.

"Six California specials," Rose said, setting the plates in front of everyone.

"Eat up," Reverend Crenshaw said.

"This looks marvelous," Viola said.

She hadn't taken her eyes off the door. She seemed to be willing Peter to walk back through it.

Before too long, he came through the door again and rejoined the party. He was less than enthused about the breakfast in front of him, but if Viola liked it, he would find a way to like it too.

"Dig in, Vi!" Lester said. He spat a chunk of chaw under the table before setting to work on the food before him.

"Anything else?" Rose asked as she set the last plate down in front of Betty.

"Not just yet," McDaniel said. "Not just yet."

"IN TIMES LIKE THESE"

By nightfall, the land around the tent was full of cars and trucks and the occasional tractor. The rows of weathered chairs were filling up quickly with stout, sturdy bodies with curious minds. The women in their pretty dresses and the men in broad plaid shirts and slicked-back hair sat politely waiting for the service to begin.

Some of the older folks in the tent that night were aware of what they might witness. Some remained skeptical while others were joyful to the point of anxiety. There was little for most of the audience to be anxious about in their lives, so however the evening turned out, they were grateful for the distraction.

Peter peeked through a small hole in the curtain. It probably wasn't the brightest thing he could have done at the moment, having never been on stage as a performer. The little kid inside of the young man began to tremble. His feet became like clay and he couldn't move.

He knew he couldn't back out now, not with Betty and Viola counting on him. He didn't care much about Crenshaw and McDaniel, but he couldn't let down Betty or Viola.

He could have used a little more rehearsal, but he was technically ready. Still the terror of burning something unexpected, or God-forbid an audience member, threatened to consume him. The very thought of being in front of this many people made him nauseous. He thought about his mother back home in Orton's Cove and her grilled cheese sandwiches and endless skeins of material.

The bulging, uneven seams in the musty cloth would have never gotten past her little white sewing machine. She demanded only the best from herself—Peter knew it was up to him to give his best. Even though she wouldn't know, he would.

He did everything he could to turn his mind to the task at hand until it was finally time to face the crowd. He looked at his palms for a moment as if to punish them for the fine mess they had gotten him into. But then he praised them, and pleaded with them. "Please, don't let me down now."

"It'll be okay. You'll be wonderful," Viola said, approaching him from the darkness backstage. "I'll be right where you can see me at all times."

She kissed him on the cheek before pushing him onto the stage and positioning herself stage right. Peter was still looking at where Viola had been standing when Betty approached him from his blindside. She pinched his sides hard enough to make him squeal. He slapped his own hand over his mouth as he turned and faced her. They shared a quick laugh together. Then it was over.

"Are you excited?" Betty asked.

"I guess I am," Peter replied looking down at his shoes then looking at the slit in the tent that Viola had escaped through. He wished he had followed her.

"You're going to be fine," Betty coached. "Just do it the way you've been rehearsing it with Mr. McDaniel and by this time tomorrow we'll be counting money to send back to Orton's Cove."

"I'm just," he shivered.

"You'll be fine. I'll be right where you can see me at all times." She kissed his cheek and exited the same way as Viola, positioning herself stage left. He watched the flap of tent material blow in the breeze. He thought about his mother again.

"You must be Peter," a woman's voice from behind him said.

Moments from a clean getaway. He looked into the face of the strikingly beautiful woman who had just spoken to him. "Yes, Ma'am," he gulped.

"I'm Fiona."

"It's very nice to meet you, Ma'am," Peter said extending his hand.

"Your palms are sweaty," Fiona said. "Are you nervous?"

"A little," he said softly.

"Well, don't be," she said. "You'll do just fine. Don't you worry about a thing. I'll be right where you can see me at all times." She kissed him on the cheek and exited the way the other women had, positioning herself in front, at the edge of the audience.

Once again, Peter stared blankly at the flap of material.

"Peter?" Lester asked coming up from behind him.

"I'm fine," Peter said quickly. "I'm not nervous at all. I'm ready. Let's get this dang show going!"

"I was just going to ask if you wanted a chaw."

"No, thanks, Lester, but I could use a cigarette."

"You got time; just don't smoke in the tent. Don't ever smoke in the tent. Sneak out that little slit there but don't be gone too long."

"That one?" Peter asked, pointing to a hole in the cloth that Lester confirmed was the best way out.

Peter slipped out into the dimming light of evening and pinched a cigarette from his pack. He lit it and drew the smoke deep into his lungs. He rolled his head back on his shoulders as he exhaled, sending the thin clean smoke up into the clouds. He did this again— and again.

He rubbed the flimsy matchbook between his fingers as he rolled his head around on his shoulders. His eyes scanned the perfect night of perfect stars and he was suddenly less anxious.

Crenshaw's voice boomed throughout the tent. Peter listened closely for his entrance cue while he smoked his cigarette. He thought about Luther and Joellyn, Old Man Kaucky, and Frank, the usher at the Rialto. What he discovered in these few moments before he first set foot on stage was that he had very quickly grown homesick for Orton's Cove.

He was hungry. He wanted one of his mother's old-fashioned grilled cheese sandwiches. He wanted a float at the soda fountain.

He wanted to rewind. Even as he watched the cigarette he flicked toward a mud puddle tumble in the air, he wanted to recall it, to have one last sweet drag of tobacco.

But, he was being summoned.

Peter slipped back into the tent where he heard the crowd responding to Crenshaw's bellowing. Crenshaw was pouring it on thick with damnation and revelations. He was walking through the proverbial lion's den and the pits of hell to bring these sinners to their salvation. But, he was moving quickly through his presentation. Too quickly perhaps.

Perhaps inspired by Deacon Feller's daughter, or by the idea of who might be lurking around, Crenshaw whipped through the service with power, passion and uncanny speed. He thought it best to give the spotlight to Viola sooner rather than later. She would—in turn—give the duly warmed up crowd over to Peter.

Peter could hear Viola warming up. Her voice sounded like an angel's, but her singing had a very different effect on him. Parts of him were confused—parts were embarrassed. All of him was happy to hear her sing.

Viola could tell Crenshaw was racing the devil to get off stage so she knew she had to be ready when McDaniel called her name.

"In times like these," Viola sang softly, "You need a savior. In times like these. You need an anchor." she sang, almost to herself. The words rolled off of her tongue and up to Heaven on the prayers of the people gathered in the tent.

When the crowd was sufficiently warmed up and on the edge of their seats, Crenshaw introduced Viola. She made a spinning entrance onto the plywood stage. Her arms were spread out and the edges of her dress were lifted by the wind. She looked like an angel that had been plucked right from a Christmas tree.

As her heavenly voice filled the room, blanketing the clapping hands and tinny tambourines, Peter could see Viola's silhouette through the curtain. The more her voice poured out, the more Peter struggled not to cry.

"That rock is Jesus," she sang. "Yes, he's the one. That rock is

Jesus. The only one."

The angels danced with Viola that night, as they did every night. She swayed and shook and rocked back and forth. There was nothing but the music and the love of the Lord in that little girl. She was wondrous to Peter. She was wondrous to everyone.

When Viola's act was complete, she whirled off the stage and the lights were dimmed. Crenshaw made his way back in front of the congregation and raised his arms to the heavens. As a slim spotlight illuminated the man, he stamped his foot down hard and incited a cheer of "Amen! Amen! Amen!"

On the third "Amen," Peter emerged from the curtains and took his place—beside Crenshaw—in the spotlight. As practiced, Peter spread his arms up to his side, as if they were newly sprouted wings. Then he extended them out over the audience.

On the final movement, Peter's hands went straight up into the air. He stretched his fingers back as far as they would go and aimed his palms at the opening in the tent—just as they had planned. The flash of light was quick, as white balls of fire shot forth and some of the sparks showered down on him and Crenshaw. He repeated the motion and the next balls of flame burst wider and further, and showered more sparks over the pair in the spotlight.

"Praise him and his strength," Peter yelled. "For he brings you..." Peter stalled. He had forgotten the next line.

"Righteousness." Crenshaw whispered.

"Whiteness," Peter yelled loudly.

"Not 'whiteness' Peter, 'righteousness'!" Crenshaw whispered louder this time.

"The Lord brings you *righteousness*!" Peter yelled.

A woman in a red smock passed out in the front row. She was caught by two men who set her down on her chair gingerly before returning to their excited form of worship.

Not to be outdone, another woman, this one bigger and in a blue smock with a matching hat, passed out. She was in the third row. Thankfully, there were a few men there to catch her. She was laid gently in her chair and was soon forgotten about.

Peter looked at Viola, then Betty and then Fiona, before he settled on Viola for an extended moment. They were all smiling and clapping. Crenshaw motioned for him to leave the stage, but Peter was in no hurry.

The young man was overcome with emotion. He thrust his hands toward the sky one more time, sending a red ball of fire over his head, and the head of the reverend. It landed in front of the writhing congregation and fizzled. Crenshaw leapt from the stage and stepped on it quickly.

As the last of the sparks were stamped out, Peter walked off stage, through the split in the curtain. He couldn't have wiped the smile from his face with a baseball bat. Peter had tasted success for the first time in his life and he thought—maybe—he liked it.

Peter thought about all of the people he left back in Orton's Cove who hadn't even noticed him before this. He had decided—a long time ago—that not being noticed was worse than being hated. Now he might get noticed—and not hated by the kids at school. His head buzzed with the possibilities.

Viola was there to greet Peter when he snapped back to reality. Her hug was so full and so warm, Peter got nervous. Viola sensed this, as well as the physical effect the hug was having, and she backed away gracefully.

Betty and Fiona arrived simultaneously and congratulated Peter. He was sweating and shaking and laughing. He was also trying to hide the effects of Viola's hug but no one else noticed. They were all just happy that his performance had gone so well.

Peter reached for Viola and hugged her again. She smiled at him for a moment before letting go this time. Betty sensed the connection and finally noticed his reaction to this hug. She decided it better not to hug him—not now anyway.

"You were wonderful," Fiona said. She started to hug him, but when their bodies touched, she got the message Betty had successfully avoided. She looked at Viola.

"You really were, Peter," Viola added.

"They were passing out in the aisles," Betty said.

"Was I really okay?" he asked, reaching for Viola.

"You were colossal," Fiona said, stepping in between Peter and Viola.

"Magnificent," Betty added.

"Yeah," Viola said, smiling innocently at Peter. "Really incredible."

"Don't you have one more song, Viola?" Lester said, as he joined the little group.

"Yes I do, Lester. I'm sorry."

"Go ahead then," he smiled at her. "They're ready for you now."

Lester started to give Peter a hug, but Fiona intercepted him much to Peter and Betty's relief.

"HONESTY, HUH"

That night, as the exhausted but exhilarated group sat around the small table in Peter's room at the Valley View Motel eating take-out chicken and counting the wrinkled dollar bills, Reverend Crenshaw asked Peter to join him outside. Crenshaw led Peter leisurely across the porch. He stopped, looked up at the drooping basketball net before slowly turning toward Peter.

"Son," he said firmly. "When we make a plan, I want you … nay, I expect you to stick to the plan. There is no room out there for improvising. Am I making myself clear?"

"Sorry, sir," Peter said.

Peter put his head down and walked away. Neither of them saw Viola come to the door. She stood quietly with her hand over her mouth. Crenshaw turned on his heel and walked past her and back into the room. Viola watched Peter walk away across the pockmarked ball court. She didn't say a word.

Peter walked around to the front of the hotel and sat down on the front steps. He lit a cigarette with his right hand and let his thoughts wander to the simplicity of Orton's Cove. He longed to drink a Dr. Pepper with Luther and talk about nothing. He missed the lumpy stools at Old Man Kaucky's place. He started thinking— again—this trip may not have been his best idea.

He looked at his hands and wished he could give someone else the power so he could go home, where he belonged. He was sure there was a payoff to having these hands but he wasn't sure what it was yet. He'd just as soon not find out.

Thoughts of Viola dancing across his mind embarrassed him as he sat alone under the flickering streetlight. It wasn't that he hadn't had these thoughts before, but he was nearly 17 and she was just 14 and it just didn't seem right.

He hadn't had many thoughts like this since he met Miss Kosan when she first came to Orton's Cove to teach kindergarten. He was in the seventh grade and for a woman her age, she was not much taller than he was. She had short curly dark hair and always wore short skirts with nylons.

He and Luther made it a point to stop by her classroom every day after school to wash the chalkboards or bang the dust out of the erasers. She would sit at her desk and grade papers while the two star-crossed boys tidied up every inch of the classroom sneaking furtive glances at her perfectly tanned legs or her deep brown eyes —mostly her legs. Sometimes the smell of her Fabergé would waft across the room filling their heads and stirring other organs.

In the evening, the boys would sit on the curb outside of Old Man Kaucky's and sneak cigarettes and plan out their futures. They would take turns inventing extravagant lives with Miss Kosan as their wife or lover. If there was ever a time in his life that Peter showed anything that even resembled imagination, it was when he and Luther sat on that curb and talked about Miss Kosan.

Sometimes, if the spirit moved them, they would sing popular songs— only they substituted Miss Kosan for the name in the song. This yielded such classics as, "With a Little Help from Miss Kosan," and "Midnight Train to Kosan," and who could ever forget "Sunshine on my Kosan."

Because of these exercises in song, Peter began to imagine himself as a great musician who was going to make records and have fans all over the world who loved his music. He and Miss Kosan would travel in his private jet and travel to far off lands and they would go backstage and they would smoke cigarettes with all the other rock stars.

Peter actually tried to write her a song that was all her own, but he couldn't find many good rhymes for Kosan. He thought about using her first name, but Marjorie doesn't rhyme with very much either. These two issues were exacerbated by Peter's inability to focus on anything for too long.

Mostly Peter and Luther were content to smoke cigarettes and sing their little songs and dream about the day they would graduate junior high and be ready to ask Miss Kosan for a proper date.

At the Thanksgiving Turkey Trot that year, Miss Kosan walked into the school auditorium for the big dance. She was holding hands with a tall, dark man in a shiny, blue suit. Peter and Luther recognized him from the used car lot out on the highway. The fathers called him Romeo.

Romeo didn't smile much. His lips were paper thin and flat against his face. The boys thought this was strange because Miss Kosan was always smiling. He didn't dance much either. Luther was going to ask Miss Kosan to dance, but Romeo scared him. Peter didn't have the nerve to ask Miss Kosan to dance. He was grateful for the guy's presence, even if all he did was stand by the punch bowl guzzling the sticky sweet red confection while Miss Kosan talked with the other teachers and some of the students. Mr. Harvey asked him who he liked in Sunday's football game. Romeo just turned away as if he hadn't heard.

When the dance was over, Romeo took Miss Kosan by the hand and led her out the door. Peter followed them out—keeping a safe distance. They paused for a moment in the parking lot. Romeo tried to give her a kiss. She offered her cheek instead and after a quick peck, they got into the car.

Peter saw the whole thing and told Luther about it, but Luther wouldn't believe a word of it. He knew, or thought at least, that Miss Kosan was saving her kisses for his graduation day.

That Friday, when Peter and Luther showed up to help Miss Kosan, their work was already done and Romeo was sitting on her desk. He glowered at them until they left. His thin lips pressed together tightly.

The following Friday, Luther and Peter's work was done again and there was Romeo almost daring them to enter the room. He sat still, perched on Miss Kosan's desk. He glared at Peter and Luther, with a dusting of chalk dust on the front of his pants.

The more Romeo came around, the less Peter and Luther were given access to Miss Kosan. By the time Christmas break came around, Miss Kosan was banging the dust out of her own erasers. Romeo didn't need to hang out at the school anymore. He had accomplished his goal and Peter and Luther had moved on—at least in action if not in mind.

❀

Peter knew this whole arrangement was temporary. He understood that he would eventually be going back to Orton's Cove, and he didn't want Viola to get hurt. He was determined to keep his thoughts—and his feelings to himself.

"Can I join you?"

The voice startled him. Peter looked up. Betty was standing next to him.

"Uh, yeah," he replied.

"I hear Crenshaw was kind of rough on you back there," she said.

"I shoulda known better," Peter responded.

"Still..."

Peter looked into Betty's eyes as he scratched his head for a moment.

"Listen, Peter," she said pulling herself closer to him. "I told your mother I would watch out for you and that is what I am going to do. But there's something that you need to understand."

"Yeah?"

"Let's start by talking about Viola Rogers."

"What about Vi?"

"I wasn't born yesterday. It's clear how you feel about Viola,"

Betty said.

Peter tried to say something, but Betty wouldn't let him interrupt her.

"All I want to say, Peter, is you should follow your heart. If you like her—if you *really* like her—let her know."

"But," Peter was trying to process what Betty was saying. "What will we do when this is all over? What'll I do come fall?"

"All I'm saying is be *honest* with yourself and with her and no one will get hurt."

"Honesty, huh?" he smiled. Peter considered the possibilities. A smile grew on his face. Maybe he didn't have to keep his feelings to himself after all.

"In the second place, Peter, do not let Reverend Crenshaw bully you around," she went on. "You need to remember that you are the show. You are who people are going to be coming to see. If you feel like you want to throw a little extra fire, than by all means do so!"

"But how did you..."

"I saw you guys through the window. The way you walked away, I assumed he'd said something nasty. He's jealous," Betty said. "If you get all of the attention, then how is he going to get women like Deacon Feller's daughter to come back to his room with him?"

"Was it really him?" Peter asked. "I was always taught to not trust a man who puts cream in his coffee."

"I was coming out of my room as he was posing the unfortunate girl in a lawn chair. He's not what he seems."

"I guess not." Peter said.

Betty continued. "Mr. McDaniel loved what you did tonight, and he's the real boss around here. Do yourself a favor. Have some fun with this, Peter. We don't know how long our little adventure is going to go on so we might as well enjoy ourselves."

Betty got up to go to her room. "Just be sure you don't lose track of yourself, Peter Campbell."

She started to walk back toward her room. She paused and turned back to where Peter was sitting. She dropped a thick envelope into Peter's hand.

"What's this?" he asked squeezing the envelope.

"It's your share from tonight's revenues. I went over the balance sheet with Mr. McDaniel and Lester. This is your cut. Tomorrow we can go to the Western Union around the corner and wire some of it home to your mother."

"Thank you, Betty," he said. "Do I give you some of mine? How does this work?"

Betty said something about her cut being about more than money. "I have what I need. You take care of your momma," she added. "We'll figure it out after the next revival."

Peter watched Betty until she disappeared around the corner. His thoughts of Viola began to occupy his mind again, only this time he didn't feel rushed or like he had to hurry up and decide what to do. He needed to be honest, like Betty said. Honesty takes time.

Peter rested his elbows on the stairs behind him and turned his face to the sky. *Mine glow brighter* he thought to himself. He felt a smile begin to curl up the corners of his mouth.

Closing his eyes, Peter took a deep breath of the moist air and held it for a moment before letting it go. The smile was for no one. He let the air out of his mouth slowly.

Good night, Miss Kosan, wherever you are.

"CAN I JUST SAY 'WOW'"

Clifford Robinson was a struggling meteorologist by day, but when the sun went down, the topography maps were rolled up and put aside. The computer monitors were dimmed. The radios silenced.

The night belonged to Clifford Robinson. He would slip into his best, blue suit and gray slicker. His heavily pomaded head was topped with a Stetson pork-pie hat. The gray felt crown was flawless. He took the 777 bus to Puddin' Tap where an ice-cold beer and a hot microphone would be waiting for him.

Walking through the dingy little bar, hat now in hand, Clifford's hair reflected the sickly yellow lights that bounced around the room without any pattern or consistency. He waved to Mavis Ketchum and anyone else who looked up at him as he made his way to the stage.

He pulled a little scrap of paper out of his jacket pocket and handed it to Arne, the big, loud guy running the sound system.

"Evenin', " Arne said taking the slip.

"Same to you," Clifford said with a wink.

"I asked you to stop winking at me, Cliff," Arne said half-heartedly.

"Sure, baby," Clifford said.

Clifford turned and walked back to the bar. He ordered a Budweiser—no glass. He was ready to sing.

Clifford only sang Sinatra at Puddin' Tap's karaoke night. This was Garth Brooks country. The blue glow from the little television set cast an eerie pallor on his bony face. He watched the words roll by him as he approximated movements that could have been mistaken for dancing.

If he were in Chicago or some big city where all the tough-guys think they're Sinatra, his act likely would have gone unnoticed. There were plenty of creaky-voiced pathological Sinatra-clones to go around in any big city. The hat and slicker get up made no difference out there. He was just another guy who didn't own his life.

At Puddin' Tap, the identity crisis wasn't as much of a problem as Clifford's choice of songs. The first time Mavis Ketchum heard him sing "The Lady is a Tramp" she was shocked at the language. How could a gentleman say those things about a lady? The next time when he came into the *Gas-n-Go* for his cigarettes, she wouldn't even look him in the eye.

The rest of the crowd at the Puddin' Tap tolerated Clifford when it was his turn to sing. Arne was very careful with his rotation of Clifford's songs, especially after midnight when the Howard brothers were there, or when Mavis Ketchum and the girls from Hal's Used Car Lot were there. You can never be too careful, especially where the Howard brothers are concerned. One wrong note and there was no telling how one of them might react. Everyone at Puddin' Tap knows enough to stay away from the Patsy Cline catalog if they want to have a peaceful evening.

Clifford's first choice for the evening was "The Way You Look Tonight". He dedicated it to his *girlfriend*, Loretta. None of the regulars had actually met this Loretta, they weren't even sure if she existed. The only thing they were *pretty* sure of was that Clifford had never traveled more than two miles from his bar stool in his entire life. The holes in Clifford's stories didn't diminish his passion for singing the song, even if this wonderful woman did only exist in his mind.

He was wrapping up his song when Fiona and Viola entered the dingy little bar.

When Clifford saw the two girls, he perked up considerably. Even his tempo quickened; his spine stiffened and his song began to unravel. The Howard brothers followed Clifford's gaze to the two girls. They ran their fingers through their hair in vain attempts to look less like they normally looked. Even old Puddin' made an effort to tuck in his tattered Hawaiian shirt.

Lester and Peter came in a few moments later and joined the girls at the table. The appearance of the two young men knocked the wind out of some of the local sails, and by the time McDaniel and Crenshaw joined them, the Puddin' Tap regulars were pretty much back to normal. Everyone except Clifford.

Clifford didn't look at women as personal conquests, or the men as competition for that matter. He saw his audience had doubled. They were fresh faces and fresh ears for him to impress with his song stylings.

He took many long bows despite the fact that the group had only heard the last few notes of his song. They hadn't even heard him sing.

"This place is…nice?" Viola said to no one in particular.

Looking around at the leering men at the bar and the other tables, Viola instinctively shuffled her chair closer to Lester. Betty moved closer to Peter. Fiona sat next to Betty and reached for a big plastic songbook.

"Who'd like what?" Crenshaw asked.

"Whatever's clever," Lester said flipping through the songbook looking for a song for Viola to sing.

Crenshaw walked to the bar. McDaniel escaped to the bathroom. Viola sat with her hands in her lap looking at Peter who sat with his hands in his lap looking at her. Betty and Fiona were looking through a songbook and giggling about the Howard brothers who were visibly itching to approach them.

"Are you going to sing, Peter?" Betty giggled.

"Nah," Peter responded. "Fire's my thing." He never took his eyes off of Viola.

He didn't even look away to light his cigarette. He simply

wrapped the end of his cigarette in his hand and ignited his palm.

Betty encouraged Peter to save his talents for the stage.

"I'll sing," Viola said quietly. "If Peter wants me to."

"That'd be swell," he said sighing a cloud of dirty blue smoke.

"Me first," Lester said.

Lester walked to the bar and filled out the sign-up sheet. He delivered the slip to Arne who was finishing a stirring rendition of "American Trilogy". Visibly excited, Lester sat back down at the table.

He had—undoubtedly—one of the most beautiful voices ever to whip a crowd into a joyful frenzy. Having spent his childhood singing with McDaniel in tents and churches around the country, Lester had developed a love for the craft.

As he got older and Mother Nature proved aesthetically unkind, Lester stopped singing in the tents and the churches for the most part. He never lost his passion for singing, but rather than sing in public in front of a paying audience, he sang at home. He sang in his car. He sang in the shower or when he when he was outside doing yard work. Lester sang because it was the only pure joy he had ever known.

Unlike so many people in Lester's life—music never let him down and never broke his heart.

He had recently discovered he had a knack for singing Fiona to sleep when she was restless. He sang because it truly was the only pure joy he had ever known, but was just never comfortable singing in a well-lit venue ever again. Lester didn't mind occasionally singing in a dark bar or restaurant now and again where the lights were rarely sharp or true, where no one could make out the faults of his face and he had trouble making out theirs.

Crenshaw brought a thick black plastic tray of drinks to the table and began to distribute them. The beer bottles were sweating and the ice in the sodas tinkled. Betty smiled when she saw the Reverend had remembered her request for cherries.

"Alrightee," Arne yelled into the microphone. "Looks like we have a new singer here tonight. Kinda looks like we have a *couple* of new singers in the house tonight. We're going to start with…" he struggled to read Lester's scrawl in the dim light. "Leslie?"

"That's Lester," he said standing and making his way back to the front of the bar.

"Hi, Lester," Arne said, noticing the contours of his face as he got closer. "Where ya' from?"

"Here and there," Lester said, softly.

"Are you ready to make your Puddin' Tap debut Lester?" he asked, adding a smirk.

"I guess I am," Lester said.

Arne left the stage and Lester positioned himself in front of the microphone at the edge of the spotlight. He did not tell Fiona that he would be singing *their* song, but when the shimmery bells rang out through the tinny speakers she knew exactly which song Lester would be performing. He waited for the words to appear on the blue television screen. He didn't need them, but they were a pleasant and familiar diversion from the emotions that the words held for him. He was still getting accustomed to "saloon singing" but it was all or nothing at all.

"You're my lamb. You're my angel." he started.

Fiona listened to Lester sing like it was the first time she had heard the words. Every syllable was filled with an expression of love.

The faint penumbra from the streetlight just beyond the window backlit Lester, creating a familiar silhouette while the electric glow radiating from the karaoke monitor gave his face a soft blue tint.

"I'm not a thousand miles away," he sang.

By the time Lester approached that last few lines of the song, every person in the room was hypnotized. Even the Howard brothers were visibly touched by Lester's performance.

As the final note rang out, Lester set the microphone into the stand and walked back to the table. Mavis Ketchum and one of her girlfriends were clutching the collars of their dresses and weeping openly. Betty was misty eyed—thinking about her father back in Orton's Cove. Peter put his arm on the back of her chair in an awkward attempt to comfort her. He understood what she was feeling. He thought about his mother all alone in the big old house. Even Puddin' was moved by Lester's performance.

"Can I just say '*WOW*'?" Arne barked into the microphone as the applause filled the room. The volume was disproportionate to the number of people present.

"Why ain't he still singing in the show?" Crenshaw whispered to McDaniel.

"Look at that mug," was the response.

"We gotta find a way to use that to our advantage," Crenshaw whispered.

McDaniel looked at Crenshaw and said, "This from the guy who wrote the book on taking advantage." Crenshaw took offense, but he could see the truth in the facts.

McDaniel softened. "He is amazing, isn't he?"

Lester sat back down at the table and Fiona wrapped her arms around him. He blushed a bit and ducked his head but she caught him and gave him a big kiss.

Viola and Betty watched the skinny man in the pork-pie hat, with the slicker over his shoulder, saunter past the table and slip the little scrap of paper into Arne's hand then glide back to his seat at the bar.

Viola stood up and stepped around the table and approached Arne. She handed him a slip as well.

"What do have we here?" Arne popped into the microphone. "Are you a singer too, Princess?"

"I sing a little," she whispered.

"You sit down, let me get Clifford up here, then you'll be next." Arne smiled broadly at the tender child.

"Yes, sir," Viola said, making her way back to the table.

"Don't call me 'sir,' " Arne said. "I work for a living." Arne busted out in such an uproarious laughter he startled everyone at the table. The rest of the patrons were used to it and didn't even seem to notice.

"Now, Clifford. Come back on up," he said when he finally caught his breath. "You got a tough act to follow, and you're coming before a pretty young lady, so mind your manners."

Clifford—hat now on his head and slicker over his shoulder—sidled back to the microphone and winked at the table where the strangers sat. Clifford tipped his hat as the swirling sounds filled the air and he stepped into the blue glow of the television monitor. The illusion, it seemed, was perfect—until he opened his mouth.

"The summer winds. Came blowin' in. Across the sea..." he croaked the words out like they hurt his throat. Perhaps it didn't hurt *him*, but they certainly hurt the crowd. There was not one line that wasn't burdened with accuracy of tone or timing. When he was done singing, people were applauding for the end of the performance. Clifford believed otherwise. There was no harm in that.

As Clifford strolled past the revivalists, he leaned in between Lester and Fiona and said, "I'm a meteorologist by day. How about that?" He winked and walked back to his seat.

Lester knew a man who did not understand his shortcomings when he saw one. It was best to let a man believe what he wished to believe.

Arne stepped in front of the microphone and adjusted the height for Viola.

"Alright," Arne started. "Everyone please give a warm Puddin' Tap welcome to Viola. Come on up, young lady. The stage is yours."

Viola moved hesitantly. She almost hated to be too far from Peter for more than a few minutes, but she wanted to sing for him, like Lester had sung for love. She would use the song to tell Peter, and everyone else, just how she was beginning to feel about him. She didn't even notice the microphone Arne offered her. She didn't need it. She fixed an intense stare on Peter and the words poured out as the music started.

"Maybe I hang around here. A little more than I should. We both know I got somewhere else to go..."

Arne watched in amazement as the young girl wrapped her entire being around every note and lyric without restraint. Mavis and her girlfriends were racked with heavy sobs. Puddin was even seen wiping the corners of his eyes with a damp old bar rag.

Viola sang her tender little heart out and for one moment, the Puddin' Tap was a suburb of Heaven. When the song was over and she sat back down, Viola surprised everyone when she took Peter's hand and held it. Betty smiled at the two of them. McDaniel and Crenshaw shared a specific uneasiness. This could either be the greatest thing in the world, or it could end up in teenage heartbreak. Either way, Fiona seemed to approve and that was all Viola really cared about—beyond Peter's reciprocation.

Peter was thrilled—but a little anxious. He looked to Betty who smiled broadly at him and Viola. Little beads of sweat began to form around his hairline. One dripped down his forehead and into his eye. Fiona smiled at them as Peter blinked the sweat away.

"Now it's your turn," Arne said to Betty. "Your friends can sing. How about you?"

"I...I..."

"Come on, Darlin'" he laughed as he approached the table where they all sat. "You can do it. It's only karaoke."

"Alright," Betty giggled, standing and smiling at Peter again. He smiled back at her.

"You'll do great," Peter said.

Arne asked Betty if there was a song she'd like to sing. She was awkward, unsure of herself. She pulled out the slip of paper she had filled out but had kept concealed in her lap. She gave it over hesitantly. Arne turned and headed back to the front of the bar.

Betty started to get up and then she sat back down. She looked around nervously. Everyone at the table encouraged her to get up and sing. They coaxed and cajoled until she got up in front of them and grabbed the microphone.

"Ready, Betty?" Arne said. He let out that howling laugh once again. "Ready, Betty? That rhymes... Get it?"

"I guess so," she said. "I've only ever sang in church before."

"You mean you've never done this before?" he asked sarcastically.

"Never in a bar, only in church, or with the school choir."

"Just think of this as our little church," Arne howled.

The music started. It startled Betty, but she resolved to give it her best shot. "At first I was afraid. I was petrified. Kept thinking I could never live without you by my side..." She closed her eyes and belted out the words.

It was painfully obvious Viola and Lester were the singers of the group. It wasn't that Betty was categorically bad; it was just she sang in a key different from the one that was playing. Her key, or keys, happened to be uniquely their own. However, what Betty lacked in ability, she compensated for with enthusiasm. It didn't take long before she was dancing, her eyes still closed, throwing her head back and forth. She put her arms out to the world and twirled around carelessly until the microphone cord wrapped around her and she had to stop.

As the song came to an end, she was just coming out of the knot. She handed the microphone back to Arne and floated back to her chair on the audience's applause.

"That was wonderful," Arne said diplomatically. "Maybe we can get Betty back up here again before the night is over."

Peter wiggled his eyebrows as if to suggest it would be fun.

"Okay," she gushed. "Maybe."

"But now," Arne said. "I want to sing a little song. I'm sending this one out to a special little lady... She knows who I am!"

Crenshaw couldn't have cared less about Arne's singing of an Elvis classic. He stood up and asked if anyone at the table wanted another drink.

"I got it," Fiona said, standing up. She took everyone's order and brought the black plastic drink tray with her to the bar. She gave Puddin the order. While she waited for the drinks, Clifford approached her.

"I'm Clifford," he told her. "I'm a meteorologist. I just sang, up there, a few songs ago."

"So I heard," Fiona said. She looked over at Lester who was calmly watching the interaction with one eye and Arne's performance with the other.

"You know, a *weather* guy," Clifford said.

Then it dawned on Fiona, "Ah, that's why you sang 'Summer Wind' isn't it?"

"I'd sing 'Ride the Wild Lightning' if they had it." He laughed at his own joke.

Puddin set the drinks on the tray.

"How about 'Fire and Rain'?" Fiona said. She laughed gently for Clifford's benefit as she turned to walk back to the table.

"Hey, that's a good idea. I wonder if Frankie ever did that?" he asked her.

"I don't know," she called back.

Clifford scurried back to his seat and ripped the book open. He scanned the pages—reading as fast as his lips could move.

Fiona set the tray on the table. Betty was happy to see that Fiona had also remembered her cherries.

"Excuse me, sir. Do *you* sing?" a female voice asked McDaniel.

It was Mavis Ketchum hovering over him. She smelled of beer and Spaghettios. McDaniel was a lonely man, but he had hoped he would never become that lonely.

"No, madam. I surely do not," he answered.

"Do you dance?" she belched.

"No, madam, I surely don't," McDaniel replied.

"Don't call me '*madam*'. I'm just one of the girls," Mavis laughed. "My name is Mavis." A speck of orange-brown pasta jumped out of her mouth, landing on the white lapel of McDaniel's jacket. He casually flicked it off with a pudgy index finger and smiled. McDaniel was looking at Crenshaw for the save.

"Mavis, well that's a beautiful name," Crenshaw said, standing up. "I'm Reverend Harland J. Crenshaw."

Mavis stretched out her hand. "Mavis," she repeated. "Mavis Ketchum."

"It's my pleasure to make your acquaintance," he lied as he escorted her back to her seat by the bar.

McDaniel watched as Crenshaw flirted with the woman, he whispered in her ear and tickled her elbow lightly before easing his way back to the table.

"What did you tell her?" McDaniel asked Crenshaw as he returned to his chair.

"I told her that I would be honored if she would spend a little time with me after hours," Crenshaw said.

"Are you crazy?" McDaniel asked.

"She's drunk," Crenshaw said quickly. "There's no chance she'll remember the invitation, and we'll be gone by sunrise."

"But…"

"She was clearly not your type, and I didn't want to be embarrassed, or worse, have her feelings hurt."

"But what if she does remember?" McDaniel was panicked for Crenshaw's sake.

"A kiss is still a kiss," Crenshaw said leaning back in his chair as Arne's song ended.

Lester was good-naturedly racing Clifford back toward the host and the microphone. Both men had their request slips extended. This put Arne in a difficult position. If he took Clifford's slip first, he risked offending guests, not to mention the people who didn't want to hear Clifford sing again. If he took Lester's slip first, Arne was in the position to offend Clifford who, despite being an irritating man and a mediocre meteorologist, was still a regular customer.

Lester allowed Clifford the win, graciously.

"The man knows talent," Clifford said to Arne.

Arne read Clifford's song and then looked at Lester's request and said, "We'll get your song on next, Lester. Are you ready, Clifford?"

"I am," Clifford said throwing the coat over his shoulder and grabbing the microphone.

Arne walked back to the karaoke control board. Clifford closed his eyes and looked down at his feet for a moment as the music began to fill the air.

The little meteorologist began his assault on the opening lines, "Just yesterday morning they let me know you were gone."

"LOOK AT THIS MUG"

The insect lights snapped, claiming more innocent lives. The enclosed screen house served as a conference room for the small party who sipped iced tea and talked quietly to one another.

All around them outside was inky wet darkness only broken up by the dim lights from the rental cabins. According to the signs, the beach was closed, as was the game room and the dining hall. Crenshaw had convinced the owner, a hollow-chested man in horn-rimmed glasses, to let them use the little room to unwind and plan their next move.

Crenshaw's mood had lightened, if only because of the distance the day's travel had put between him and Deacon Feller's daughter. Lester was happy for the opportunity to sing for Fiona even if it was in a saloon. McDaniel was worried about Mavis Ketchum and little else.

Fiona dozed peacefully on the plastic cushion in the cast iron easy chair. The brightly colored cushion reflected large purple orchids and offered sticky comfort. The neon yellow flower arrangement in the middle of the picnic table seemed to help keep everyone else awake, but she had already enjoyed two beers and that was all she needed to fall comfortably asleep.

Crenshaw and McDaniel sat across the small table from Lester and Peter. Road-worn maps surrounded the gaudy flower arrangement and weathered spiral-bound notebooks in various states of disarray.

Peter moved the arrangement to the floor of the meeting room.

Betty and Viola were the only ones not in attendance. They were sleeping easily in the firm cedar-smelling beds in their cabin.

"We had a little fun tonight," Crenshaw said, his watchful eye scanning the dark for any sign of Mavis Ketchum.

McDaniel shifted his weight, which unbalanced the entire meeting space. He quickly adjusted and steadied the table. "We'll head east in the morning," McDaniel started. "If we stick to parkways and state highways, we're likely to find a plethora of welcome mats waiting for us out on the open road."

"That's the dang plan?" Peter asked. "If that's the plan, I don't like it."

He was proud of himself. This was something he and Luther used to say to each other when there was work to do and one of them felt the other had an easier load. It was all in fun, but now he missed Luther. He missed his mother. He preferred the slow anonymous life in Orton's Cove. His one consolation was Viola.

"Do you have a better plan?" McDaniel asked, scratching his fleshy chin.

"I'm not the manager, but shouldn't we decide which towns we're going to stop in and how long we're going to stay?" Peter said, in an uncharacteristic display of logic.

He quickly lit a cigarette and watched the bluish smoke disappear over their heads.

"Towns change," McDaniel said. "Strip malls go up; cinemas with 14 screens get built. The genius of this business is pulling into a town and smelling the air and knowing if this town is going to welcome you with open arms, or send you packing."

"McDaniel is right, Peter," Lester said. "Back when I was in the show we could plan for days and days and then get to the town and we land right in the middle of some civic event and no one would be able to see us. Or the town was gone all together. Or the town was the same but the people had changed. There's always going to be people who want their spirits lifted, but maybe not as many people that want to be entertained. Today, there's too many distractions.

Too many arcades, cinemas, miniature golf resorts. The same towns that were successful two years ago might have changed. You just never know."

"And there are too many carnies out there making it difficult for a respectable revival to remain respectable," McDaniel added.

"You said something just there," Crenshaw said motioning toward Lester. "You said when you were in 'the show'. What happened that you aren't in the show anymore?"

"Look at this mug," Lester said, pointing at his own face.

"What about it?" Crenshaw insisted. "It's your voice that matters."

"I don't think so," Lester said. "There have been too many years and too many miles."

Lester's mind wandered back to his final show—remembering the night as if it was yesterday, although it was many years and even more miles away.

❀

McDaniel was traveling with Lord Kirin, the fire-eating midget who spoke in tongues. Mae Anne Doyle, known as the Farmer's Daughter, who sang hymns and played the concertina, was accompanying them.

Mae Anne Doyle had been like a mother to Little Lester. That's what they called him back then—Little Lester—with his bright eyes and his angelic voice.

Together this small, but passionate, band of entertainers scoured the countryside bringing joy and salvation to every farm and field where the old Dodge would carry them. In those days, they were welcomed in every burg and hamlet they happened to visit.

It was a beautiful show every night. In those days, McDaniel spent time preaching to the congregation. He was slimmer and more at ease in front of a crowd. His voice was full of lusty reverence that reached out and caressed the sinners assembled there before him.

Mae Anne, who would sing soothing renditions of traditional hymns, followed McDaniel's ardent sermon each night accompanied by an ancient concertina. McDaniel found the old instrument at a farm auction. He thought of Mae Anne the moment he saw it, so he splurged on her—one of the most talented and caring performers of the tribe.

Shortly after McDaniel presented the concertina to Mae Anne, she taught herself to play the instrument. Mae Anne could be seen by the light of the fire almost every night—long after everyone went to bed—squeezing the little box and pushing the shiny buttons until she got something that sounded like music. Soon enough she was playing recognizable hymns. McDaniel was impressed—but he knew she could do it all along.

Lord Kirin performed after Mae Anne. His thick-limbed body was surprisingly agile as he bounded across the stage swallowing the ends of the flaming sticks and speaking in various tongues—real and imagined.

Lord Kirin was the third in a line of Kirin men who—after a startlingly cold baptism in the Lost River Cave—experienced the epiphany and the gift. This Lord Kirin was the last one still performing and the only one who was without actual scars.

No one was sure exactly what he was saying—when he performed— but no one questioned the fact he was speaking the language from some faraway place. Folks rarely question fire-eating midgets, especially when they can't understand what they are saying.

When Kirin's performance was complete, the audience was typically quite happy to see Little Lester take the stage. Lester would strum his old box guitar and sing. From where he stood, he could see the women clutching their breasts and swaying to his music. The men just removed their hats and let their heads fall against their sunburned chests.

As autumn turned to winter, the little troupe went on hiatus because no one was interested in sitting in a tent—or anywhere too far from their hearth—to freeze for any reason, God himself or otherwise.

The following fateful spring, they reassembled without Kirin. He had fallen in love with a bottomless dancer named Hilda who worked in a popular sailor bar on Long Island. They were married before the first thaw.

Mae Anne was there and, of course, McDaniel was there along with Little Lester who wasn't so little anymore. Mae Anne noticed the change first but said nothing. Standing there, clutching her battered concertina case, she knew she was no prize either.

The season started out like any other. They were playing to crowded tents across the South and even up into the southern portion of the Midwest. They were pitching the tents in towns they had only dreamed about playing and the coffers were beginning to bulge.

Lester seemed different somehow. McDaniel made note of it yet he didn't know what to do about it, if in fact there was anything to do. Lester's voice was still pure, but people didn't seem as drawn to him as they had been in the past. McDaniel realized that whatever was happening it would have to play itself out.

Finally, in Cairo, Illinois McDaniel realized what the problem was. As Lester took the stage, he saw the discomfort on the faces of the young ladies in the front row. Lester had realized something was happening to him too, but rather than admit that he was getting uglier with each new day, he focused on singing and playing better.

Unfortunately, what he saw in the faces of the girls in the front row that day stayed with Lester. When he tried to strum his guitar his fingers felt like clay. Then his throat closed. He couldn't breathe. He was just too ugly.

Lester was not used to this type of reception. His entire life was a series of smiles and applause and strangers looking at him lovingly as he did the only—the purest—thing he knew how to do. Lester's own joy was paralleled by the joy he brought to the people who filled the tents. Suddenly that joy was replaced with discomfort and tension. He had no words for what he was experiencing.

When he tried to describe the feeling to Mae Anne, she called it stage fright. She said it was normal. She did not want to discourage the boy. She said he would get over it, that the feelings would pass. But every time Lester opened his mouth to sing, his discomfort would cover the songs like a wet wool blanket. The scared young man tried and tried again, but all he could do now was croak pitifully. Then, one night, after a long run of dissatisfying shows, Lester's eyes filled with tears as he turned and walked off of the plywood stage.

"Jeezus!" one woman said to another, just loud enough for Lester to hear. "Did you see the mug on that kid?"

The sound of Lester's heart breaking was deafening in his ears. McDaniel and Mae Anne watched the young man drag himself to the old Dodge and throw himself onto the faded hood. For the rest of the show and the encore Lester looked out across the waves of wheat and didn't say a word.

When he heard McDaniel's voice coming out of the tent, he turned and looked at his reflection in the windshield of the car. What Lester saw was the face of a man who was once a boy—a boy who brought joy and warmth to the hearts of hundreds of people. The boy had become a man and that man would never have that childhood experience again.

"Look at that mug," he said quietly. "Look at that mug."

❀

"If you change your mind," Crenshaw said, snapping Lester out of his melancholy reverie. "We could really use your help."

"I done my part the last time Mac asked," Lester said.

"You were remarkable and we are all grateful for the results." McDaniel said.

"No disrespect, Harlan, but I can't see it happening," he said wiping the moisture from his eye. "Wowing the audience? That's Peter's job now. Peter and Viola are doing just fine. They don't—forgive me—you don't need my help. I know where I'm needed and that's just fine with me. You'll have to excuse me." With that, Lester stood up slowly and walked over to where Fiona was sleeping. He slipped his arms under her like a big gentle forklift and pulled her body out of the chair and to his chest without waking her.

"There would have to be something really big to get me back into the show," Lester said looking down at Fiona asleep in his arms. "I ain't just gonna do it to do it. I'm sure you understand."

Peter stood up and opened the screen door. Lester carried Fiona down the dark road to the second cabin.

"How's he gonna open the cabin door?" McDaniel wondered out loud.

Before anyone could hazard a guess, the light in the window went on. They watched Lester's silhouette set Fiona on the bed. A minute later the light went out.

"WHO'D YOU CALL"

The morning sun restored the happy glow to Lester's mug as he checked the ropes and the bungee cords on the truck. This was more for his own benefit than anyone else. The ladies were in the little store stocking up on toiletries while McDaniel and Crenshaw squared the debt with the owner. Moments later, the revivalists were assembled in front of the truck. They decided who was going to ride in the Caddy and who was going to go in the truck but there was still no sign of Peter.

McDaniel sent Viola and Betty to the game room to see if he was there. Lester and Fiona were dispatched to the beach area while the older men waited in case he showed up at the vehicles.

"Here he comes," McDaniel said, motioning towards the young boy, who was strolling a little too casually to where the men were waiting.

"Sorry," Peter said. "I had to make a phone call."

"Well, let's wait here until the search parties return," McDaniel said. "Then we gotta hit the road."

When Viola saw Peter standing beside the truck, the panicked look on her face was replaced by a smile that made Peter stir. Her delicate walk turned into a delicate trot. Betty didn't alter her gait. She wanted Viola to get to Peter first. She enjoyed seeing them happy.

Lester and Fiona came up behind him brushing sand off their

shoes and the cuffs of their pants.

Lester slapped Peter on the back and smiled. "You had us scared for a minute there," he said.

"Peter will ride with us today," Crenshaw said.

The scare was almost too much for him. He wasn't about to let Peter out of his sight again.

"Can I smoke in the car?" Peter asked.

"If you must," McDaniel answered.

"Can Viola ride with us?" he asked.

"I'll ride with Fiona and Lester," Betty offered.

"Fine. Fine. Let's just hit the road," Crenshaw said.

As they pulled out onto the road Crenshaw shifted around and looked at Peter. "Who'd you call?"

"A friend," Peter said cryptically.

He closed his eyes and let the sun warm his face as he gingerly slipped his hand into Viola's. She rested her head on his bony shoulder and closed her eyes.

Crenshaw turned around, but he wasn't satisfied. He didn't like the idea of the boy acting independently like that. It could only lead to trouble.

"ARE YOU READY FOR THE FIRE?"

The light mist did nothing to dissuade the crowd who was already streaming into the gray canvas tent. Excitement crackled like lightening in the air, casting imperceptible blue sparks across everything.

Row after row of anxious visitors was peppered with the usual cynics and the uninitiated. They waited for the lights to go down. Many of the people there had at least heard of the "Tennessee Twister" and they knew they were in for a potentially joyous and wondrous occasion.

For some it was a variation on their standard schedule of waking at sunrise to work on their farms, and then—after a hearty breakfast—going back out into the fields to work. In fact, for most of the people who came out to the tent, the only interruption to farming was eating.

The "Tennessee Twister" was a highly anticipated distraction from their routine.

Suddenly—though—there was talk about the boy with the flaming hands. This was something they could barely comprehend. For the most part, they were happy enough to hear Viola sing. The people out here had become accustomed to being fed tall tales from white suits in shiny Cadillac cars. These tall tales usually met with limited degrees of skepticism. Rural folk learned to take everything they were told by a man in a suit in their stride.

In the corner of the tent, clearly detached from the crowd, stood Gavin Crickle. His sharp, shiny suit hung perfectly on his rail-thin body and his chiseled features were rarely compromised by a smile or a frown.

Earlier that week when his secretary, Patricia, showed him the newspaper clipping about the young girl's singing, he was intrigued. Not normally the sentimental type—he saw money signs where most people saw beauty—he sensed this little singer could be his next epic payday.

It took him very little time to clear his calendar and grab a plane out of the Big Apple to small town America to see the girl they called the "Tennessee Twister".

Judging by the intensity of the crowd, Crickle was already beginning to congratulate himself on his shark-like instincts which told him that he had made the right call. He had left Brad Pitt at a table at Sardi's, but this kid would surely be worth it.

He could see, before he even laid eyes on her, that she possessed the necessary skill to manipulate these bumpkins—to bend them to her subtle will. She had the power. He would teach her how to wield it.

He also sensed *she* was naïve and could be manipulated herself. He just had to get past her handlers who might be a little less gullible. He didn't see them as being any match for him. Gavin Crickle just needed to figure which angle to play as soon as he figured out who he was going to play it on.

First, however, he had to see for himself. He had to be certain that this little girl possessed something that no other 14-year-old girl did.

He had shuffled a lot of things to be here. Pitt was the least of his concerns. He prayed this wasn't a waste of his time. He pulled a heavy dark cigar out of the packet and snipped the tip. He let the little brown stub fall to the grassy floor of the tent. Completely oblivious to the disapproving faces, he lit the stogie with the Zippo Bruce Willis had given him for his last birthday.

The bare bulbs inside the tent flickered once then dimmed as

Crenshaw stepped out into the small pool of light in the center of the sagging plywood stage. He rubbed his hands together and hesitated before addressing the crowd.

"Ladies and Gentlemen," he started. "Boys and girls. Grandmas and Grandpas. When I look out at all of the faces assembled here tonight, I am reminded of a story about a man who walked along the shores of the great sea and reached out to the fishermen there."

He said, "I think you all know this man, and who those fishermen were because you've all heard the stories. You all know that that man was our Lord Jesus Christ and he was gathering souls to help him spread the word—*His word*."

"Amen!" someone called out from the back of the tent.

"Amen is right, brother," he smiled. "Tonight, I walk along the shores of this great community gathering souls to do the Lord's work. His work here in the community must be done as well as his work all around the world."

The practiced speaker paused for a moment to let the monumental concept slip into the collective consciousness of the congregation. There was not a wasted moment or movement in Crenshaw's delivery. Everything was perfectly and economically timed and executed.

"Tonight," he started up again after the appropriate pause. "You will witness the lovely Viola Rogers, the girl some people know as the 'Tennessee Twister.' She will amaze you with her voice as she beckons the angels to join us in praise.

"You will also meet Peter Campbell who has so much of the Lord's love within him that it manifests itself in flames that shoot from his very hands."

"We'll see," someone laughed out loud from the back of the tent.

No one else laughed.

Gavin Crickle forgot about the cigar and gave Crenshaw all of his attention. Was he really about to see a kid shoot flames from his hands? These people had to be either very good at their special effects, or they were banking on the yokels not being very bright.

Even Crickle knew better than to try and scam the meat-and-potatoes families of Middle America in their own back yard. Crickle estimated that if, in fact, there were no glitches, this might be the most important trip of his career. Everything else would be there when he got home. Patricia would see to that.

"I give you," Crenshaw said with a wide sweep of his arms, as he stepped out of the spotlight and Viola whirled her way out onto the stage. "The angel you know as the 'Tennessee Twister'—Viola Rogers!"

"Faith of our fathers sitting there..." she began.

Her voice gave life to a hymn that even the most dedicated Christian would agree had no soul whatsoever. "In spite of dungeon, fire, and sword..." Her alabaster arms scraped against the doors of heaven as she spun herself around and offered up the words. They floated above the crowd until they found a soft heart in which to nestle, or a hard heart to soften.

She segued into 'I'll Fly Away', which Lester loved so much. It only took two choruses to incite the crowd to sing along with her. The bellowing bass vocals of the men assembled on the line "In the mornin' Lordy!" where appropriate. The audience joined in a uniform—if somewhat deafening—level of applause when the song was finished.

Then Viola started to sing 'Amazing Grace' and a sweet gentle hush filled the tent. "How sweet the sound. That saved a child like me..."

This was the last song of Viola's part of the revival and it happened to be Fiona's favorite. It was also a favorite of the congregation and Viola happily sang all four verses, and then repeated the first verse accompanied by the audience. There was barely a dry eye in the county.

The voices were strong and clear and uninterrupted except for the muted electronic beeps that came from just outside the tent. Gavin Crickle had slipped out between the folds and dialed the home office.

"Patricia, it's Gavin," he whispered into the telephone that was about the size of a matchbook. "Put Kellogg on the phone."

There was a short pause.

"Listen Buddy," Crickle said. "Just listen."

Gavin Crickle walked back into the tent and he held the phone out in front of himself. The receiver was aimed at the stage and Viola's voice slipped into the little black hole and journeyed across the cosmos careening from one satellite to the next until they trickled delicately out of the plastic speaker on Kellogg's desk.

Patricia looked at her boss's boss who sat transfixed on the little machine and what it was emitting. She had seen Jack Kellogg go toe to toe with some of the biggest names in the entertainment industry and walk away smiling, but now sitting there listening to the ancient hymn he was getting misty-eyed. This kid had an effect on him like she had never before witnessed.

That night over dinner, Patricia told her husband that Jack Kellogg showed signs that he might be a human being after all.

Right now they both just stared at the speaker box and listened to the angel who seemed to be singing only for them.

"Was blind but now I see…"

When she finished singing, Viola disappeared into darkness behind the folds in the curtain as Crenshaw emerged from the back of the tent, propelling the thunderous applause into another uproar of approval.

Kellogg looked at Patricia. She took the hint and disappeared quickly.

"Now you all know that the Lord giveth," he said.

"And the gubment taketh away," this from the back of the room.

Everyone laughed.

"Work your magic, Gavin," was all Kellogg said.

The line went dead.

Crickle slipped back out into the night. He had to find the little girl and have a quick face to face—at any cost. Moving around the side of the tent, he could hear Crenshaw speaking about donations. The money was for the Lord, no doubt, but the Lord had apparently sent this preacher to collect and hold it for Him.

"Now," Crenshaw said. "I would like to introduce Peter Campbell." And as much as it pained him to praise the boy who had singed his face, Crenshaw added, "This boy is a joy to behold. The Lord speaks through Peter Campbell and you'd best be listening! Are you ready for the fire?"

The crowd roared and jumped to their feet. Maybe there was something to this after all because if it were a fake, there would be serious trouble. There is nothing worse than a pissed-off bean farmer, sweating in a revival tent on an Indian summer night, when work is being neglected.

The recorded music began to play, but the weak pool of light remained deserted. Crenshaw looked around the tent, but he couldn't find Peter anywhere.

"The boy must be experiencing stage fright," he said as he slipped out of the stage light.

What he saw just beyond a little group of pick-up trucks panicked him.

Peter, who was supposed to be on the stage, was arguing with a beanpole of a man in a nicely tailored suit.

"What on earth?" Crenshaw called out as he approached the men. "Peter, you're supposed to be on stage, NOW!"

"This guy wants to see Viola," Peter said, pointing to Gavin Crickle.

"Look," Crickle said. "I don't want any trouble. I am an entertainment agent and I was called here to witness a young singer—Violet? Vanessa? I'm sorry I can't read my notes. I liked what I saw and I wanted to know who was handling her."

"Her name is Viola and no one handles her," Peter shouted. "Besides, I already called the dang William Morris Agency. So just get lost."

Gavin showed Crenshaw a bent white calling card. By now Fiona and McDaniel had joined the discussion. Crenshaw looked at Crickle's calling card for a moment before reading it out loud, "Gavin Crickle, William Morris Agency. Should I go on, Peter?"

"Whyn't you say that in the first place?" Peter said to Mr. Crickle.

"I tried to but...never mind," he laughed, offering his hand to Peter. "Can I meet the little angel now?"

"When we are done for the night, you can join us for our late night meal," Crenshaw said. His eyes glowed with dollar signs. Crickle's suit had to cost more than Crenshaw's entire wardrobe. This might be a good night for everyone, he thought.

Fiona spoke up. "Peter, don't you think you should get back to the tent and give these people what they paid for?" Fiona was nothing if she wasn't practical.

Walking back toward the tent, everyone hesitated for a moment when they heard a familiar voice accompanied by a familiar guitar. The revivalists peered through the opening of the tent and saw Lester in the stage light.

"I walk to the garden alone..." Lester sang.

McDaniel looked at Crenshaw who was looking at where Fiona had been standing. She broke into a graceful pace toward the stage. The sweet music traveled from his guitar directly into her heart. She didn't even try to stop the tears that rolled down her flawless cheeks.

Lester's voice elevated like smoke from a sacred fire. "And he walks with me. And he talks with me. And he tells me I am his own. And the voice I hear. As I tarry there. No other has ever known..."

"Look at the mug on that guy," a man whispered to his wife.

"Hush now," she replied. "The man is singing." She replied wiping a tear from her eye.

"WHERE'S MY BREAKFAST"

Gavin Crickle was a privileged child by any standards. His father, Dick Crickle, was one of the savviest power brokers in Hollywood, at a time when no one was exactly sure what a power broker was.

His mother, Francine, was a relatively anemic ballet dancer who was believed by some to be the illegitimate daughter of Errol Flynn, although any real proof of this lineage has never actually surfaced. Francine never denied or admitted to it, but it made great cocktail party conversation.

There was never a time in his life when Gavin did not get exactly what he wanted at the precise moment he wanted it. Whether it was a toy as a child or a sports car as a teenager, Gavin never got used to the word 'No'.

Growing up, Gavin had a nanny. She was a lovely old woman from Argentina named Consetta. She doted over him as an infant, then later as a toddler. As he grew older, he became increasingly dependent on her, even for the mundane things most people take for granted.

If there was ever a time Gavin knew any form of disappointment, it was at the hands of Consetta and justice was quickly served.

It was on the eve of his tenth birthday when Consetta fell ill. The doctors told Dick and Francine that Consetta needed to rest for a least a week. He was very firm when he insisted that it be uninterrupted bed rest. Nothing he could think of would be important enough to disturb the saintly woman's rest.

The next morning as she lay quietly in her bed, rubbing the rosary beads between her wrinkled pink fingers, some of the neighborhood children celebrated little Gavin's birthday in the yard below her window. They played pin the tail on the donkey, and they bobbed for apples. They shot spitballs at the clown who tried miserably to do some feeble magic tricks for them.

Consetta smiled to herself as she drifted off to a deep and satisfying sleep. The laughter of children, especially little Gavin, was music to her ears. It was love's symphony and nothing made her happier.

The following morning as the sun peered through the window and washed itself across her love-creased face, she tried to pull herself out of the bed. She knew she shouldn't, doctor's orders, but she also knew her little angel would be waiting for her in the kitchen.

Consetta felt bad enough about missing the party. She couldn't stand one more day without Gavin to dote over and to spoil.

The bowl in front of him sat empty and the television screen he stared at was blank. His scowl let her know he disapproved of her sleeping later than him—especially the day after his birthday.

"Where's my breakfast?" he whined.

"One minute, Gavin," she said cheerfully.

"Why isn't the television on for me to watch my cartoons?" he grumbled.

"I'm sorry," she said as she crossed the kitchen to hit the little white button that was no more than a few feet away from where Gavin sat.

She pulled the large yellow box of cereal from the shelf and poured the bowl full for him before turning and shuffling to the refrigerator for milk. By the time the old woman turned around, her little angel had capsized the bowl spreading the little golden nuggets of cereal across the spotless kitchen floor.

"No Sugar Pops," he grunted.

"What would you like then?" she asked sweetly.

He said nothing. He gazed intently as the cartoon cat chased the cartoon mouse with a hammer. The mouse was quicker and smarter, but Gavin always liked the cat better.

She brought down a bright red box and set it next to him. Without pulling his eyes from the television, he swept his arm across and set the box tumbling to the floor.

Next came the green box, but it met with the same fate. The white box was last and the old girl caught it in mid air. This got the little guy's attention. His eyes lit up, but it wasn't with excitement.

"I'm going to go back to bed, Gavin," Consetta said. This time she had to force the sweetness into her voice. "When you are ready to eat, you come and get me."

She walked back up the stairs leaving her little angel to explain the piles of cereal all over the floor, to say nothing of actually having to prepare his own breakfast. She was tired, weak. She needed her rest.

That evening, Francine crept into Consetta's room and lowered herself gently onto the bed. She laid a fragile hand on Consetta's arm and whispered to her.

"Consetta?"

"Yes, Mrs. Crickle," Consetta hadn't been sleeping so much as massaging her rosary beads.

"What happened in the kitchen this morning?"

"The boy was excited," Consetta smiled. "It was nothing. He'll grow out of it."

"I'd say it is something," the boy's mother started.

"Do not worry, Mrs. Crickle," Consetta went on. "The boy didn't mean it."

"I'm not so worried about the boy, Consetta. I am worried that you left that mess in the kitchen and didn't bother to clean it up. What do you think Dick would have done if he came and saw that mess?"

"Mrs. Crickle?"

"I called our friend down at the INS and they will be coming for you in the morning. I just think you'd be happier at home than here. Don't you miss Brazil?"

"But, Mrs. Crickle," Consetta began.

"No matter, I just can't have that level of irresponsibility in my house when I am out. Gavin is far too precious to me," she said.

"You are sending me to Brazil?" Consetta couldn't believe what she was hearing. "If you want to fire me, then fire me. This I will understand. Why would you send me to Brazil? I am Argentinean."

"Peru—Ecuador—whatever. I think Brazil will be just fine. Anyway, it was Dick's choice, not mine," she said curtly. "I will have Mr. Anderson wake you in the morning to supervise your packing. Mr. Floyd from the INS will be here at nine. No hard feelings Consetta?"

"But I'm a citizen of the United States," Consetta objected weakly. "I was born in Grand Rapids, Michigan."

"Okay, then," Mrs. Crickle smiled. "So Brazil it is."

The old woman just closed her eyes and returned to massaging her rosary beads.

When Gavin Crickle saw the reaction of the congregation in the tent—their need to connect with this child—he knew that nothing was going to stop him from cashing in on Viola. If Peter wanted trouble, Crickle could dish it out. He was going to get that little girl to Hollywood if it killed her.

"I ONLY SING GOSPEL, SIR"

Gavin was waiting at the diner when McDaniel and Crenshaw entered. Betty, Lester, and Fiona followed them in. They all sat at a large table and settled in as the waitress brought a pot of coffee and started pouring it for anyone who had turned their cups over for her.

"Where's Violet?" Gavin asked.

"Viola." Fiona corrected.

"She's with Peter," Betty said. "They'll be along in a minute."

Betty beamed; she was proud of her handiwork. It was she that engineered their little rendezvous. She had seen enough of Peter watching Viola and Viola watching Peter. Even though they had barely even progressed to holding hands, they needed some alone time. Now she basked in the glow of their happiness.

"I'm a very busy man," Crickle said.

"If you gotta go," Lester stated flatly, "then go ahead on."

"I didn't mean to be rude, I'm sorry. I'm still on L.A. time."

"You'll have to forgive Ol' Lester," McDaniel interrupted. "He's what you might call 'pragmatic' if you know what I mean."

"I understand," Gavin responded easily.

Crickle could almost visualize this meeting—this girl—translating into large piles of money and he was not about to let that opportunity slip away.

"It's my fault," Crickle said. "Always in a rush."

Deep down, Crickle believed that he deserved more Academy Awards than many of his clients. He was not only a better actor; he was quicker on his feet.

"Hey… There is no fault here. You're among friends," Crenshaw said, trying to lighten the mood. "Tell us about California."

Just then, the screen door creaked and Viola and Peter walked in together. Peter stopped at the table behind them to flick the ash from his cigarette into an ashtray. They sat down across from Crickle.

"I'll get right to the point," Crickle said. "I am in the position of making your little songbird a very popular and wealthy little songbird. With the right songs and proper music arrangements, coupled with the necessary video and corporate sponsorship exposure." Crickle paused, for effect, then looked squarely into Viola's eyes. "You could be the next Whitney Houston."

"I only sing Gospel, Sir," she said quietly. "Sometimes I sing other things but mostly I only sing Gospel."

McDaniel and Crenshaw exchanged amused looks. Lester and Fiona exchanged relieved glances. Betty just smiled at Peter who was smiling at Viola. Crickle was the only one not enjoying this transaction.

"I don't think you're plugged in here, Honey," Crickle said shifting in his seat.

"What he's trying to say is–" Crenshaw started.

"I can speak for myself, Mr. Crenshaw," Crickle interrupted.

"Reverend." he corrected quietly.

"What I am saying is that you need to get into the loop with me on this one, Vi-baby. If you dump this musty tent show and come back with me to LA, we'll make so much money that you can give it to any church you want. Wouldn't that make you happy?"

"My name is *Viola* and this tent and the people in it are what makes me happy, Sir," she said. "No disrespect intended."

"Are you trying to tell me that traveling around like a gypsy with these rednecks is your idea of fun?"

The thin line of sweat that had betrayed him only once before now made an unwelcome appearance on Crickle's perfectly coiffed brow. Crickle shifted his weight uncomfortably as he looked from face to face as if they were a bad dream his father could buy his way out of.

"That's about enough of that," Peter said.

He snubbed out his cigarette and reached for a fresh one. He drew a tight focus on the skinny man's bony face. His glare never wavered. This was his golden moment.

"Do you think I didn't see that little trick with the fire? You're a fake. She's the real deal." Crickle said firmly.

Peter stood up slowly. Viola pulled him down into his seat.

"What the hell are you gonna do *James Dean*? You think I'm afraid of you? You got a better offer here for your little *friend*?" he paused. "Oh. I see what's going on. You're all shakedown artists. Okay, I can appreciate that. Everyone wants a slice of the pie before Violet leaves. That's fine. Let's talk turkey. Who's first? You, kid?" Crickle pulled out his checkbook and a pen laughing quietly to himself.

"No one wants your money, Mister," Lester said. "And for the last time, her name is *Viola*!"

"Are you the father?" Crickle snapped. "If you're not the father, then I'd like to speak with a parent. I'm talking serious business here."

Lester adjusted himself in his chair but didn't stand up. He didn't need to. The look on his face was enough to scare a man.

Crickle was very aware of Lester's presence. He was in too deep, and he knew he had to see this thing to its conclusion.

"He's my friend," Viola whispered.

"That's because you don't know any better," Crickle spat out too quickly.

His glare frightened her and she leaned a little closer to Peter.

"So who speaks for her? Whose name goes on the line that is dotted," Crickle asked. He always loved that line, but he had to admit, it sounded better coming from Alec Baldwin.

"Y'all ready to order?" the waitress asked. She had come up to the table quietly. No one noticed her. She seemed to defuse the situation—if only for a moment.

"Yes," McDaniel said, looking at the menu. "I'd like…" McDaniel started.

"We are not ready to order," Crickle barked.

"You don't have to be rude," Crenshaw said, in time with the waitress.

They looked at each other and smiled.

Crenshaw knew who he wanted to bring home that night. Her name was Elizabeth. She was a divorcee who lived around the corner from the restaurant. She had a fat one-eyed poodle named Ringo waiting at home for her. But there was no one else.

"Where am I?" Crickle asked rhetorically. "Is this Night Gallery? Am I in hell? Where is Rod Serling?" Crickle's agitation level was spiraling upward at a deadly speed. "Do you people have any idea who I am?"

"If I'da known you were the one they were-" Peter started and then stopped himself as quickly.

Crenshaw eyed Peter warily.

"Nothin'," Peter mumbled to himself.

They all shook their heads and looked at one another for clues. None of them had ever seen him or heard of him before. The only knowledge they had was what was printed on his bent little business card. Peter pulled the card out of his pocket and flipped it onto the table.

"Mister," Lester started. "No one really cares who you are. We were doing just fine before we met you and will do just fine long after you're gone."

Despite the fact that the mountains of money were slipping away before his very eyes, McDaniel was heartened by Lester's statement. It rang of longevity for the crew, which translated into different piles of money—immediate piles of money. These piles might not be as big, but there would be less people claiming a stake and the money would spend the same.

"Peter is right," Crenshaw added quickly. "We regret causing you any inconvenience, but Viola is going to stay here with her family."

"We'll see about that," the angry Crickle said. He stood up so quickly the chair fell over behind him. "This isn't over!" he said as he stormed out of the restaurant.

Later that night, sitting on the side of the lumpy, pink bed, Crenshaw pulled off his shoe and let it fall to the ground. He looked over at Elizabeth, lying next to him. He sighed.

"Come on, Sweetie," she giggled. "We got all night. Are you ready to see what I can serve up for you?"

He smiled at his reflection in the mirror before sliding under the covers.

Elizabeth's dog, Ringo, moaned quietly once as he laid his head on the cool tile floor. All was well for some folks that night.

"IS THIS GOING TO BE OKAY"

The locals called it the Chop Chop House. It was barely a house, more a weathered decaying wooden shack where the old Korean woman everyone knew as Miss Chop Chop butchered whatever animal was brought to her.

Miss Chop Chop spoke almost no English. At least no one remembers ever having heard her speak any English, except for the words "Chop Chop." The men would throw the geese, or the ducks, or other assorted woodland creatures up on the Formica counter for her to dress while they stepped outside and smoked cigarettes and talked about trivialities to pass the time.

Miss Chop Chop had the dexterity of a surgeon and she kept her work area equally clean. The outside of her humble hovel was less than inviting, but inside was as clean as any operating room and it smelled of garlic and lilacs rather than bottled disinfectant.

No one was really sure where Miss Chop Chop came from or how long she had been there. Generations of men had hazy memories of their grandfathers bringing them to the little shack after a successful hunt.

They would lean against the ageless oak trees or squat in the tall grass smoking unfiltered cigarettes listening to the musical rhythms her cleaver made on the table. Her precision was orchestral and the men reveled in the music.

When the sounds stopped, they re-entered the little building and gave her a few crumpled dollar bills. Some of the more skilled hunters were known to shoot an extra bird for her. She nodded gratefully and uttered something in her mystical tongue.

Miss Chop Chop was seen in town once a week shopping for the essentials, candle oil and rice mostly. Cigarettes were her one vice. She went through cigarettes the way an adolescent goes through sweet smelling chewing gum. Other than her weekly shopping sojourn, Miss Chop Chop stayed completely to herself. She saw no use in trying to talk to people who wouldn't understand her anyway.

Her contentment came from climbing the old walnut tree behind the Chop Chop House. She enjoyed perching herself on the highest branch she could reach where she could smoke cigarettes and look out over the rolling hills and smaller trees. It was from this vantage point she saw the tent being erected and the chairs being unloaded. She lit another cigarette, from the tip of the one she had been smoking, and watched as the fat man in the white clothes and the slender man in the black clothes directed the movements of everyone around them.

There was the big, strong looking man who appeared to be whistling happily as he moved from chore to chore. Miss Chop Chop saw a young boy milling about, not really doing anything. Even from this distance, his slouching shoulders gave him away. She decided he was the sullen type.

There were two young girls in the back of the truck not being very helpful at all. The older girl laughed out loud and looked around at all of the activity taking place just a few feet from where she sat on the back of a truck talking to the other, much younger girl.

The younger one radiated beauty so innocently Miss Chop Chop felt her soul being hurtled back in time, to a place where her own daughter had once brought her happiness in the same innocent and radiant way. This was before the train came through town and carried the young girl far away to the university where she learned all about statistics and algorithms. Somewhere along the learning curve, she seemed to have forgotten about the Chop Chop house and the woman living alone there.

There was another woman who was doing more physical labor than any of the men. This woman made Miss Chop Chop smile. She knew a lot about these strong women who work hard and are grateful for the opportunity to do so.

Miss Chop Chop climbed down from the tree and scurried back into her shack. There she pulled the glossy white cardboard box out from its place under her modest cot. She opened the box slowly and pulled the pink satin dress out and held it to her cheek. She was careful not to get any dust on the dress.

Miss Chop Chop packed the dress away in that box years ago. She decided to wear it to the tent tonight. She had every intention of seeing what the beautiful young girl did.

As quickly as the tents went up, the group was surrounded by white media vans with bold red lettering on the side. Neither McDaniel nor Crenshaw could decide what to focus on, the set up or the tide of media. What was worse, was that it was too early for this level of attention. This much attention meant a palm—or two— would have to be greased.

Men in baseball caps and wool sweaters began pulling cameras and microphones out of one of the vans while a young woman in tight jeans and a T-shirt walked around with a little black device in her hands.

The device—a light meter—hung around her neck when she wasn't using it. The harmless little instrument was used to read light levels, but to Peter and Lester it could have been a scanner for detecting lethal toxins in the air.

"I'm looking for Peter Campbell," a little man with a wiry beard and wild hair said to Betty as he approached the revivalists' truck.

"He's here," Betty said. "Somewhere." She looked around, nervously, hoping to spot either Crenshaw or McDaniel. "Can I help you with somethin'?"

"My name is Hack Granville and I'm with CNN," the man said offering her his card. "I tried to make it out yesterday, but there was a tremendous fire in Riverside County and I ended up covering that. I hope I'm not too late."

"Too late?" Betty asked.

"I'm curious to see why this revival is different from any other that travels around the countryside. Call me a skeptic, but I've seen enough of these dog and pony shows to be a bit jaded."

He moved around the truck slowly finding himself eye to eye with Viola who had slipped up behind Betty. Viola smiled at him briefly and the pang of something familiar rushed through his heart.

"You will be glad you came, Mr. Granville," Betty said. "I can promise you that."

"I already am," he said, softly to himself.

"Hello, friend," McDaniel boomed as he waddled over to where the stranger was talking to the girls. "Clayton McDaniel at your service. And you are–"

"Hack Granville, CNN," the man replied, offering a business card and his press badge. "I got a call from a Peter Campbell."

The light went on over McDaniel's head. He didn't hear the rest of what the man had to say. Peter was finally catching on. Maybe the boy *is* ready. Either way, there is no bad publicity. He made a mental note to congratulate Peter later.

"As you can see," McDaniel started. "We are very busy right now, but if you can work around us, we can surely work around you."

"That'll be fine," the newsman said. "If you'll excuse me…"

Hack nodded to the girls, then to McDaniel before rejoining his crew in setting up cameras and checking power cords.

"Is this going to be OK?" Betty asked McDaniel.

"Much better'n that, Betty," McDaniel chuckled. "It's going to be downright dandy."

"I JUST SORT OF FELT LIKE IT"

Fiona couldn't take her eyes off Lester who was busy making short work out of an overstuffed sandwich and a Kayo. Some of the local women had prepared a picnic basket full of sandwiches and apples and crackers and Kayo.

"What?" Lester said through a mouthful of corned beef on rye.

Fiona wiped a dab of brown mustard off his chin. Her smile never wavered.

"What, Baby?" he asked again.

"You sang the other night in the tent, Lester. You sang again and it was beautiful," she wiped a tear from her eye.

"Oh, that," he said. "Do we have any more Chicken in a Biscuits? Or is it Chicken's in a Biscuit? What're they called?" he asked.

"Baby, you sang in front of people again and it was the most beautiful thing I have ever heard. What made you do it? What made you sing? Did Mr. McDaniel make you sing again?"

"Nope. What?" Lester slowed down his chewing for a moment.

"I know he hooked me by having you sing," Fiona said softly. "It's okay."

"Okay then," Lester sighed relief.

"So who did you sing for?" she persisted.

"The kid," Lester said. "Hand me another Kayo, please?"

Disturbing Lester's lunch was not really dangerous so much as futile. There was little that could distract him from the act of eating and while most of his communication was typically limited to grunts and nods. He tried to be more attentive for Fiona, but the corn beef was melting in his mouth like butter.

Fiona pulled another brown can out of the basket and opened it for him. She set it in front on the table and removed the empty one. She pulled a fresh napkin out of the basket and—after wiping the corner of his mouth—she set the napkin down next to his plate.

"The kid?" she asked.

"That's part of it," Lester said. "The kid has never even been out of his hometown and here he is traveling around with us doin' his... his hands."

"And..."

"And—well—he pretty much showed me where my place was."

"And..."

"He's good like that."

"You said the kid was part of it," she pressed. "What was the other part?"

Lester hesitated. "I just sort of felt like it..."

"You just sort of..."

"Sometimes the feeling takes you over and you have no choice," Lester said. "Are there anymore corn beef sandwiches?"

"Yeah, baby," Fiona said pulling another sandwich out of the basket for her man.

"Aren't you eating?" he asked.

"I'm not hungry, Lester," she said. "You can have mine."

The smile returned to her beautiful face.

"Puttin' up that tent is hungry work, Fiona," Lester said.

"You take your time and eat as much as you want, my beautiful man," Fiona answered.

Lester smiled at her for a moment before taking a long sip of his frosty Kayo.

"ARE YOU PROUD GOOD PEOPLE?"

The tent was filled beyond capacity. Between the camera crews and the curious locals, there wasn't room to fit one more body in. Hack Granville sat at the back of the room sucking on an unlit pipe.

Miss Chop Chop was in the front row. Her hair was swept back in a tidy bun and the dress, although a little tighter than it was decades earlier, was now illuminated by the stage lights spilling across her pristine dress. The men who recognized her nudged each other and pointed. No one remembered ever seeing her in anything but the patched-up black shawl and butchers smock. No one realized how simply beautiful she was.

Crickle was in the last row. He had adopted a less conspicuous look. Denim trousers and a plaid shirt replaced the shiny blue suit. He was wearing a battered straw cowboy hat that covered his $150 haircut.

Crenshaw started the sermon as he walked into the little pool of light. "I have very little to say tonight. We *all* know why we are here. Do I need to tell you?"

"Do tell. Do tell," Miriam O'Shea called out from her place in the fourth row.

"Let me just say this," Crenshaw said somberly. "God resists the proud, but gives strength to the humble. Are you proud? I said *Are you proud* Good people?"

"No sir."

"Not me."

"No way."

The voices came from throughout the crowded tent.

"Well, you know what," he was into his wind up. "I am! I am! I am proud to be a servant of the Lord. Say it with me: '*I am proud to be a servant of the Lord.*' "

The braver voices shouted while the timid whispered, but it only took three chants to get nearly everyone in the room chanting. "I am proud to be a servant of the Lord."

When the newsman caught himself saying it, he stopped and looked around to see if any of his crew had noticed him. He needn't have bothered as they were all saying it too.

"Here she is," the Reverend swept his arm across the chanting crowd. "Viola Rogers!"

As Viola entered, the crowd noise died down. There were a few muffled sounds, but the quiet eventually consumed them all—if only for a moment.

Viola positioned herself in the stage light modestly. Then she began to sing.

"Seek and ye shall find. Ask and it shall be given." She slowly began to swirl around the edges of the pool of light. "Knock and it shall be opened. Seek and ye shall find."

She repeated the chorus. Only this time, Lester joined her on stage.

He deftly dropped his words into her open spaces.

"Seek," he sang.

"If you seeketh you will findeth..." Viola added.

"Ask!" Lester inserted.

"If you asketh you'll receiveth..." Viola sang.

"Knock,'' he went on.

"Knocketh and it shall be open. Seek and ye shall find."

As the two voices wrapped around each other in a glorious embrace, they moved through the tent and cascaded between the rickety wooden chairs. Viola whirled around Lester who stood still but raised his arms in an attempt to bridle the passion and bestow it upon the crowd.

Sooner than planned, Viola moved to the back of the tent and left Lester on his own to sing his verse one last time, alone in the stage light. Which he did and when Lester finished, the applause, resonated in his tender ears like he remembered from his childhood. The cheers and the prayers shook the canvas walls of the tent. And for the first time in a long time, Lester felt like he was home.

Crenshaw shuffled back to the stage light and held his arms out as if to embrace the congregation. His face was a beacon of love and everyone in that room became a desperate ship in an unforgiving sea.

When he began to speak, the crowd fell silent.

"We learn in Second Timothy that God did not give us a spirit of cowardice, but rather a spirit of power. When you meet Peter Campbell you will see exactly what that power is."

Crenshaw took another quick exit as Peter entered from the opening in the curtains in the back of center stage. Peter stood for a moment—alone—and looked around at the unfamiliar faces.

The young man examined the eager faces of the people gathered there. The people who wanted, needed something to believe in. To witness firsthand the power of the love that lived within the tent that night.

Peter slowly raised his right hand, then his left. He reached up toward the highest point in the tent and stretched. The first balls of fire to leave his hands were deep red. This surprised Viola and Fiona, and someone in the audience screamed. The red flames were Peter's favorites. He loved when they flashed red, white and blue.

He extended his left arm and his right arm out. Then he stretched again. The balls of fire flowed out a royal blue. Peter felt himself smiling deeply. This made him feel almost as good as when Viola made him smile. He concentrated on the energy he was releasing. It was working—just like he'd practiced it.

No one could believe what they were seeing, but the concentration and the colors were working. When he put his arms out in front of himself, the balls of fire were white-hot. He could have guessed it was coming, but he was still grateful and a little shocked when he saw it.

Viola ran and grabbed McDaniel and Lester. Crenshaw heard more of a response than normal, which prompted him to take a peek in the curtain. He couldn't believe what he was seeing and he'd seen Peter's fire before.

Peter squeezed his eyes as tight as possible and concentrated on the colors he wanted to create. He finally put his arms back up over his head. The balls of fire finally spit out in perfectly alternating red white and blue.

Viola loved the look of satisfaction that blended with pure love illuminating Peter's face while his fire warmed the crowd's hearts as well as their imagination and joy.

The congregation cheered and screamed like a crowd at a sporting event, inspiring Peter who looked in Crenshaw's direction. Crenshaw smiled and nodded. The cheers were his cash register rings and business was booming.

Peter gave one last stretch, bathing the first three rows of true believers in harmless red sparks that changed to blue and white. Now Peter's eyes were wide open. His own handiwork was dazzling him.

Miss Chop Chop stood up on her seat and began to clap but she had to stop every now and again to catch the tears streaming down her face. Her rough hands caressed her face as she took a long deep breath. She let the air out slowly.

"DEAR MOM"

Maria's family was the first Mexican family to settle in Orton's Cove. Like so many great explorers before him, Pedro Beltran had set out to find his older brother, Pablo, in San Diego when he took a wrong turn that led him to the quaint little town.

Pedro and his wife, Vanessa, bought a small frame house with the money they had brought with them. The plan was to use the money to open a *taqueria* with Pablo, but as Pedro's roots took hold in Orton's Cove, he decided it would be wiser to purchase a home for his family.

It would have been less expensive to eventually build a taqueria in Orton's Cove and he wouldn't have to listen to his brother's incessant chattering about his fictitious date with the legendary Charro.

Maria was Pedro and Vanessa's only child, but as parents, they could not have had better luck. She was as sweet as she was pretty and she was as quiet as Pedro expected a woman to be. Maria's one transgression is that when she came of age—she had no desire to work at Beltran's Burrito Bistro. She could barely bring herself to eat a burrito—let alone prepare one. She was made for a more delicate work.

Maria's passion was designing and making clothes using her sewing machine. She was often seen at school in dresses and skirts that turned the heads of the boys. Each piece was created, not in vanity, rather with meticulous love for the craft of tailoring.

She was leaving the school one sunny afternoon in a particularly striking jumpsuit when Alice Campbell saw her from across the street. The woman, who was there to pick up Peter to take him to a doctor's appointment to lance a boil on the back of his neck, called the young girl over and inquired about the unique suit.

By the end of the week, Maria was working for Mrs. Campbell after school and on weekends. When the work was slow, or they were done for the day, the elder seamstress would pull out some of the books of designs she had made when she attended Orton Central.

Things were far different in Alice's day—the designs were more conservative—but Alice was proud of what she had accomplished in her youth and Maria was glad that she was able to see the work that Alice had done. The design books were a bridge between the two women—bonding their friendship.

Together the women created gowns and blouses and other items of feminine apparel they sold at all of the town's craft sales and church bazaars. There was rarely a time that one of them didn't see one of their designs at the grocery store or in church or at the weekly school bazaar.

Now—with Peter gone Maria had become Alice's main companion. They were working on costumes for the Independence Day parade when Walter brought them the mail. Alice walked out to the front porch where she sorted through the same tired pile of bills and junk mail. Near the end of the pile, she noticed familiar handwriting on the envelope.

"Maria," she called from the front porch. "Get the lemonade. There is a letter from Peter!"

Maria scooted out onto the porch with two sweaty glasses of the sweet yellow fluid. She set each one on the table and sat quickly next to Alice on the bench.

Dear Mom,

I am sorry it took so long to write this letter but Mr. Crenshaw keeps me very busy.

"Reverend Crenshaw," Alice said excitedly, looking up from the page.

We are traveling around and seeing lots of stuff. Betty is fine. She is a great girl, Mom. I have some new friends too. There is Lester who used to do what I do except with singing. He is a nice guy and everyone likes him a whole lot.

"I'm sure they like you, too, Peter," she said, wiping a tear from her eye.

Then there's Fiona, she's beautiful. You'd like her. She's a lot like your friend Audrey from over the Bingo hall. She's Lester's girl.

"That's nice," Maria said.

Lastly, there is Viola, she's kinda my girl. She can sing like a bird and dance like a cyclone and I think I want to marry her except she'll probably be famous one day and I'll always just be Peter Campbell from Orton's Cove. When this thing is over, no one will even remember me.

"Everyone will remember you, you silly boy," Alice said. She had to look away for a moment.

Anyway, I hope you are having a good summer. Say Hello to Maria and Luther and Joellyn and everyone in Orton's Cove.
Love, Peter

Quite by accident, she looked back into the envelope and noticed a slip of green safety paper that could only be a cashier's check. She slid it out and turned it over in her hand. It was made out to her in the sum of $1,000. There was a little note attached to it which read "This is from Peter's earnings, Love, Betty"

Alice looked at the check, over and over again. She continued to count the zeros as if this was the largest amount of money she had ever held before, it may as well have been.

"That's nice," Maria whispered.

"My boy makes me so proud," Alice gushed.

She wrapped her arms around the gentle Mexican girl and hugged her. The young girl hugged back with a mighty strong hug for such skinny arms.

"Let's get back to work," Alice said. "We still have to make the pants for Uncle Sam. Many people are counting on a sharp dressed Uncle Sam!"

"NIGHTHAWKS…"

No one noticed Gavin Crickle creeping around outside the cafe. He looked like another hayseed to anyone who didn't know better or look closer. He walked back and forth in front of the large plate-glass window with his hands jammed into the pockets of his blue jeans.

From his place on the pavement, he couldn't hear a word anyone at the table was saying, but he could see by their faces they were laughing. They were laughing out loud in huge hearty gusts. He felt they were laughing at him and that was unacceptable.

They kept raising their glasses and clinking them together as if they had something to celebrate. They were drinking coffee and soda pop, but their enthusiasm vexed Crickle.

An older looking Asian woman wearing a shiny pink dress entered the café. She dropped a large package in front of the big guy in the white suit with the large white hat. The package was wrapped in butcher's paper. She turned to walk out the door when the big guy in the white clothes called the rotund waitress over.

He handed the bundle to her and said something pointing out into the street.

The waitress took the bundle into the back. Then the man in white waddled out the door—trying to look confident and failing miserably. He was in pursuit of the Asian woman. He bumped into Crickle but didn't seem to notice.

The man in white caught the Asian woman a few steps from the door where they exchanged a few pleasant words before they both turned and headed back to the café. The man in white paused for a moment when he reached Gavin Crickle, but was unsure where he knew that face. He smiled and tipped his hat and escorted the Asian woman into the café.

Gavin Crickle paced back and forth in front of the restaurant with his hands in his pockets. His mind raced like never before. He knew he couldn't go back to Tinsel Town empty handed—but he also knew he had no leverage with these people. These bumpkins seemed not to know—or care—what he could do for them, or what they could do for him.

When the bus pulled up and the television crew began to pour into the café, Gavin made a seamless getaway into the inky darkness of the night. The crew filed in and took seats where they could find them. They saved a seat for Hack Granville at the main table.

The rotund waitress started putting out pitchers of water and extra flatware. The man in white and the older looking Asian woman took their seats at the end of the table.

"HERE'S TO YOU"

The people in the other booths and even up at the snack bar had been sending sodas and coffees over to the table where Crenshaw held court. Their generosity made them feel as if they were included in the gathering of the celebrities who had just performed for them.

Peter sat directly to Crenshaw's right, smoking cigarettes with a silly smile plastered on his face. Viola sat next to Peter. She was holding his hand. Across from them sat Lester and Fiona. Betty sat next to Fiona. McDaniel sat at the other end of the table. He would be happy for even a momentary respite from Crenshaw's constant oration.

The white porcelain platters of food were circulating around the table levitated by hands that passed them to other hands. As each plate went around, the food diminished quickly. As soon as one was empty, another one replaced it. There was no discernible traffic pattern for the plates.

"Here's to you," Crenshaw said raising his glass. Crenshaw was looking at Peter. He hoped some of the frost between them had thawed over the course of their time together.

Everyone toasted loudly and happily.

"And to you," Lester said.

Lester was looking at Fiona. He loved how she loved him.

Everyone toasted loudly and happily again.

"Cheers," Peter said.

Peter was looking at the waitress who was bringing a heaping bowl of mashed potatoes out for them. Everyone laughed and then they drank again.

No one heard Miss Chop Chop enter, but when she materialized at the head of the table with the bulging bundle in her hands, McDaniel and Crenshaw both shouted, "Here's to you!"

The sweet woman blushed.

"For you," she demurred. "Fresh. Fresh."

She set a large package on the table in front of McDaniel and bowed gracefully before heading back out into the night.

"Was she calling me fresh?" Crenshaw roared.

"She must know something we don't know," McDaniel laughed. Then to the waitress, "Lily, could you please have the cook prepare whatever this is. We have a hungry news crew on their way in. Oh, and make sure the man pacing outside the window gets something to eat. He sure looks hungry."

Lily took the package and disappeared into the kitchen. McDaniel jumped up and followed Miss Chop Chop out the door and down the street. He bumped into the skinny hayseed, but was too focused on the woman to notice.

"Excuse me," he said trying to catch up with her. "Excuse me, Miss?"

She stopped and turned around slowly. Her body faced him, but her delicate face was pointed in the direction of the ground. Her hands locked in front of her; she waited for the man to catch his breath.

"Why don't you stay and eat with us Miss?"

"My name Liu," the woman said. "People around here say me Miss Chop Chop,"

"Hello, Liu," McDaniel said. "I'm Clayton. Clayton McDaniel. My friends call me Mac. I would be delighted if you joined us for dinner."

"That would be very nice, Mr. Mac," she said. "Are you sure that it would be okay with your friends?"

"The more the merrier," he laughed and offered his arm, which she took.

She allowed him to walk her back to restaurant.

It was on the way back he noticed Gavin Crickle, but couldn't quite place how he knew the young man. The face was familiar, but the context was all-wrong. It couldn't have mattered any less to him anyway; he concentrated on the woman on his arm. He smiled and tipped his hat as he continued past.

They walked in just moments ahead of the news crew and sat down at the table. Peter and Viola moved down a chair so Liu could sit next to McDaniel. The woman never took her hand off the crease in his elbow the whole night, which was just fine with him.

It was Viola who figured out who the skinny man lurking outside was. By then it was too late. She had watched him pace back and forth in front of the restaurant. Viola knew she should have said something but she was afraid to spoil the festive mood. Eventually, her attention turned back to Peter.

"TALK TO ME, ASH"

Hack Granville had had a promising career in professional football. As a running back for Iowa State, he was considered to have a lock on the Heisman trophy until he blew out his knee at his senior homecoming game.

Rather than let the injury sideline him completely, he shifted his focus and changed his major and ended up graduating with a degree in communications and a minor in theater.

Hack's father Joe grimaced at his portrayal of "Puck" in A Midsummer Night's Dream in that steamy auditorium one week before graduation. It wasn't that the performance lacked style and charisma; in fact he had to admit the kid was pretty good. It was the tights and the slippers the elder Granville had a problem with. The pads and the helmet were much easier for him to deal with. They were surely much easier to tell his friends about.

Hack's mother Nancy was so proud of him, she sat through every performance from beginning to end. No one mentioned the fact she had never been to one football game. She took great comfort in the knowledge there was little chance of him getting a concussion or a torn hamstring performing Shakespeare.

After college, Hack tried his luck out West where he drifted into small television roles interspersed with various production jobs. It was the perfect time for a single guy to be living on the West Coast. He worked enough to keep himself fed and played enough to keep himself alive.

This all changed—as these things always do—when Hack met Ashley Kerr. She was a sound technician for an independent film studio that had hired him to direct a short documentary. The Chamber of Commerce for the vastly changing Haight-Ashbury neighborhood was anxious to change their image. They decided that a PBS-style documentary—if handled well—would do the trick.

Hack used to watch the glow from the monitor in the editing room reflect on her face. It was this image, the repetition of watching her that he just couldn't stand anymore. If he was going to get any work done, he had to make some kind of arrangement with Ashley Kerr.

By the time the Haight-Ashbury project was aired on public television, Hack and Ashley were sharing a cozy little flat in a building populated with struggling actors and budding filmmakers. They were married in a small civil service the following spring.

When she announced she was pregnant, Hack realized it was time to head back to Iowa where their child would be reared in a more sensible environment. Los Angeles was fine for him, it was even fine for him with Ashley, but it was no place to raise a child. So, they packed up what they couldn't sell or give away and drove Hack's old Nash Rambler back to the heartland.

Hack took a job selling cars with his father and made grainy little 8mm films on the side. Ashley stayed home and raised Anthony and worked part-time in the Des Moines Public Library. Neither of them was happy, but they went through the motions because it seemed like the thing to do.

Maybe it was the tone the shriveled, old woman took with him while test-driving the blue Buick. Maybe it was another day without a lousy sale. Maybe it was seeing his lovely wife so completely unhappy. Something changed inside of Hack and this change was revealed one rainy, achy Friday evening in late April. He quit his job at the lot and ran all the way home. The heavy air weighed him down—but the feeling of knowing he was doing the right thing carried him through.

When he walked into the house, he found Ashley sitting on the couch. It was clear she had been crying. He sat down next to her and wrapped his arm around her shoulders. She settled into his embrace.

"I'm sorry, Hack," she said through her sniffles.

"For what, Ash? What's the matter?" he asked.

"Forget it," she said in a way he knew he could never forget it.

"Talk to me, Ash."

"It's just–" and the floodgates opened again cutting her off before she could finish her sentence.

She buried her face in his shoulder and cried. Her body hitched with each sob.

"I know that you want to stay here but…"

"What on earth are you talking about, Baby?" he said.

"Look!" She produced a white envelope from the folds of her blouse.

It was a telegram from the east coast.

Hack read it once. Then he read it again. Then he set it down carefully on the table and stood up. It was more of an uncontrolled contortion than a victory dance, but Ashley knew what it meant.

"You mean you'll take the job?" she asked.

"I guess I'll have to. I'm unemployed."

"Is New York going to be a good place to raise Anthony?"

"Wherever we are is a good place to raise Anthony," he said pulling her up from the couch. He repeated his gesticulating contortions; only this time he embraced his wonderful wife and they danced together.

"The pay can't be great," she said.

"It's the ground floor," he said. "All I've ever wanted was to be in on something from the ground floor."

"Are you going to call them tonight?" her excitement was growing.

"I'll call them tonight and we'll leave as soon as we can," he said. He laughed and hugged her deeply. "Did they say what CNN stood for?"

"I guess we'll find out," she replied.

"Soon enough," he said.

It didn't take long for Hack to inject his own brand of know-how into every project that came across the board. By the end of his sixth month, Hack was directing segments on everything from travel tips to local weather.

He also worked as a writer and a producer, when he was needed. It was his early segments on what would later become known as the "Gulf War" that brought prestige to the station and elevated Hack to the position of executive producer.

The former used car salesman eventually got to pick and choose his assignments and he retained total creative control over each segment that he produced. When the call came in from this Peter Campbell, he was intrigued and decided to see for himself what it was all about.

"TAKEN CARE OF"

The sky was clear and the moon was sharp and slick except for the area that seemed to be smudged by God's careless fingers. Peter and Viola sat on the granite steps of the fancy hotel while the adults attempted to decide their fate. Neither one could speak.

Inside the green-carpeted conference room, Hack Granville paced back and forth, alternating his attention between the black telephone in his hand, and the two men who were sitting nervously on the stiff leather couches.

"I hope he knows what he's doing," Crenshaw said.

"I'm sure he does," was McDaniel's quick response.

"Yeah, but he's–"

"Why don't you go find yourself some company," McDaniel said quickly. "That might relax your nerves."

"This is so easy for you; you have Miss Liu. I have no one," Crenshaw said. "Besides how can I think about anything right now except for what's best for the children?" Crenshaw was agitated. He never once cared for the children except when his pockets might be about to be empty.

"They're hardly children," McDaniel scoffed. "And since when does anything but your libido and your wallet matter to you anyway?"

Having said this, McDaniel fell into an uneasy silence.

Hack waved at them and covered his mouth.

McDaniel folded his fingers across his belly and let his head roll back on his fleshy shoulders. Crenshaw stood up and began to pace in synch with the frustrated producer.

The scene looked like something out of an old silent comedy the way the lanky preacher shadowed the stocky television man. With choreographed grace, they avoided colliding but things did get a bit tricky at the narrow end of the room. One close call too many and Hack was motioning for Crenshaw to take his seat. For his part, Crenshaw tried to ignore the unspoken request, but Hack gave him a look that clearly told him that defiance was not an option.

"I hope he knows what he's doing," Crenshaw whispered to McDaniel.

"Shut up," McDaniel whispered back.

Hack hung up the phone and sat down across from Crenshaw and McDaniel. He placed his hands carefully in his lap. He looked from one man to the next, then back to the other.

Hack didn't say a word for quite some time—at least it felt like a mild eternity. He just sat and looked back and forth between the men. Occasionally he would stop and look down at the shiny surface of his polished shoe, or out the window to a spot no one could discern, but then it was back to the men sitting across from him.

Finally, Hack spoke. "We need to get as much footage on this as possible, and from as many angles. It has to be very clear, for Peter's sake. This cannot have the appearance of a dog and pony show with great special effects. What that boy does is pure, and it's real and it is vital to our success—and to his—that it translates that way for the viewing audience."

"Understood," McDaniel said.

"We have to get Viola into a studio where she can record what she is doing. Video alone won't do her voice justice," Hank continued.

"That can be a bit expensive," Crenshaw sputtered.

"Taken care of," Hack responded.

"What else do we need to do?" McDaniel asked Hack. "What about Lester and Fiona, and us?"

Hack thought for a moment and responded. "Lester will do the voice over segments and Fiona will be a technical advisor. We also need her constantly apprised of what we are planning with the girl as Viola is a minor."

"And us?" Crenshaw repeated the end of McDaniel's question.

"We will find a place for the both of you; unless you want to just sell their contracts outright."

"There are no contracts," Crenshaw said in a weak moment of honesty. "There is nothing, but a handshake and our word. We also promised to take care of Peter's mamma."

"We'll leave it up to Peter and Viola then," Hack said.

"Not me," McDaniel said. "I'm out. I've grown very genuinely fond of those kids, but this has to be where my trolley stops. You two go on ahead, just promise me you'll take good care of those children. This is getting too big for me."

Hack and Crenshaw looked at each other for a moment. Neither could believe what they were hearing. They both realized what Peter was about to become and they had every intention of being there every step of the way, with or without Clayton McDaniel.

"What are you talking about, Mac," Crenshaw asked.

"I'm done, boys," he said happily.

His relief was obvious.

"I never expected it would get this big. Those are some good kids out there—really good kids, but I'm tired—I'm good and tired and I think it's time for Clayton McDaniel to take his little Lady Liu on a long, lazy vacation."

McDaniel was more afraid of what they—or the attention— might turn Peter into and didn't want to be around to witness it. Surely, somewhere, there was a mediocre musical combo waiting to be swept from virtual obscurity by the tireless entrepreneur.

"We'll say our goodbyes in the morning," McDaniel said.

He stood up and strolled out of the room. He was whistling a familiar tune which neither Hack nor Crenshaw could place.

"PEOPLE WILL COME FROM ALL OVER"

Talley's Corners was an impossibly small spot on even the most detailed map. A stray grain of salt would eclipse the little blemish if you were to unfold a map on the Waffle House counter. That was all about to change in ways neither Reverend Crenshaw nor Hack Granville would be able to fathom with any acuity, not initially anyway, for a long, long time.

Originally, the town of Talley's Corners was nothing more than an intersection where two scarred one-lane roads met, before going on to find greater, more inspiring highways.

Edmund Talley and his family lived in the farmhouse that stood proudly on the northwest corner of the main intersection, where the rising sun shone into his bedroom window every morning. His barn, with its skyscraping silo, was located just off the driveway that led out onto the southwest corner of the intersection.

Before too long the corner across the street to the east would hold a small bunkhouse for the migrant workers. The southeast corner of the intersection was where Edmund Talley decided to build a school for the children of the workers as well as the families that were beginning to settle in the area.

Edmund's wife, Gladys Talley, spent her days in the dusty little schoolroom teaching the children arithmetic, ABCs and reading, with the help of her trusty leather Bible.

Edmund worked side by side with the workers. He never expected them to do anything he wouldn't do. He worked as hard—or harder— than every man in his employ. This was his father's way and it was his way. He expected it was the Talley way.

In the evening, when the weather permitted, Edmund gathered the workers and their families in the front yard on the northwest corner where he played the accordion and everyone sang hymns. Their voices reached heaven with no distractions, back in those days.

When it became clear to the benevolent landowner that the migrants had no intention of migrating, he offered to let them earn their own parcels of land on his expansive property. The men who took him up on his offer built little, wooden shanties on their plots of land and moved the family out of the bunkhouse and into the shanty as soon as it was possible.

Their exodus made more room in the bunkhouse for new migrant workers who would eventually either earn their stake or stay on at the bunkhouse. Whatever fate they chose, the Indian summer evenings brought the residents out to sing and drink apple cider with the good man and his learned wife.

Owen Mixon was the county surveyor. He had little to do, but he took his job very seriously. He had handled all the transactions for the Talley family and their workers. He saw to it that all the paperwork was in order. The file folder of deeds had grown thick over the years.

With every season, Edmund Talley purchased a little more of the County's land. When it came time to assess the property for tax purposes, Owen Mixon labeled it Talley's Corners as a point of reference.

It was Owen Mixon who suggested building a small church next to the schoolhouse. Not long after the church was built, Edmund Talley III became the region's first grocer. His shop was built on the other side of the school.

Generations of Talleys were educated in that school—fed from that grocer—and sang inside that old church whenever weather commanded. Otherwise they'd be gathered in the crabgrass around the silo, singing praise and praying for a good crop.

Things being as they were, with new highways brought in, new people and growth was inevitable. By the time Edmund and Gladys Talley went to the great beyond, an entire community had sprung up around them.

Most of the old was gone and most of the new was built with loving hands. The silo stood to remind people why they came and who was there before them. The old church was still there, too.

❀

By the time Crenshaw directed the convoy to the quiet intersection of Talley's Corners, the small town was incorporated. It even had its own zip code.

The convoy didn't attract much attention. People were passing through town all of the time, especially in the autumn when the scenery was breathtaking. The palette of colors each leaf created gave the impression that the entire countryside had been hand-painted just for the occasion.

It was the big white panel truck with the crane mounted to the roof that caught more than one resident's eye. It didn't help matters that the first person out of the truck was a cameraman with long wavy red hair pulled back in a ponytail.

A crew of young people who were clearly from another town, perhaps another planet, followed him off of the truck. They were all wearing shorts, either khaki or denim, bulky sweatshirts or t-shirts, and baseball caps from various teams or production companies.

The last one out of the vehicle was Hack Granville, the paternal figure who the townsfolk figured would be responsible when it came to the young crew. His manner of dress wasn't much different, but he had a more mature look about him, and he was the one talking to the priest.

"Unless I miss my guess," Crenshaw said. "We are in the heart of God's country. This is Talley's Corners where the Good Word is the backbone of the people."

"Do you really think that this is the best place to capture the show with a live audience?" Granville asked.

"People will come in from all over," Crenshaw said. "When there is a revival of any sort in little towns like this, a massive audience is guaranteed."

No one noticed the dusty black Ford pull up on the far end of the parking lot. The driver's face was chiseled and his features were fine, only they looked a little older—more pinched—now than they should have.

"Let's go see Mayor Mixon," Crenshaw said, indicating over his shoulder toward what Granville correctly assumed to be the middle of town. "His grandfather is one of the original settlers of this fine little town."

"Good information to have," Granville said raising an eyebrow.

"Picked up a few brochures at the rest area where we got off the interstate," Crenshaw said.

"You have the makings of a newsman," Granville said.

"Thank you. I think," Crenshaw responded.

The crew, having finished their stretching and smoking, waited for their assignment. Despite their casual appearance, they moved like a squad of well-trained soldiers, everyone responsible for his or her role.

"If we see a restaurant on the way, we're going to stop and eat. I'll catch up with you."

"Good enough," Crenshaw said.

The town hall was only a few minutes down the street. Along the way the revivalists passed a Pup-n-Pop and a Dixie Chicken stand. Lester pulled over and let everyone out under the bright red and yellow awning, which was lit by a neon chicken. He let Peter and the ladies out of the car.

"Y'all wait here for Mr. Granville and the crew," Lester said. "Me and Reverend Crenshaw will be back in a few minutes."

"Can I get you anything, Les?" Fiona asked.

"Maybe a couple of buckets of chicken to start feeding the crew. When you see us coming back down the road, order another two."

This final directive sounded like Crenshaw. Lester rarely worried about food. Crenshaw always worried about someone getting over on him.

They pulled away leaving Peter and Viola at the curb. Peter was lighting a cigarette while Viola rocked back and forth and tried to look down the road. Fiona and Betty went in to warn the folks at the chicken stand to prepare for a horde of hungry people.

"Don't go far," Fiona called out to Peter and Viola as they ambled away from the chicken stand. "And don't be gone long."

Fiona kept one eye on them as they walked toward the little drug store, across the road from the chicken stand. Betty ordered three buckets of chicken, one pound of cole slaw, and two pounds of baked beans.

The young girl behind the counter smiled, hiding her braces with her left hand, and took their money as the white van pulled up. The crew disembarked the van and settled in on the aluminum picnic benches. Betty passed out napkins and paper plates. Fiona took a head count to order soft drinks. The crew ate noisily. The succulent sound of smacking lips and greasy fingers rubbing together was music to the old stubble-faced man who was frying the poultry as fast as they could eat it. Suddenly he was back in Normandy in a smart green uniform cooking for the boys.

Peter and Viola returned in time for the second wave of greasy red and yellow cardboard chicken buckets to make their way out of the little window and onto the table. Peter chose to sit three tables away from the crew.

Viola immediately began helping Betty deliver soft drinks and coleslaw. Fiona stepped out toward the road to see if she could see Lester and Crenshaw.

The dirty black Ford slowed down for a moment and the driver stared through her with the darkest eyes she had ever seen. They were set deeply in his bony skull. Fiona knew she had seen him before; she just couldn't place where. She shivered once, before turning back to the task of feeding the crew.

Thankfully, just then, Lester pulled up and let the engine die as he and Crenshaw piled out of the car and waded into the happy crowd of diners at the chicken stand. Crenshaw saluted to the old cook and winked at the young cashier as he lowered himself onto the bench and began to eat.

On his second bite of a drumstick he noticed Peter was sitting alone. He looked around and saw that Viola was helping serve the food. He began to get up but Peter's expression was neither inviting nor encouraging. He sat back down.

"Why don't you join the others?" Viola asked as she set a large cola and a clean ashtray in front of Peter.

"I'm okay," Peter said.

"Are you sure?" she persisted. "Would you like some company?"

"If it's you," he said smiling.

Viola loved it when Peter smiled. It didn't happen very often so when it did, her young heart was filled with joy.

She walked back and, after putting a few pieces of chicken on a limp plate, she rejoined Peter at the table where she ate quietly as they watched the crew deplete the stock at the Dixie Chicken.

"Viola," Peter said softly. "What happens when this thing ends?"

"It doesn't have to end, Peter," Viola said.

"Someday I'll go back to Orton's Cove and you'll go back to Tennessee," he said, focusing on an inflatable chicken that was suspended over the table. Anything was better than having to look into her eyes just then.

"Couldn't you take me to Orton's Grove?" she asked.

"Is that what you'd want?"

"Wherever you want me," she said.

The young man blushed fully. He looked at the young woman for an extended moment before getting up and walking over to the other table. He reached in between the sound guy and the boom girl and grabbed a bucket of chicken and a tub of beans.

He walked back to where Viola sat waiting with an extra plastic fork and a handful of moist towelettes. He didn't say another word until the bucket held only bones and the beans were just a fond gastrointestinal memory.

"DON'T FORGET TO SMILE"

True to Crenshaw's word, the turnout for the Talley's Corners meeting was a colossal event. The tent was even more packed than he had predicted it would be. The shiny faces of the eager congregation lit up as row after row was filled until the tent swelled beyond capacity. Crenshaw could hardly contain himself.

The benches were full at least an hour before the show and a dozen more were added in the front and back of each section. The inside walls of the tent, where people typically stood and watched, were filled three deep.

The camera crew, with all of their necessary paraphernalia, was wedged into every open space possible with extra lights and microphones hanging and dangling everywhere they could be attached. Hack Granville and Crenshaw paced the width of the tent along the outside wall. They intended to stay out of sight as long as they could.

Peter, Viola and Betty walked out in the field behind the tent, toward a massive oak tree.

"Don't forget to smile," Betty told Peter. She was becoming quite the stage mom.

"And stand straight," Viola added, mimicking the act.

"Mr. Granville said that you should not look directly into the camera," Betty went on.

"But don't look like you're trying to avoid it," Viola inserted.

"Who wants a cigarette?" Peter offered half-heartedly.

"No, thank you," Betty said.

"Me neither," Viola said, but she smiled at him just the same.

Peter ignited his cigarette using his hands, for practice.

Before long, they heard Crenshaw's oration booming out of the slits in the canvas tent. There was nothing that could block his voice as it poured out of the crowded tent and floated up into the early evening sky.

Crenshaw was now shouting. "And when we ask ourselves what do we do with this faith, when we ask ourselves what we do with this great and wonderful gift. The answer is simple; we share it."

"Amen," Mrs. Bloodworth called out.

"Amen," little Zak Bloodworth called out, because he was in the habit of repeating everything his mother said.

Crenshaw felt overwhelmed by the size of the crowd and by all of the lights and the cameras. But he was in no hurry to relinquish the stage. He strutted back and forth and continued his sermon.

"By sharing our gifts. By offering ourselves to others, only then can we truly see our gifts for what they are!"

The crowd murmured in approval.

"These gifts are the divine love of our Savior, Jesus Christ!" with the last few words, he almost (and very theatrically) collapsed on the floor.

The first guitar chord rang out as Crenshaw shuffled off of the stage as Lester was entering from the seam in the curtain.

"Amazing grace. How sweet the sound..." he began to sing.

Crenshaw hesitated for a moment. He looked at Lester who was singing one of Viola's songs. Not a big fan of improvisation, he was quick to forgive Lester if only because the audience was already beginning to sing with him.

"I once was lost..." Lester continued.

Crenshaw bowed his head and walked away. Perhaps television cameras were a good enough reason to come out of retirement. He had to admire Lester in spite of himself.

"Twas grace that taught my heart to fear..." and the entire

congregation was singing along with him.

Lester encouraged the crowd to give in to the experience any way they were comfortable. He threw his head back and reveled in the singing that filled the room and lifted him up out of the tent and deposited him gently at the golden gates of Heaven.

They repeated the last verse and fell quiet when Zak Bloodworth jumped up on his chair and began to sing, "Amazing grace how sweet the sound…"

Every camera found him with such accuracy there would be very little, if any, editing to do later. Not a soul made a sound as the little boy repeated the first verse and his mother cried softly into her hands.

Lester led the audience in a full and hearty ovation for the little boy who sat down as if nothing out of the ordinary had happened. He put his little head on his mother's lap and looked up at the big man with the guitar. Their eyes locked for a moment. Little Zak Bloodworth smiled.

As the applause finally lulled, Lester opened his arms and said, "Ladies and gentlemen, God bless that child. Now I give you …" Lester began to call her the Tennessee Twister, but then thought better of it, "Viola!"

Viola came out onto the stage and bowed her head. Slowly she lifted her face to the eager crowd and began to sing, "I don't know how to love him…"

As the words flowed from her, she moved to where the little Bloodworth boy was sitting. She took him by the hand and led him throughout the tent. They squeezed their way through the throngs of people as she sang to those immediately around her, and those on the opposite side of the tent.

"I never thought I'd come to this. What's it all about?" she sang as she towed Zak Bloodworth up to the stage with her. They spun around on a cloud of joy, hand in hand.

As Viola's song came to an end, she curtsied politely to Zak who bowed like he had seen in the Fred Astaire movies his mother watched. Then the boy returned to his mother's side again.

"Day by day..." Viola started her next number. "Day by day..."

She began to clap her hands over her head. Zak followed suit. Soon the tent was full of joyful people clapping their hands and singing along. Viola made her way back to the stage.

"To see thee more clearly..."

Hack watched on the monitor and barked instructions into the microphone connected to the little headphones that the crew wore. There was no way that he was going to miss one second of what he couldn't even believe he was witnessing.

"Day by day... day by day..." Viola went on, picking up the tempo. "Oh, dear Lord, three things I pray..."

She glanced over at Betty and Fiona, swinging their tambourines and singing every word right along with Viola.

"Three things I pray..." they sang loudly.

"To see thee more clearly... To love thee more dearly..."

The crowd was on their feet—Zak ran back to the stage where he could stand next to Viola one more time. He was beaming with unspeakable joy.

Viola showered the people with her love, which was her music, which was limitless. As the song spun into its climax, the cameramen zoomed and focused and recorded as many of the beaming faces as possible. Hack pulled back from the microphone. He knew this was the time to let the crew work their magic.

Without warning, the volume dropped. Silence enveloped the room save the dulcet tones of the beautiful Viola, "Follow thee more nearly... Day by day..."

She continued the denouement moving through the crowd, shaking hands touching the shoulders of the men as they sat down not voluntarily as much as out of necessity. Viola walked Zak back to his seat next to his mother before she disappeared into the folds of material at the back of the stage.

Gavin Crickle decided this would probably be his last chance to get the girl. Even if it wasn't, he had had enough of the quaint pastoral country life. He longed for cracked sidewalks and overpriced sushi.

As Crickle watched the young girl make her exit, he slipped out of the tent and ran along the wall that faced the highway. He was quite sure no one would expect to see him coming from that side.

She was standing where he could see her, but not where he could see Peter watching him. He took a casual step in her direction. Then another step. Then another.

"Here's the dang green, Mr. Money-man," Peter said jumping out from behind the tent.

He aimed his hands at Crickle as he closed his eyes tight and pushed. The green balls of flame looked like sour apples falling horizontally out of a tree. Gavin could do nothing but try to cover his eyes.

Viola screeched but she couldn't pull her eyes away from the crouching man. A strong wind came up and lifted the cowboy hat—still flaming—off of his head and sent it rolling out onto the quiet highway. The wind that took it away flipped it end over end.

By the time the lights were through flashing, Crickle's eyebrows had suffered serious damage along with his retinas. Peter stood in front of him, or at least a form he assumed must be Peter.

The acrid smell of burnt flesh and singed hair filled the air that circulated around them. He held his scorched face in his hands. Miraculously, he didn't make a sound. His mouth opened and closed a few times, but he didn't make a sound.

"You better get in there, Peter," Viola said pushing him into the tent. "Reverend Crenshaw sounds like he's almost done."

"Stay right by me," Peter answered grabbing her by the hand. His palms were warm. They felt good to the touch.

Peter walked with her to where Lester and Fiona were standing. "Don't let her out of your sight," he said. "She'll explain."

Peter stepped out onto the stage and was greeted by thunderous applause. At this point, even the crew was feeling emotional about the whole thing. The lenses on their cameras fogged up and the sound people had to work to stifle the sniffles. Hack made a quick contact with his crew to be sure everyone was still on task.

The young man looked back toward where his beloved stood, safe in the arms of her mother and Lester. He was watching her when Crickle staggered in through the back of the tent and made his way up the aisle, using chairs and people's backs for direction as much as for support. He stood facing the stage where Peter was standing.

He held his blistered face in his hands. The smell was unmistakable. Many of the men who worked in the slaughterhouse were all too familiar with the scent of burning flesh. The ones who weren't used to it were repulsed pretty quickly.

A collective gasp swept through the room when Gavin turned and faced the crowd. He dropped his hands long enough to reveal the terror that was once his face. He pointed to Peter who stood in the center of the stage not saying a word.

"He did this to me! He is not a messenger of the Lord!" Crickle growled in an unearthly voice. "That boy is the spawn of Satan! Look what he did to my face!"

Peter stood his ground and faced his accuser who had fallen to his knees and begun to cry. Peter slipped his hands into his pockets. Two officers from the Talley's Corners police department pushed their way through the crowd, stopping between Peter and Crickle.

"What's going on here?" the taller one with the bad complexion asked.

"Ask him," Peter said, sullenly pointing toward Crickle.

"I'm asking you, boy," the cop persisted.

"I ain't saying nothin', officer," Peter responded.

Peter started to walk off the stage to where Lester and Fiona were holding Viola. Crenshaw quickly joined them there. They made a small protective shield for Peter. He never made it there.

"You aren't going anywhere!" the shorter, darker officer said grabbing Peter by the arm.

"I wouldn't do that, Bumpy," the taller one said. "We don't know what this kid can do."

In response, Peter gently tugged himself loose. He extended his hands in a submissive manner—palms down—that indicated they might as well cuff him. Peter had no intention of resisting formal arrest, just as surely as he had no intention of being accused of anything more than what he had already done.

Betty was entering the tent as they were walking Peter down the aisle between the astonished faces, which had developed into shameless gapers. She rushed to Viola's side.

Viola cried hysterically. Fiona cried less, but she was still shaken. Lester went to retrieve the car while Crenshaw pulled out his wallet. He began flipping through cards. With any luck he might know an attorney in the area.

"It's going to be alright, Vi," Betty whispered as she hugged her young friend.

"These small town jails can be awfully dangerous to a stranger," she whispered.

"I think Peter can handle himself," Betty said.

When the paramedics arrived, they strapped Crickle onto the gurney and rolled him out of the tent. Even through his singed eyelashes and crispy eyelids, he never took his eyes off Viola.

"FOUR CIGARETTES WOULD BE NICE"

By all accounts, Evers Ciderman Jr. had a pretty lousy childhood. He never denied that the lousiness of that time was entirely of his own doing. If there was ever a black cloud in Talley's Corners, Evers Ciderman Jr. brought it to town the day he was born. He hung that heavy dark cloud over the ramshackle sheet metal shed the Ciderman family, such as they were, called home.

❁

Evers came into the world with his hands balled into tiny little fists and a sneer that graced countless black and white school pictures year after year. His mother doted on him in his infancy, but as a toddler Evers was beginning to carve out his niche.

As he grew older she found it more difficult to dote on the angry little child. He was merciless with the neighborhood kittens and parakeets that he caught in his pudgy pink fingers.

He was nine years old when he mastered the Zippo lighter. From that time on, no one in Talley's Corners could leave their pets unattended for any length of time.

Miss Swan left her miniature poodle, Bobbin, outside long enough to answer the phone. She returned to the sound of the yelping dog doing his own version of Stop! Drop! and Roll Over!

She didn't actually see Evers but she was sure he was responsible.

Evers' father's countless attempts to discipline the boy were in vain. There was nothing he—or anyone—could do that would change the direction the boy was heading in. No punishment was powerful enough. No beating had any impact on the boy.

When word got out that Evers' parents were planning to leave Talley's Corners the citizens of the little town breathed a collective sigh of relief. They packed up one night and left without a trace. The morning found Evers alone in the shed. There were some canned goods and a short note but that was it:

Happy Birthday Ev,

Take care of yourself.

Mom and Dad

Evers Ciderman turned 12 years old that day.

His parents took Evers' younger brother Cleo with them. They were petrified Evers' hatred and anger could poison the toddler. The day his parents left became a pivotal turning point in his life. Their final action set the rest of his life in motion.

That was also the day Evers Ciderman had his first run in with the police. The first in a string of arrests that would get him bounced to every foster home and juvenile hall that would accept him, until he was 18 years old and forced either to try and make a way for himself or land in a proper prison.

❀

It was no surprise to Officers Bumpy Bridges or Tom Waxel that when they swung the cell door open for Peter, that an ancient Evers Ciderman was already sitting there in the cell. He leered at the young boy before spitting on the floor.

"You know you can't do that in here," Bumpy said to Evers as he unlocked Peter's cuffs.

"Looks to me like I can," Evers replied.

This was followed by a ghastly attempt to clear his throat before the old man spit on the floor again.

"Evers Ciderman," Tom called from outside the cell. "Why you gotta be so ornery? And in front of our new guest."

Bumpy secured his cuffs back onto his belt and stepped out of the cell closing the door. The two uniformed officers walked out of the holding area, leaving Peter to fend for himself with the crazy old expectorator.

"Name's Evers," he said calmly. "Ain't you kinda young to be in here, boy?"

"I guess I am," Peter answered quietly.

He watched the man intently.

"Don't worry 'bout me, son," the man said. "I just act that way for their benefit. I'm really just a rotten old egg, when you get down to it. What's your name?"

"Peter. Peter Campbell. Do you mind if I ask why you're here?"

"Bad luck and endurance," the man cackled, pulling a wrinkled cigarette pack out of his shirt pocket. He noticed Peter's eyes light up.

"You want one?" he asked.

"My friends will have mine. When they get here, I'll pay you back," Peter said reaching for the flattened cigarette.

"That's right you will," Evers said matter-of-factly. "Two to one."

"Fair enough," Peter said accepting the flame from Evers' match and drawing the smoke into his lungs.

"Tonight's transgression includes punching old Cussy Clark in the teeth. Shattered the new dentures and everything." Evers smiled.

"What'd he do?" Peter asked.

"Who?"

"Cussy Clark."

"Cussy Clark is a she," Evers laughed. "She was cheating. Stud poker."

"You punched a lady in the face?"

"That a tough old broad ain't never been confused with no lady," Evers said flicking his cigarette ash into the spotless stainless steel toilet. "She woulda probably kicked my ass if Bumpy's brother wasn't there with us. He hates violence."

"Bumpy's brother?"

"He's not a cop, Bumpy's brother. Hell, I don't imagine I'd even be in here except that we was gambling."

"So you're in here for punching an old lady in the face?"

"And gambling and public intoxication and reckless stupidity. What about you? What brings you to this little chunk of God's country?"

"I lit a guy's face on fire," Peter said.

"You lit a guy's face on fire and you're judging me for punching an old broad who cheats at cards?"

"He was trying to snatch my girl," Peter said defensively.

"I imagine I'd light a guy on fire if'n he tried to snatch my girl too." Evers stretched out his legs and leaned back on his bunk as Peter told him the whole story.

As Peter was getting to the part about Gavin's face igniting, Bumpy came back into the holding area with a pot of coffee and two cups.

"Sorry, guys," he said. "We're out of cream and sugar."

"Never trust a man puts cream and sugar into his coffee," Evers said as he accepted the empty cup with a nod. He cleared his throat loudly.

"Save your spit, Tom's on a call."

Peter looked from his disheveled cellmate to the short dark policeman. "Our Mr. Ciderman doesn't like Tom very much. It has something to do with a certain Miss…"

"Come on now, Bumpy," Evers sneered. "You know that's jest an act."

Peter accepted his cup. Bumpy poured Evers' coffee first, then Peter's. Bumpy slipped out of the cell and pulled an extra cup off of the rack. He poured himself a cup.

He set the coffee pot on a small table between the bunks before he walked out of the cage that held Peter and Evers. They sat and drank coffee and smoked cigarettes watching Bumpy go through his paces.

"So, just what did happen out there, boy?" Bumpy asked.

"His name is Peter," Evers said.

"Right, Peter," Bumpy coughed into his sleeve. "Can you tell me what happened?"

"I'd rather not, if it's all the same to you, officer," Peter responded.

"Call me Bumpy," the man said. "I was asking off the record."

"He told me," Evers laughed looking Bumpy straight in the eye.

"You told him and you won't tell me?" Bumpy whined.

"I'd just rather not talk about it anymore is all," Peter said swinging his legs up onto the stainless steel bed that was bolted to the wall.

He leaned his back against the wall and crossed his legs comfortably.

"If you change your mind, just holler," Bumpy said as he headed back out into the next room.

"I'll do that," Peter said.

"Bump's a good enough guy," Evers said. "I know he doesn't like it when he has to arrest me, but I keep reminding him that it's his job."

Evers pulled out two more cigarettes and flipped one toward Peter.

"That makes four you owe me. Anyway, I try to tell Bumpy that we all have our stations in life. Mine is to be a pathologically small-time low-life and his is to be a vigilantly law-abiding citizen. You know protect and serve."

"Do you like being in jail all the time?" Peter had to ask.

"It's about the only home that I have ever known. Shoot, I knew when I sat down to play cards that old Cussy was a cheater, but I played anyway cause I knew what I would do with her when I caught her."

"What about your family?" Peter pressed on.

"I was born into this world with a chip on my shoulder so big that the doctor thought I had two heads. The things I did to relieve the pressure of that chip made my family go away from me. By the time the years had eroded the chip down to a sliver, I was set in my ways."

"But you can change," Peter offered earnestly.

"Why I wanna do that?" Evers asked. "I got everything here that I could ever need. Besides, an old cheetah don't change his stripes."

"Isn't that spots?"

"Whatever. Point is I made my mark in this world no matter how small that mark is. You're in the process of doing what I already done. I only hope you take a smarter way around to gettin' where you gotta go. Does that make sense to you, Peter?"

Peter nodded and set the empty coffee cup on the table between the bunks. He looked at Evers for a minute before reclining against the wall. He locked his fingers behind his head.

"You know, Mr. Ciderman..." Peter started.

"Evers," the man on the other bunk interrupted.

"You know, Evers," Peter began again. "When Viola, that's my girl, looked at me when I was protecting her, it was the best dang moment of my life."

"I do know the feeling," Evers said. "I know it all too well."

They lay quiet for a moment on their separate beds across the cell from each other. Peter gazed at the ceiling but it was Viola he saw dancing through his mind.

❀

This was a night that the wolves were quiet and the moon howled. The storm raged around outside the little shed. Any sane man would have made do with what he had in the house. Evers Ciderman Jr. was out of beer though and that was a situation that he was not prepared to handle.

He knew from experience that it was no more than 100 yards from his front door to the front door of Talley's Tavern. He pulled on his heavy wool coat and walked out the door. The lightning lit his way until he got to where the streetlight struggled to cut through the darkness.

Through the downpour, he could see the front door of Talley's Tavern. The porch lights were dim but familiar. The flickering neon was a beacon in the night.

When he pushed the door open, he was greeted by a blast of warm moist air. The air smelled like stale beer and old cigarettes. This was a smell that Evers had grown to love over the years.

Evers ordered two six-packs from Nick, the bartender. He stood and watched the couples and the ladies dancing around the little bar. Everyone was laughing and having a good time. No one even seemed to notice the big man waiting for his beer.

Lulu Waxel eventually walked up to Evers and asked him to dance. He remembered vividly it was Lulu who asked him to dance, not the other way around, as Tom likes to believe. He would have never asked one of these women to dance. Evers Ciderman Jr. was smarter than that. He was going to get his beer and go home.

Lulu pushed the issue and Evers finally gave in. He held the woman in his arms as they spun around to the last few strains of a song he had never heard before that night. Some of these days a passing glimpse of a chord or a refrain from that song would bring him back to that night—to Lulu's arms.

Nick motioned that Evers' package was ready. He also gave Evers the warning look about dancing with Lulu. When Evers tried to break loose of her grasp, she refused to let him go. He tried again but she refused again. She let herself be dragged back to the bar. She laughed and waved to her friends as she went.

"There's a storm out there, Miss Lulu," he said when he got to the door.

"A little water never hurt no one, Mr. Evers," she giggled in reply.

Evers looked back at Nick who was shaking his head, "No," Evers just shrugged and pulled Lulu into his coat. He pushed the door open with his foot and they walked out into the storm.

The combination of her warmth and the pounding rain was intoxicating for Evers as they traversed the parking lot and got to the door of his shed.

The power was out—which was not an uncommon occurrence for Evers' place. He lit up the interior of the little shack with candle nubs he saved for these occasions.

Lulu looked a little older—a little worn—in direct light but the candle light softened her and made her that much more beautiful to Evers. He grabbed two bottles of beer and pulled the tops off.

He handed one beer to Lulu and kept the other for himself. The tough guy was relaxing into the couch. He wrapped a thick arm around Lulu. She slid an arm around him as well.

They alternated their activity between kissing and drinking. They were both skilled in the activities and were enjoying time together.

She finally fell into his arms where she would have likely stayed all night had it not been for the pounding on the door. Evers was startled which quickly turned into suspicion because he never received visitors. Besides, who would be out there in this storm in the middle of the night?

When he opened the door, he was met with a cold wet fist in under his right eye. He fell back so hard, he was sure he broke his shoulder. He tried to count how many people were entering his home. There were three pair of blue dress pants with black shoes and two pair of greasy overalls with work boots.

They circled him and began to kick him as often and as hard as they could. There was no compunction about where they kicked him. They unleashed a torrent of kicks to every open part of Evers' body.

When one ran out of breath, another took over until everyone was completely exhausted and they had dragged Lulu by her hair out of the storm and into a waiting car.

One by one, the attackers puffed their way out into the night leaving Evers there on the floor to die. He pulled himself to his knees. The flood of salty tears washed most of the blood off of his face in uneven streaks.

Despite the beating he had just received, he wasn't hurt as badly as he thought he was—or should have been. It was his heart that took most of the brunt of the attack that night. He crawled over to the space on the couch where she had been sitting; he placed his head on the overstuffed cushion and cried himself to sleep.

❀

"I reckon your friends will be here soon," Evers said.

"Don't worry," Peter said. "I'll get you some dang cigarettes."

"It ain't the smokes, Petie-boy," Evers said. "Just be grateful, say a prayer that you got friends. I can't blame anyone but myself only I don't imagine I would be here tonight if I'd ever had even one friend."

"And Cussy Clark wouldn't be sitting home with a dang ice pack on her face," Peter offered.

"That's right, son," Evers laughed quietly.

The picture of the smoke stained old hag with the Zip-loc bag full of ice pressed against her mouth made Evers smile. Strangely, they fell silent again.

The next sound they heard was Bumpy opening the door to the holding area. Peter could see Lester and Crenshaw signing papers while Bumpy brought the ladies into the back.

Viola gasped and ran to the iron bars that separated her from Peter. Betty and Fiona stood on either side of her and comforted her while Peter touched his finger to hers through the spaces between the bars.

"Are you okay, Peter?" she asked.

"I'm fine," Peter answered.

"Can I get you anything?" this from Betty.

"Four *dang* cigarettes would be nice," Evers answered over Peter's shoulder.

"Did you happen to grab my cigarettes?" Peter asked the women.

Fiona handed the dented pack through the bars. Peter tapped the top of the pack against his index finger and caught the cigarettes as they fell into his now open hand. He handed Evers six cigarettes.

"Thank you, Sir," Evers said putting six cigarettes into his own pack. "But I think you miscounted."

"Call it interest on a loan," Peter said.

Bumpy led Lester into the holding area. Crenshaw waited just beyond the door. As he unlocked the cell door, Peter slipped out and into Viola's trembling arms.

"She's definitely worth whatever you have to pay for lighting that old boy's face on fire," Evers said quietly to Peter. "Say, just out of curiosity, what kind of lighter did you use?"

Peter turned and ignited a small part of his palm. The glow illuminated the cell and the old man's face for one moment, before dimming. "It wasn't no dang lighter," Peter said.

Bumpy began to swing the door shut again when Peter grabbed it with one hand. He kept his other arm around Viola. Peter stood there for a moment looking at the man in the cage.

"I don't know if you care or if this even makes a difference now," Peter said. "But you should know that now you have at least one friend."

Evers turned over on his bunk as if he hadn't heard the boy.

Peter led Viola out of the holding area. Betty, then Lester and Fiona followed them.

"Nice kid." Bumpy said.

"Yeah…" Evers replied.

Bumpy locked the door again, gently.

"YOUR LOVE BELONGS TO ME"

Gavin Crickle was still shaken up when he left the hospital. They bandaged what they could and applied salve to every exposed area where there should have been skin on his face.

He considered signing a formal complaint against Peter but that would mean that he would have to stay here to testify, or come back for the court date.

He figured he would get home as quickly as he could and locate William Goldman to write a made-for-TV movie about his recent experience with Viola and Peter. Good ratings would justify the agency's expenses without bringing the girl home with him. He needed to get the project green-lighted before one of those CNN flacks got their chance.

He also thought about finally getting a chance to make that buddy-chick flick with Uma Thurman and Oprah Winfrey. These bandages would go a long way currying favor—and possible sympathy—from producers and other contract negotiators.

As he drifted in and out of a fitful sleep in his seat in an overstuffed business class seat, he heard a child's voice singing a song someone used to sing to him when he was a little boy.

"Well I'm the Sheikh of Araby. Your love belongs to me..."

He thought he was dreaming. The little girl couldn't be on the airplane. He had lost her. He had seen her get into the truck with the ugly man and the pretty girls. After all he been through had they ended up on the same plane? Couldn't be, but he could hear a child singing.

The sweet little voice continued to float around the cabin. The sleeping passengers were not bothered by it and the ones who were awake seemed to be soothed by it.

Crickle stood up slowly and began to walk down the aisle in the direction the voice was coming from. He slowed at each row and peaked in to see if the child was sitting there waiting for him to offer her the opportunity of a lifetime.

He got to the last row and crossed through the galley and started making his way down the other side. He moved like a clumsy panther down the aisle trying to locate where the voice was coming from.

He arrived at the other end without finding the voice so he cut across the narrow hall where the bathrooms were and he began to move back toward his seat. That was when he found her. She was sitting right in front of him all along.

Crickle laughed to himself cracking the charred—and slowly healing skin. The pain was excruciating but he had his girl. She was right there. Crickle had won—again. She was no Viola—but she was surely trainable.

When he popped his burnt and bandaged face into her little face, the child let out a blood-curdling scream that panicked every passenger on the airplane.

Crickle couldn't have imagined what his bony face must have looked like to the child. The bandages and the salve and burnt flesh horrified the child so intensely; she had to be taken forward to first class where the thin blue curtain separated her from the hideous monster.

When the plane touched down, Crickle slithered off with his head bowed and lost himself in the teeming crowd at the airport. Eventually the little girl's mother convinced her she would be safe and they were able to get off the plane and go home.

The little girl never sang again.

"A BOY NEEDS HIS MAMMA"

Alice Campbell had to take the phone off of the hook. It rang constantly. It was as if everyone she knew just happened to be watching CNN when they broadcast the Talley's Corners revival.

Truth of the matter is that most of the people in Orton's Cove were switching from Babe's Bassmasters on channel 32 to Hick's Happytime Hoedown on 34 and their slow moving fingers lingered on 33, which was the CNN station in Orton's Cove, just long enough to catch some of the action.

She wasn't sure exactly what she should do. The only thing she was sure of is a boy needs his mamma. She reconnected the phone and called Maria. By nightfall, they were heading west in Maria's brother's Pinto station wagon.

"A boy needs his mamma," she said as the sun began to fall behind them.

Maria nodded in agreement.

They decided to work their way down to Talley's Corners and hopefully, pick up Peter's scent there. She tried not to cry and Maria did a great job of distracting her by singing "Michael Row The Boat Ashore" and doing "Row Row Row Your Boat" in rounds.

The occasional tear got swept across her face as the wind rushed in from the open window.

"I'LL MAKE YOU A DEAL"

While he was waiting for Peter's release, Crenshaw made some phone calls. The first was to the Talley's Corners Inn to cancel their reservations. He wanted to get out of town as quickly as possible. There was nothing here for them now. He would send someone back for whatever they could retrieve but he knew he had to get the kids out of there.

The second call was to Hack Granville's answering service to inform him which direction they would be traveling as well as to assure him he would still get exclusive rights to the story. He also wanted Hack to know that the newsman would be contacted as soon as decisions were made regarding finishing out the season.

The Gavin Crickle incident may—eventually—play itself out as a boon to their little traveling troupe. If that turned out to be the case, Crenshaw wanted to keep the door open for future broadcast opportunities. He had to admit to a certain lecherous affection for the pretty young ladies in Hack's crew. When he closed his eyes he could recall them buzzing around in their khaki shorts and ironic baseball caps.

A sigh of relief escaped his heavy chest when he saw everyone come out of the holding area. Peter's hesitation and consequent re-entry into the room gave him a start but Peter was back quickly and he was wearing what looked like a real smile.

"Let's go," Crenshaw said leading everyone out the door.

Standing on the front steps of the building, Lester shoved his hands deep into his pockets and rocked back and forth on his feet for a moment. Fiona looked at the ground with her hands slipped into the back pockets of her jeans.

"Is there a problem here?" Crenshaw asked.

"Well…" Lester started.

"We're talking about packing it in for the season a little early," Fiona said too quickly.

"What the…" Crenshaw started.

"Well, with Peter getting arrested and all…" Fiona saw how what she said affected Peter. "I'm sorry, Peter. It's not like that. We love you, and we love that you love Viola, but we just aren't sure that this is the safest environment for her."

"I understand," Peter said.

It was his turn to put his head down as he walked away from the group.

"How could you?" Viola whispered to her mother.

She turned and watched Peter walk away for a moment before running after him.

"You understand, don't you, Reverend?" Lester asked.

"I guess I do," the Reverend said. "But shouldn't that be Viola's choice?"

"She's a child, Reverend," Fiona said.

"I'll make you a deal," he said smugly.

Betty stood nearby and watched. She was never sure what she was seeing or what it meant with Crenshaw, but she kept an open eye and an open mind. She was starting to understand the way he dealt with people, but she still had miles to go.

Fiona and Lester were a little more used to the routine, but they had been friends for a long time and decided to give Crenshaw the benefit of the doubt.

"Let's get those two kids back here and offer them an ultimatum; Viola can go home now, and take Peter with her, or she can stay on the road with us. We can finish out the season and make some bigger decisions come August."

"How can you make Peter stay with her?" Betty interrupted. "I know for a fact that he wants to get back to Orton's Cove. He won't admit it but he misses his mamma."

"I didn't say that I could," Crenshaw said. "I am just willing to bet that Viola would rather be with Peter on the road, than just be with him at home. She knows she was meant to do the Lord's work. Peter is the bonus package."

"So if she says that she wants to go home, and that she wants him to come with her, you'll walk away?" Fiona asked. She wasn't a loud woman, but she surely was a strong woman.

"Until next season," he said smiling.

"And if she wants to stay?" Lester interjected.

"Then we pull ourselves together," Crenshaw said. "We drive through the night until we get to Beaver Falls. I'll make a few calls and we can have what's left of the tent picked up from here and delivered to us there. Once we are back in our rhythm, the season will be over before we even realize it."

"What about Peter?" Betty asked. "Doesn't Peter have any say in this?"

"Of course he does," Crenshaw said. "Let's take care of one thing at a time."

"Viola. Peter," Lester called out to the figures that were standing under the streetlight.

They turned and began to walk slowly back to the steps. The light from Peter's cigarette bobbed up and down as he walked, hand in hand with Viola.

"We have a proposition for you," Crenshaw said. "In *light* of this evening's events, no pun intended, we have been discussing the idea of ending the season early."

Betty was nearly as shocked as Fiona was. Lester didn't really notice, but it appeared that Crenshaw was going to present this in a completely unbiased way. He wasn't going to attempt to sway Viola, just lay out the options for her and let her decide for herself.

"We know that you and Peter have grown very fond of each other. So we, your mother and I, decided to leave the fate of the season in your hands. Would you like to continue as we are? Or would you like to go home?"

Betty and Fiona looked at each other quickly but Crenshaw clarified quickly.

"Now you understand that if you go home, Peter will be more than welcome to go home with you. Lester and your mother have agreed he could live in the attic above the barn until you two can be married."

"Nice touch," Fiona thought to herself.

"I don't remember that part." Lester thought to himself.

"This guy is good. He is *really* good," Betty thought to herself.

"I want to do whatever makes Peter happy," Viola said proudly.

"Peter?" Crenshaw asked.

"I don't know," he said quietly. "Can we talk about it in the dang morning? I'm tired."

"Of course we can," Fiona said. "I'm in favor of getting back to the hotel for a good night's sleep. We'll be fresh in the morning and we can talk over breakfast. There is no harm in missing one day."

"I hope we can get a room this late," Crenshaw said. "I canceled our reservations at Talley's Corners Inn because I thought that we were in a hurry to leave here. I have rooms for us at the Beaver Falls Red Roof Inn."

"I don't think I'll be able to drive all the way to Beaver Falls tonight," Lester said. "Why don't we go back to the tent and sleep there. I don't think anyone is going to care—not tonight—not really."

"We'll be fine," Fiona said. "We can sleep under the stars like in the old days."

"I think it'll be fun," Betty said.

"Can we have a campfire?" Viola asked.

Everyone looked at Peter for a minute.

"Dang," Peter said.

"Maybe that wasn't the best idea," Viola said.

"You know, in the old days, I usually found a hotel once everyone was asleep," Crenshaw said as the group walked toward the car.

The idea of sleeping on the cold, hard ground was not very appealing to Crenshaw. What was even more disheartening was not having the chance to meet a young disciple to help him relieve some of the stress of the evening.

Crenshaw wished he had some idea whether the CNN crew had decided to stay in town.

"TELL HIM THE BEST PART"

The morning light found almost everyone sleeping soundly wrapped tightly in sleeping bags and quilts that Lester had gotten from the Dodge and scattered around on the old plywood stage.

Crenshaw had hitched a ride into town with an old farmer on a big tractor at dawn. He needed to make a few phone calls in private. He was confident that the season would be finished no matter what he wanted or thought was best. He just needed to get the Beaver Falls situation settled.

Between calls he paced around the small diner, choking back a cigarette. He had *liberated* the pack from Peter while Peter was sleeping. He sipped the chicory coffee, which somehow relaxed him. Still he paced and smoked and waited for his contact in Beaver Falls to call him back.

A chubby little woman in the flowery dress and plaid apron moved around and about him in a flawless dance from table to table as she set out salt and pepper shakers and sugar bowls. If she minded the cigarette, she gave no indication of it.

Occasionally, Crenshaw held his coffee cup out which she filled without even looking as she pirouetted past him. Somewhere along the way, he had learned he really liked the flavor of black coffee and no longer diluted it with confections.

Crenshaw was surprised to see the Dodge pull up outside. He

watched as everyone piled out. They were a ceaselessly happy group. Before they even entered the diner, Crenshaw snubbed out his cigarette and pushed the ashtray away. He didn't want Betty or Viola to see him smoking. He didn't really like anyone to see him smoking so when he did, which was very seldom, he kept himself out of sight from family and friends.

Peter approached him with a glare in his eyes that startled the older man. He palmed the cigarettes off to Peter with a look that begged for a chance to explain—later. There was also a five-dollar bill rolled up in the pack.

Peter made a quick exit. Viola followed him. He stopped on the sidewalk in front of the diner and lit a cigarette. Peter glared at Crenshaw—all the while Viola beamed up at Peter. Peter eventually led Viola down the street out of Crenshaw's line of sight.

The phone rang. Crenshaw jumped but the chubby lady beat him to it.

"Talley-Ho!" she said. "This is Beryl. What can I do you for?"

There was a pause.

"I think he is, lemme check," she said.

She placed her hand over the receiver and addressed Crenshaw, "Are you Reverend Crenshaw?"

"Yes, I am," he said reaching for the phone.

She didn't seem to notice his reach.

"Yes, he's here," she said into the receiver. "Of course you may talk to him."

Beryl handed Crenshaw the receiver. She brightened up when she saw the group settling in. She brought everyone menus and a pitcher of water.

There was a pause before Crenshaw began to speak.

"I am sorry, Mr. Granville," he said sharply. "I have given them the option. If they choose to end the season early, then who am I to stop them?"

"That's why we use contracts in this business," Hack replied from his room at the Beaver Falls Red Roof Inn.

He was a patient man, but he felt like the preacher was stonewalling him.

"Your business perhaps, but my business is different," Crenshaw replied.

"Just keep me informed," Hack said. "That's all I ask. If your word is as good as you want me to believe it is, please remember our agreement."

"If they decide to finish out the season, you will be the only call that I make. Fair enough? I did promise you exclusives which you will get in whatever form I can provide them."

The diner was beginning to fill up now. The curious citizens were sneaking peaks at Lester and Fiona. They were glad the fire-boy wasn't around. Reverend Crenshaw slipped a muffin into his pocket and made his way between the tables to the front porch.

He took the short step off the porch and walked to the end of the building. He turned to his left and there they were. Peter was leaning on a small pile of chopped wood next to Viola. Crenshaw wasn't surprised to see them there together holding hands and whispering to each other.

"Good morning Peter, Viola," he said moving across the red dirt yard and settling himself on to the tree stump used to hold the wood that was about to be chopped. "How are you two this fine morning?"

"Reverend Crenshaw," Peter said as he eased himself up and walked to where the preacher was sitting. He watched the man pull a muffin out of his jacket pocket and pick most of the lint off it before taking a deep bite.

"What is it, Peter?" the man mumbled between crumbs and blueberry chunks.

"I want us to do one more meeting. I want to do it here, in this town. I don't want to go to no dang Beaver Falls. Viola wants to do it here too. After that, she's going to go back home with Lester and Fiona and we're going to send Betty home to Orton's Cove."

"And what about you, Peter?" Crenshaw asked.

"I'm going with you to do as many revivals as I can before the first snowfall. I gotta make some money for my mamma. But as soon as we done, I'm going back to Orton's Cove to finish school."

"Tell him the best part," Viola said as she stood up and joined Peter on the porch.

"After I graduate, I am going to move to Tennessee and live in the attic above the barn until me and Viola can get married."

"I have to admit that this all comes as a bit of a surprise, but if this is what you both want…"

"It is," Peter said.

"Yes, it is," Viola answered.

"There is one condition though," Peter said. "My friend, Evers Ciderman Jr. has to be there tonight."

"Mr. Ciderman?" Crenshaw asked. "Isn't he the man that you were in jail with last night?"

"Yes, he is, Reverend," the boy responded.

"Can I ask why you want him there tonight?"

Peter didn't say anything. He didn't have to. Peter was not the type of guy that asked for much so when he did, the people around him were likely to give it to him.

"I need some coffee, Reverend. Do you want a fresh cup?" Peter asked.

"I'll get it," Viola said.

She disappeared into the diner, letting the framed screen door slam behind her. When he was sure she was out of earshot, Peter took a seat on the swing next to Crenshaw.

"Please understand how much I appreciate what you done for me, sir," Peter started. "My mamma's been puttin' away all that dang money that we been sending home and we both really appreciate it. I just don't want to see anything bad happen to my Viola."

"I understand," Crenshaw said. "You know we may have a little trouble getting permits for tonight, after last night and all."

"I don't think we will," Peter said. "Now I know I ain't as bright as you but I'm thinkin' that there might be a handful of people here who didn't make it to the revival last night. They might feel cheated if we left town and didn't give them a chance to see what their neighbors are talkin' about."

"You know, Peter, you may be brighter than you think you are," Reverend Crenshaw said with a laugh.

"You know, Reverend" Peter laughed softly. "Maybe you're not such a bad guy after all."

"You never can tell," Crenshaw smiled.

Viola came back out onto the porch with the two cups of steaming black coffee. As she handed each of the men a cup, she told Peter he had a phone call. He took his cup and went inside. Viola took his place on the swing.

"I appreciate you doing this last show with us tonight, Viola. I really do," Crenshaw said. "I know how much this means to you and I want you to know that I think you, and Peter, are doing the right thing."

"Thank you, Sir," she said.

Peter rejoined them wearing a tremendous smile. It was the biggest smile either of the people on the swing had ever seen.

"That was Mamma on the dang phone. She and Maria are just down the road a piece and expect to be here by nightfall."

"Maria?" Viola and Crenshaw asked at the same time.

"She works for Mamma," Peter said not noticing Viola and Reverend Crenshaw were curious for different reasons. "They have been driving non-stop, Maria told me. They were worried because of what they saw on the dang TV and she wanted to make sure that I was all right."

"That's great news Peter," the Reverend said. "And now, if we are going to have a meeting tonight, I'd better start making arrangements. I have to call Mr. Granville, or course. I have to cancel Beaver Falls. I have to check on permits…"

"Please don't forget about Mr. Ciderman, Reverend," Peter said.

"I'll see what I can do," Crenshaw said.

Crenshaw walked back up onto the porch and pulled the screen door open and stepped inside. He held the door with his left hand and eased it shut so it wouldn't slam. They watched his form melt into the dense opaqueness of the screen. The image faded slowly.

"CAN I KISS YOU"

Hack and his crew were more than a little surprised to find themselves back in Talley's Corners. This locale was not what they had planned for. Hack couldn't understand why Reverend Crenshaw would want to face an audience that would, more than likely, be angry—if not completely hostile.

He only hoped the rest of the media had taken Crenshaw's bait and were en route to Beaver Falls. While he would admit it was hardly ethical to let the wrong information slip into the right hands, things could have been worse.

Hack watched his crew work. The tireless young bodies ran the wires, set up the cameras, checked the light levels and generally made certain—then double certain—that everything was set for the night. They had learned to be prepared for whatever the night might bring.

No one was more surprised than Hack, when he saw the caravan of network news crews pulling up around the tent, like covered wagons. The snappily dressed anchors sat in long-legged directors' chairs having hair and make-up sessions while their crews jockeyed for camera and microphone positions.

Sensing Hack Granville's obvious tension over the intrusion, Crenshaw's trot became a full run, which was punctuated by his stream of apologies and denials.

"I swear none of these people got their information from me," he said breathlessly. "Please believe me, Hack. I told everyone we were sticking to schedule and would be opening in Beaver Falls. There is really nothing I can do now!"

"Don't worry, Reverend," Hack said. "We brought this on ourselves. Our coverage of last night's meeting was so good we're the ones who brought the vultures out. In a way, it's good to know that someone is watching."

"Then you aren't angry?" Crenshaw collapsed with relief.

"I didn't say that," Hack laughed. "But there's not much that any of us can do about it, is there?"

"I'll make sure that Peter and Viola pay more attention to your cameras than any of these other cameras," Crenshaw said defiantly.

"Just have them do their best," Hack replied.

"Whatever you say," uttered a relieved Crenshaw.

A young lady in a Patriots sweatshirt and khaki shorts walked up to where the two men were standing and offered the producer a clipboard. The preacher took that as his cue and he left them to talk. The tent was already filling up and he had to make sure Viola and Lester were ready. He needed to check on Peter as well. He wanted to make sure Evers Ciderman Jr. was sitting in the front row so Peter could see him straight away.

Peering out from between some folds in the tent, Lester and Fiona saw the crowd was appreciably bigger than the night before. Someone had opened up the back wall of the tent and people were spilling out into the pasture.

Viola and Peter ducked in and out of the parked cars looking at the license plates hailing from just about every state in the union. Places Viola had seen in her travels. Places they had talked about visiting. Places they had only dreamed about.

Peter listened as she told him about the precious red dirt in Alabama and the endless rows of corn in Iowa. The Mammoth Cave in Kentucky was one of her favorite and more spiritual places. She also loved hiking up Lookout Mountain in Tennessee. Along the mountain paths stood many historical markers. Viola loved to read all about their historical significance and witness the natural beauty.

"One time, when we were driving through Tennessee," she started. "I wrote a little poem about how beautiful everything was to me."

"I'd like to hear it," Peter told her.

"It's kind of silly," she blushed lightly.

"I still want to hear it," he persisted.

"Are you sure?

"Yeah," he said.

"Okay, Here goes…

> *If there is something prettier*
> *Than this place called Tennessee*
> *I don't think I'll believe*
> *Until it's something that I see*

See I told you it was silly," she said.

"Dang, Viola. That was the prettiest poem I ever heard in my life," Peter told her. "Real pretty, just like I bet Tennessee is. I can't wait 'til I live there."

"Thanks, Peter," she said. "We'd better get back to the tent. I want to meet your mother before the revival starts. Reverend Crenshaw is going to come looking for us pretty soon if we don't head back. After last night, he's a nervous wreck. I think I saw him smoking a cig…"

"Viola," Peter interrupted her and grabbed her hand. "Can I kiss you?"

"Of course you can, Silly. You don't have to ask."

The sweet young angel puckered her lips and squeezed her eyes shut. She aimed her perfect face at Peter's. He puckered up too and let his lips brush softly against hers. The kiss was as quick as it was light but Peter felt the thrill rush through his body as he tried to walk—nonchalantly—back toward the tent.

"BRING OUT THE FREAK"

C renshaw stepped out onto the stage and felt it sag beneath his weight. He made a mental note to purchase a new one for next season. The sea of faces surprised him for a moment but he recovered quickly and raised his arms out in front of him.

He saw Alice Campbell and the girl who must be Maria slip into the back row of the crowded tent. He smiled to himself. Crenshaw knew the drill. He put his head down and mumbled a silent prayer before lifting his face slowly to heaven. The words were inaudible but the invocation was clear. The crowd fell silent.

Finally he leveled his face and looked directly into the loving face of Alice Campbell. She smiled and waved. He winked, almost unnoticeably.

"Good people of Talley's Corners and from across this great country of ours—across all fifty states I welcome you to witness the work of God through these children and the beauty they create."

"What happened last night?" a voice yelled from the back of the tent.

"The world belongs to the children for they are the ones that create the beauty that make the vagaries of this world bearable."

"Tell that to the guy with the crispy face," another voice yelled.

Reverend Crenshaw ignored *that* voice also, but Alice looked around her to see who could be so disrespectful.

"It was Jesus who said 'Suffer the children that they may come unto me.'"

"So that a freak could light them on fire," the first voice yelled.

The crowd was beginning to divide their loyalties. There were those who came out of need. There were those who came out of curiosity. Then there were those who came to make trouble.

Alice came out of love and had no intention of sitting idly by while some hayseed made a mockery out of the revival. She stood up quickly and spoke to the back of the tent. She wasn't sure to whom she was actually talking to but everyone got her point.

"You need to go home and ask your mamma why she never taught you manners," she started. "I'm sure she had a good reason and we'd all like to hear it. In the meantime, you would do well to be respectful when you are in a tent of the Lord."

"This ain't no tent of the Lord, Lady," the second voice said. "This is the lair of a fire-spitting demon and we come to see him do his little trick."

"I assure you that this is not a place of trickery," Crenshaw intervened. "You will all see, soon enough, how the Lord speaks to you through young Peter Campbell."

"Bring out the freak!" a man shouted.

"Yeah, Padre," another man shouted. "Bring out the freak."

"We want to see the freak," a woman called from the third row.

When everyone looked at her, she put her head down and giggled to herself.

The sea of faces that had been so serene, quickly turned into a roiling mass of anger—a mob of vehemence. They were calling for Peter and they were not to be denied.

The more they taunted, the more the shame tore at Alice Campbell. Peter's mother fell crying into Maria's arms. Maria stroked the woman's hair and whispered comforting words to her. She held the woman close to her to protect her from the cyclone of bile that was swirling around the room.

"People! People!" Crenshaw called out, but they only got louder.

When they noticed Peter standing in the center of the stage, they stopped. Crenshaw turned around and saw the boy standing behind him. The rage he held in his red-rimmed eyes made the preacher shrink away.

"I didn't want it to be like this," Peter said to no one. "I didn't want it to end like this."

Peter raised his hands slowly and opened his fists with steady deliberation. He looked out past the people, out into the night that had fallen around them.

"Peter!" Reverend Crenshaw pleaded. "NO!"

But it was too late.

Peter was too far-gone to hear him. The fury had built up in him and, as it spewed out of him, it wrapped itself around him, protecting him from their words.

Maria scooped Alice up and dragged her through the crowd and out into the open air. The mass of people closed behind them like the Red Sea after Moses.

The first ball of flame crashed off of an NBC camera and started a patch of dry grass on fire. The second ball, fueled by the hatred and the ignorance of the angry mob, exploded on the chest of a burly farmer who was laughing and pointing a fat red finger at Peter.

Frantic, the congregation turned into a crushing wave of humanity that trampled the weak as they tried to escape. Some of the men ripped through the walls of the tent while others just kicked the women and children out of their way.

The next ball of fire careened off of the support pole dropping the back wall of the tent back into place trapping many of the fleeing mass inside. They didn't seem to be shouting much anymore. The sounds were screams now, pure agony.

Outside, Reverend Crenshaw gathered up Betty and Viola and Fiona and led them to safety just beyond a small clump of trees a hundred yards from the tent. He saw Lester running toward the car to move the vehicle as far away from the inferno as possible. Reverend Crenshaw went back into the crowd to find Alice and Maria.

From this safe distance, the others watched as people jumped into cars and banged fenders and bumpers as they tried to get back out onto the main road. The screams of the voices trapped in the tent horrified Viola who buried her head in Fiona's chest and prayed it would all end. She prayed her Peter would be all right.

Evers Ciderman Jr. nodded his head and smiled. He didn't get up from his chair. He finally had a friend.

An inferno blazed where the tent once stood.

"THE SOLACE OF THE GOOD BOOK"

The sun crept up into the sky slowly as if, it too, were making sure it was safe to come out. The men and women in their big black coats and heavy rubber boots waded through the debris. Not even the most seasoned veteran of any of the county departments had seen anything like this before.

The news crews that had been covering the meeting were replaced by news crews that were covering the aftermath of the worst fire in the history of Talley's Corners. There were no apparent injuries to any of the crews as they were all on the outside looking in. This position gave the best position for escape.

A few stayed behind to help with the cleanup, but most of the news people were already on to their next crisis while this one still smoldered.

The school was closed and the hospital was crowded and the Inn was buzzing with activity. The search and rescue team had only recovered two bodies when they were looking for three. Miraculously everyone was accounted for except for three bodies. Crenshaw saw that as a sign from God, even if no one else did.

The first was Evers Ciderman Jr. A smile was burnt into the creases of his face. His teeth showed ghastly white against the darkened skin. No one, except for Cussy Clark, would mourn for him. She still owed him a punch in the mouth or two.

The second body was that of Roscoe Butler. He caught a fireball in the chest. Roscoe was a popular farmer who played the spoons and the washboard with a local Bluegrass band, the Front Porch Swingers. He farmed a small plot of land just outside of town. His wife and son Roscoe Jr. would be well provided for. The band would have to find a replacement for him though.

The third body, the one body they didn't find, belonged to the young boy from Orton's Cove who had come here to bring them the joy of the good word.

Viola cried herself sick and had to be sedated in one of the bright comfy rooms at Talley's Corners Inn. Fiona sat on the edge of the bed never leaving her side while Lester dozed fitfully in the over-stuffed love seat across the room.

Alice and Maria sat on the front porch swing and talked about Peter. Alice loved Viola, and she loved that Peter loved Viola. Alice decided to plan a trip for Viola back to Orton's Cove so that she could see where Peter came from and maybe find something of Peter's that she could keep to remember her young love. She knew she had a few of the commemorative t-shirts left in a box by the front hall closet.

Alice and Maria wrapped each other up in their embrace and took turns crying over things they remembered about Peter and things that would never be. The older woman's heart was broken so completely she thought it would never heal.

Reverend Crenshaw sought solace in the Good Book. He sat alone on the little back steps of the inn smoking cigarettes and drinking black coffee. The open book on his knee made him feel strong again. It reminded him why he chose this life in the first place.

Betty Croney walked alone through the tired streets of the bitter little town—the town that, for all its love and brotherhood, had turned ugly so quickly. The faces of the people she met would not return her glance.

Hack Granville stopped to say good-bye. He wanted answers, but it wasn't in him to make a story out of what these people—his friends—were going through. Out of obligation, Reverend Crenshaw offered Hack one last exclusive interview but the newsman turned off his camera and went home.

Both men knew that everyone had had enough.

"AND SO IT GOES"

The snow was falling lightly on the front lawns and the streets of Orton's Cove. The Christmas lights twinkled in the windows of most of the houses on Hubley Street.

The Reverend and Mrs. Crenshaw (formerly Campbell) were down at the church with Maria setting up the Christmas Bazaar. The biggest attraction, once again, would be the dresses they designed. This year, they had a bumper crop. The preacher scuttled around the linoleum floor of the church basement unpacking boxes of things to sell, to raise money to send kids to summer camp. He came upon a shirt with two open hands printed on the back. The hands on the shirt are shooting flames. Turning the shirt around, Peter's face smiled back at him. He folded the shirt quickly and stuffed it into another box of things he and Alice might want to sort through later. Then he stepped outside to smoke a cigarette under the streetlight.

Betty Croney was home baking cookies to sell for the Glee Club. The cookies were shaped like musical notes. She had taken chocolate syrup and made staff lines on the cookie sheet. The notes were arranged in such a way that if a musician were to play the cookie sheet, the song would have sounded like "Kumbaya". Her parents stood in the doorway and watched their young lady move about the kitchen singing to herself. She did that a lot these days, which was something they had never heard before. Her father put a warm hand on her mother's shoulder.

Viola was so distracted with the anticipation of her new baby brother (or sister) being born that she could only think about Peter at night when she was alone in her room. The vivid memories of their travels together play over and over in her mind like a favorite movie that she can't get enough of. She always stops just short of Talley's Corners and goes back to the beginning again. Alone in bed at night, when she spoke to God, she relayed the messages she wanted Peter to hear. Viola was pretty certain God was good about passing messages on to people.

Lester bought a karaoke machine and set it up in the house. He sang whatever he wanted whenever he wanted. He bought one new CD with each paycheck and had amassed a considerable library of music. His collection was heavy on country music, especially Conway Twitty, but he did have some James Taylor and Bob Seger because he knows that's what Fiona likes to hear. Some nights, she would join him on a chorus or two of "Against the Wind".

Fiona couldn't have been happier. She was at home with the people she loved the most in the world. She had her house, it was a home. In a very short amount of time, she would bring a baby into the world, and into her home. She promised Viola that if it was a boy, they would name it Peter, if a girl—Vanessa. Fiona missed Peter, but she prayed for another daughter just the same. Boys can be so difficult to raise.

Miss Liu and Clayton "Mac" McDaniel" decided they couldn't sit on the sidelines and watch the game. Soon enough they found an androgynous Latin pop singer who could sing cheesy bi-lingual pop songs at every shopping mall across the country. The boy was billed as "El Gato Negro" and had fans of both sexes swooning at every appearance. Mac saw the boy as a license to print money and the boy saw Mac as his stepping-stone to the stars. Some days Liu missed the Chop Chop house, but mostly she loved traveling to shopping malls with her Mac. The whole arrangement seemed to work out perfectly for all three of them.

The sign read:

"Tennessee Tom is the Original Tennessee Trader"

A young man walked into the store and looked around for a minute before approaching the counter.

"Good afternoon, stranger," Tennessee Tom said to the young man. "What can I do for you on this fine and sunny day?"

"First off," the stranger said. "I need a pack of Marlboro cigarettes in the crush proof box."

"What else?"

"I need a map of Lookout Mountain. Do you have a map of Lookout Mountain?"

"I sure do," Tennessee Tom said pulling the heavily folded map out from under the counter. "What else, friend?"

"Gloves," the stranger replied.

"Climbing or biking? I got some gardening gloves here."

"Gardening will do just fine," was the answer.

"Gardening gloves?" the man repeated.

"Yeah, or maybe those brown jersey gloves," he pulled a cigarette out and lit it.

"I got them jersey gloves," Tennessee Tom said pointing. "Right over there."

The young man walked over to the rack where all of the different types and style of gloves hung. He picked up one pair, then another. He tested them for weight, for fit, for comfort.

He finally settled on a thick pair of black nylon gloves. He carried them to the counter.

"Do you know if these gloves are fire proof?"

❀

Paul Barile is a writer/actor living and working in Chicago. He is also a film maker, a musician, and a storyteller. He is a widely published poet as well as a widely produced playwright. He teaches a variety of writing classes to children at the elementary school level as well as adults at the college level. *My Brother's Hands* is his first novel.

You can write to the author via read@lexographicpress.com, he would love to hear from you. Also you can sign up to his mailing list to be informed of news and new works, just put "Paul Barile mailing list" in the subject of your email.